WILL THERE BE LOVE?

WHITNEY CUBBISON

Will There Be Love?

Will There Be Love?

Copyright © 2025 by Whitney Cubbison

All rights reserved

This is a work of fiction. Names, characters, businesses, places, events, locales, and incidents are either the products of the author's imagination or used in a fictitious manner. Any resemblance to actual persons, living or dead, or actual events is purely coincidental.

Designations used by companies to distinguish their products are often claimed as trademarks. All brand names and product names used in this book are trade names, service marks, trademarks and registered trademarks of their respective owners. The publishers and the book are not associated with any product or vendor mentioned in this book. None of the companies referenced within the book have endorsed the book.

No portion of this book may be reproduced, stored in a retrieval system, or transmitted in any form by any means—electronic, mechanical, photocopy, recording, or other—except for brief quotations in printed reviews, without prior permission of the author.

First Edition

Paperback ISBN: 979-8-9868960-2-1

eBook ISBN: 979-8-9868960-3-8

To my mom,
who loves loudly.

"You can give without loving, but you can never love without giving. The great acts of love are done by those who are habitually performing small acts of kindness."

Victor Hugo

PROLOGUE

Gianluca, Rome

February

Gianluca swallowed the last juicy bite of bistecca alla Fiorentina, letting his mind drift to places it shouldn't. Across from him, his wife, Ophelia, and her colleague-turned-friend, Kristin, laughed and chatted in the peacock-blue booth of their favorite neighborhood restaurant, Al Piave. Kristin dominated the conversation in her bright, slightly too-loud American manner, but Gianluca barely listened, distracted as he was by the pattern of the lacy bra under her pink silk blouse.

I should at least pretend to be paying attention, he thought, forcing himself back into reality.

"And I figured, better safe than sorry, right?" Kristin said, perhaps rhetorically.

Ophelia smiled warmly. "That's one of my friend Matt's favorite expressions. He works in private security and always plans for the worst-case scenario."

"She means her French ex-boyfriend, Matt," Gianluca interjected, having caught just enough of the conversation to make a comment.

Kristin raised an eyebrow. "Oh, do I detect a hint of jealousy?"

"We were at uni together in London a thousand years ago," Ophelia explained, waving the idea off with one hand.

Gianluca returned to his mental fantasy. It was his first time meeting Kristin, the attractive and exceedingly fit blonde Ophelia had mentioned over the years, but he had been undressing her with his eyes since the appetizers. He wasn't the cheating type—he loved Ophelia and had always been faithful, but he liked to indulge his active imagination from time to time.

He watched as Ophelia stifled a yawn, rubbing her nose in a weak attempt to hide it. They were both exhausted—Ophelia from her demanding job in event marketing at the energy company Eni, and him from long shifts as head of Emergency Services at the hospital. Juggling two full-time jobs and two kids was draining. Tomorrow was his day off, and he was ready to unwind. He eyed the half-full bottle of Barolo but hesitated—he had to drive home.

"Oh my God, am I boring you to death?" Kristin asked, noticing Ophelia's yawn. "I'm so sorry. I haven't shut up all night."

Ophelia shook her head apologetically. "No, it's not you. I'm so sorry. I'm absolutely knackered and afraid I'm terrible company tonight. But I don't want the night to end on my account. You two should stay. Order dessert and finish the wine. The tiramisu here is heaven. I've been so looking forward to having you two finally meet."

Kristin shrugged and looked to Gianluca. "I'm fine to stay for a bit longer if you are."

Gianluca searched Ophelia's face for any silent clue that she meant something other than what she'd said. He found it odd that his wife wanted to leave them alone, but he did want another drink. "You sure?"

"Yes, I'll go relieve Stefania," Ophelia said, already reaching for her coat. "You two have fun. I know how hard you've both been working, so you deserve it."

"Bye, Ophelia," Kristin replied, sliding out of the booth to hug her goodbye.

Americans are always such huggers, he observed, admiring Kristin's ass through her snug camel-colored skirt. He looked up as they pulled apart and focused on his wife. "*Ciao, tesoro*[1]. See you at home."

As Ophelia exited the restaurant, Gianluca refilled their glasses. Kristin smiled, her fingers brushing his as she took the glass from him. *That wasn't deliberate,* he thought, but he decided to let his fantasy play out. What was the risk? Kristin lived in London and flirting didn't hurt anyone. Nurses and patients' loved ones were always flirting with him at the hospital, which he enjoyed but never encouraged. He gave himself permission to let his fantasies run wild, but he'd never tried to bring any of them forward into real life. It was never worth risking his family or his job.

He and Ophelia had recently celebrated their eleventh anniversary, and by all accounts, he considered their marriage to be a happy one. With two kids under the age of ten, their sex life wasn't what it had once been, but he figured that was par for the course for most couples in their situation.

"So, do you enjoy living the expat life in London?" Gianluca asked, choosing a neutral topic that would allow his mind to wander toward more risqué thoughts.

Kristin licked her pink lips. "It's a great city, but too big sometimes. Rome always feels more reasonably sized whenever I'm here."

"Size does matter," Gianluca smirked, unable to resist.

Kristin's left eyebrow rose in a pronounced arch. "It certainly does," she laughed.

Gianluca felt his balls tighten slightly and shifted in his seat. "Tell me more about your Charlie," he suggested, hoping for some detail about their relationship that could fuel his fantasy. "I heard you mention him a few times tonight."

"We met on Tinder four years ago, and I was completely charmed by his British-isms, despite having lived in the UK since

---

[1] Bye, darling

uni." Kristin flipped her long blonde hair behind one shoulder. "You know what I mean. Ophelia has the same thing. You've got to love the Brits."

Gianluca smiled, encouraging her to continue.

"He's a banker, which he hates, despite loving the fabulous lifestyle it affords us. You know… membership at Annabel's in London, et cetera. And he's got a thirteen-year-old son named Miles from a one-night stand during a misspent youth," she said flatly.

"Wow. That must come with its challenges," Gianluca acknowledged, swirling the wine in his glass. "Do you get along with his son and the mom?"

She ran her long, delicate fingers over the petals of a flower in a vase on their table, and he imagined her wrapping them around his cock. "The mom I never cross paths with. The son… well, I'm the wicked stepmom. He doesn't listen to me. I hardly bother trying anymore."

"You don't seem wicked to me," Gianluca said, lowering his voice slightly.

"I have my moments," she exhaled, looking at him through her lashes.

A wicked, sexy smile spread across her face, lighting up her wide, hazel eyes. She leaned in slightly, and Gianluca felt a jolt of electricity shoot through him, catching him off guard.

He'd only ever seen American women do this before—turn on a dime from perfectly innocent and friendly to full-on flirty with just a shift in their eyes or tone of voice. Even then, he'd only seen it happen in movies. Now, it felt as though Kristin had dimmed the lights of the entire restaurant using nothing but her powers of seduction. Italian women were much more subtle about these things.

Their silent stare lasted several seconds too long, until he forced his eyes away, feigning interest in the wall of wine bottles to his right. *Fuck me. I can't remember the last time Ophelia looked at me like that*, he thought, the tightness in his groin growing steadily.

Kristin leaned back, took a sip of wine and continued as if their flirtation had never happened. "Anyway, Charlie told me years ago that he was never going to get married because his parents are divorced, and he doesn't want to put kids through that." Her tone softened, casual once again.

Gianluca turned back cautiously, and when he did, he noticed an extra button had come undone on her blouse. The lines of her ample cleavage were now clearly visible, along with the lacy edge of her bra. He forced his gaze back up to her face.

"And I guess I'm okay with that," she continued, twisting a strand of hair around her finger. "I mean, in the States, it's odd to have kids with someone and not be married, but here in Europe, no one blinks an eye."

"Do you want kids?" Gianluca asked, struggling to decide what part of her was safe to look at. The safe zone was usually the eyes, but even that felt dangerous now.

"Eventually, sure. I'm thirty-one, so the clock is ticking, I guess."

"You're still young. Plenty of time," Gianluca assured, as images of the two of them together, in flagrante, flashed through his mind in blazing technicolor. "If that's what you want."

Kristin leaned forward again, resting her chin in one hand. That intense look returned to her eyes as she began to casually nibble on the blush-colored nail of her pinky finger, drawing his attention to her mouth.

"I want a lot of things," she murmured.

A force he didn't recognize pulled him forward, and he leaned in slightly, resting his chin on his fist to mirror her. He tried to keep the conversation aboveboard.

"Dessert? The tiramisu is excellent, and they also have a truly decadent chocolate cake."

She shook her head slowly, still nibbling on her pinky nail, never breaking eye contact.

"What *do* you want, then?" he asked, with wanton desire in his voice.

That same wicked smile crept back across her beautiful face, and suddenly, Gianluca was jolted back to reality. *Who am I right now?*

"I'm sorry," he sputtered, sitting back. "I shouldn't have asked that. You and Ophelia are friends, and I think this evening just took a strange turn."

Kristin, still leaning forward, remained perfectly still. "Ophelia and I are colleagues, not friends. And I'm not sorry for the turn this evening has taken," she said, her voice measured and certain.

Heat crawled up the back of his neck. His fantasies had kicked into overdrive, trapping his words inside him. They locked eyes until Kristin emptied her wine glass.

"I'm going to go powder my nose," she said, standing and grabbing her purse. As she passed his chair, her hand brushed his shoulder, squeezing lightly.

Gianluca watched her disappear behind the small wall of wine bottles that hid the door to the restrooms. His skin tingled through his shirt where she had touched him. He rested his forehead on his fingertips, his thoughts racing.

Does she want me to follow her? I couldn't. Could I? She lives in London, so maybe I could get away with it—just this once? Jesus, man. You're not following her into the restaurant toilets. Pull it together. You're a married father of two. You bring your family here all the time. Down boy.

Fuck me. God, I'd really enjoy fucking her.

No. Stop.

He closed his eyes, took a few deep breaths, and forced his mind to conjure images of the worst traumas he had handled in the ER—anything to get his mind off Kristin's body and what it would feel like under his hands.

Gianluca flagged the waiter for the check, and Kristin returned to the table, fresh lipstick applied, as he finished paying. He stood and gestured to the door, picking up his coat. "Shall we?"

Kristin tilted her head slightly, looking demure as she plucked her coat from the booth. Gianluca moved to help her into it, leaning in close enough to catch the scent of lavender in her hair. He felt his body pulling toward hers and used all his willpower to step back.

"Could you drop me at my hotel?" she asked. "It's The Tribune on Via Campania. Not far."

"Of course," Gianluca replied, motioning toward the street. "My car's just a block away."

They walked side-by-side in silence in the frigid night air. His thoughts spun like a tornado, his pulse pounding in his ears. Every streetlight they passed under felt like an interrogation light bearing down on him, and when he clicked his key fob, the flashing headlights and chirping horn of his black Maserati hit him like a warning.

He opened her door and rested his hand on the doorframe. Kristin slid toward him without meeting his eyes but briefly placed her hand on top of his before climbing in. As he walked around to the driver's side, he clenched and unclenched the hand she'd touched, his skin burning hot, even as his breath fogged in the cold night air. *Keep it together.*

Once in his seat, Gianluca let his eyes travel to Kristin's legs, which were crossed and angled toward the center console. A small strip of skin was visible between her skirt and the top of her knee-high leather boots, and his fingers desperately wanted to stroke it. He forced his attention to the road and pulled into traffic. It was a short ride to the hotel, up Corso d'Italia, which was bordered by the ruins of the Servian Wall, a defensive wall built around Rome in the fourth century BC. He could feel his own defenses crumbling as he drove.

"I'm so glad I finally got to meet you tonight," Kristin offered. "I've heard a lot about you over the years, and I'll admit, I even stalked you a little online. I found your bio and photo on the hospital website, which may have led me to watch a video of you on YouTube—giving a press conference in Italian about emergency room capacity during COVID, I think?"

Gianluca's mouth dropped open. "Now you tell me you're a stalker? Now that you're in my car?"

Kristin laughed. "Afraid so, *signore.* Once I saw that face, I was down the rabbit hole. You were oozing authority and power in that video. I could tell, even though I don't speak a lick of Italian."

Her mention of rabbits and licking sent his mind right back to fucking. Heat once again began escaping from every pore, and a bead of sweat ran down the back of his neck. He turned off the car's seat warmer and took a deep breath to calm his mind, but all that did was flood his senses with her scent. His grip tightened on the steering wheel.

"So, you like my face?" he asked, despite himself.

Kristin living in another country made a dalliance feel like a safe risk. There was no chance they'd run into each other at the market when he was out with his family on a Saturday. Ophelia would be dead asleep by now—she never woke up when he came home late. She was used to his odd hours and never gave them a second thought. Also, they hadn't had sex in months.

As these thoughts careened around his head, Kristin's hand moved across the center console and slid under his arm to land on his thigh.

"I like your face very much," she said, stroking her thumb along his leg. "Do you like mine?"

His pulse skyrocketed, and he started to salivate. *I want to taste her. Badly.* His forearm lightly grazed hers each time he shifted gears, but he chose not to answer, as they were nearly at the hotel. Her hand moved languidly up and down his thigh, and it took all his concentration to safely park in front of her hotel. Turning toward her, he unbuckled his seatbelt and placed his hand over hers, fixing his gaze on her mouth. He wanted to claim it.

"We shouldn't even be considering this," he finally said, albeit without conviction.

She nodded slowly, her lips parting. "We shouldn't. But we definitely are."

Gianluca turned away, looking again at the crumbling ruins of the Servian Wall, scratching at his beard with one hand while keeping a hold of hers with the other. Her skin was soft and warm against his, and he craved more of it. *If that damn wall has withstood the elements since the fourth century, I should be able to withstand this blond temptress*, he thought, shifting in his seat as his erection grew.

After a few seconds, Kristin slid her hand away from his grasp. She reached for her purse on the floorboard and pulled out a card key, placing it on the dashboard between them.

"I'm in room 405 and already soaking wet for you," she whispered, sliding her hand up his thigh, her fingers dipping cruelly toward his inseam.

He inhaled sharply as she slipped out of the car. His eyes went to the key card on the dash, and he stared at it, holding his breath. His heart pounded in his chest, pushing all his blood directly to his groin and turning him rock hard. Her lavender scent still swirled in the air. Looking up, he watched her saunter up the steps, hips swaying as she disappeared through the front doors of The Tribune Hotel.

The next thing he knew, he was knocking on the door of room 405.

PART ONE

FEBRUARY

New Beginnings

One year later

CHAPTER 1

Ophelia, Rome

Ophelia cursed under her breath, tossing one brightly colored cushion after another into the air as she searched for her phone. *Mr. Bodyguard* by The Mighty Diamonds—Matt's ringtone—trilled from the depths of her overstuffed couch.

"This is not a fun game, you cheeky monkeys," she chided loudly, attempting as always to project calm authority toward her kids, all the while knowing she lacked authority as a mother. Gianluca was the disciplinarian in the family.

As the last pillow sailed through the air and Marco and Esme tore through the living room cackling, Ophelia spotted her phone wedged under a cushion. She lunged for it and answered. "Matt! So glad you didn't hang up. The kids hid my phone again, and I just threw every pillow on my couch into the stratosphere trying to get to your call."

Matt chuckled on the other end of the line. "They're not called 'throw pillows' for nothing. Sounds as chaotic as ever over there. You okay?"

"Oh, you know me. Living the dream." She pushed her fringe back and blew the stray hairs from her eyes. "Actually, Esme just cut up my mum's antique lace table runner, which I absolutely adored, because she wanted to make snow."

"Oh man. I'm sorry. I know how few of her things you have," Matt said, his voice full of understanding.

She loved him for knowing her so well. "Yeah, I'm a bit gutted, but what's done is done. Ignore me. Tell me about Paris. How's the new job?"

"Fie, I've got a girl," he announced.

She could hear the smile in his voice, and her heart swelled instantly for her friend.

"Best news ever," she shouted, flopping onto the now pillow-less couch. "It's about time you found someone new. It's been too long since Eve. What's her name? What does she do? How'd you meet? Tell me everything."

Matt laughed. "Settle down. I'm getting there. And you'll like her, I think." He paused, his tone light but warm. "Her name's Austen Keller, and we met a month ago. For the third time. In a third country. And this time, it's going to stick."

"Austen? She doesn't sound French," Ophelia remarked with cautious optimism. Her British roots made her inherently distrust the French, so she secretly hated the idea of Matt choosing a French woman.

"No, she's American, but she lives here in Paris. We first met in Senegal about three years ago. She was my protectee, and there was instant chemistry, but I was with Eve, so nothing happened. And then we bumped into each other again nine months later in Davos during the World Economic Forum. Nothing happened then either, but we clearly had a vibe, and I was tempted both times," Matt recounted.

"What are the chances? Wow. But, of course, you're the most loyal man in the world. You'd never cheat," Ophelia stated with certainty, pulling a wool blanket over her lap and tucking it around her cold feet. Rome was known for relatively mild winters, but this February, the cold lingered.

"Very low chances indeed. And no, I wouldn't," Matt stammered. "So, anyway, I lost track of her after that but never forgot her. As soon as I knew I was moving to Paris, I thought about tracking her down, but the universe took care of that for me, and damn if it doesn't feel good."

"What exactly did the universe do for you this time, you lucky duck? Tell me about this third meeting."

"She was a guest at a black-tie event Omar attended at the Louvre last month. I got the list of attendees as part of the advance work, and she was on it. I reconnected with her there."

Omar was Matt's boss—the man who had hired him as his personal bodyguard and moved him to Paris in January. Ophelia wasn't entirely sure what line of work Omar was in, but she was relieved that it had Matt staffing black-tie events at the Louvre rather than escorting corporate executives through dodgy third-world countries, as he'd done for many of the previous years.

Matt always wore a tux well. I can just picture it, Ophelia thought, biting at a cuticle.

"You're James freaking Bond on a date with destiny—at the bloody Louvre," she exclaimed, bouncing lightly on the couch. "I couldn't like this story more if I tried."

Back in their university days at King's College London, Matt had been Ophelia's first love—though she wouldn't have called it that at the time. "Love" was a word rarely, if ever, used in the house she'd grown up in. She met Matt during her first year; she was eighteen, and he was twenty, spending a semester abroad. She thought her heart would never heal when he returned to Wits University in Johannesburg, but of course, she was wrong. Young love is easier to recover from than later-in-life love when people's expectations for their relationships become more complex. Now, after nearly twenty years of friendship and her solid twelve-year marriage to Gianluca, Ophelia felt genuinely chuffed for him.

"Thanks, Fie," Matt replied. "I want to bring her to Rome for the second weekend in March if you're around. I'd love for her to meet you, Gianluca, and the kids. How are they doing?"

"Marco is doing great. Esme's eight going on twenty-five. You won't believe it when you see her again," Ophelia laughed, while checking her calendar. "Yes—bring your girl to Rome. We're free that weekend, and I can't wait to meet her."

"Thanks. I'll talk to her about it tonight and circle back with details. Kiss Esme for me and say hi to the boys."

Ophelia hung up the phone just as she heard the front door open and Gianluca drop his laptop bag on the bench. She headed toward the kitchen, knowing he'd be there—his first stop was always the fridge. She knew his routines better than she knew her own, if she even had any. She often felt erratic, whereas Gianluca was solid and predictable. She appreciated that about him—she needed his grounding force in her life.

"*Ciao*," she said.

Gianluca was already pulling a Peroni from the refrigerator, loosening his tie.

She handed him the bottle opener from the messy kitchen drawer, then placed a kiss on his cheek.

"*Ciao, tesoro*. How was your day?"

"The usual. Work was fine. The kids hid my phone again. Oh, and Matt called from Paris. He's met a girl—an American—and wants to bring her to Rome the second weekend of March so we can meet her," Ophelia said, wrapping her arms around his waist.

Gianluca ran the backs of his fingers down her cheek. "Good for him. That'll be nice."

Ophelia stepped back and glanced around the kitchen. She loved the open floor plan that flowed into the living space. It was what Italians called "an American kitchen." When they were planning the renovation, she'd latched onto the idea while browsing Pinterest. Now, it was the perfect space to cook while keeping an eye on the kids—she could see everything from behind the kitchen island.

The sound of little feet pounding down the stairs, followed by a burst of giggles, broke her thoughts. Esme and Marco dashed into the kitchen, racing toward their father.

"*Ciao, Papà,*" they said in unison, launching themselves at his legs.

Gianluca ruffled their hair with a grin. "*Ciao, cuccioli*[2]."

Ophelia tied the lemon-print apron around her waist as Gianluca moved from the kitchen into the living room, sinking onto the couch with a soft sigh. She couldn't help but smile at his predictable routine—straight from the fridge to the couch, like clockwork.

"You two know better than to run in the house," he added, still addressing Marco and Esme. "Try to act like you're civilized. God knows you're not, but try to act like you are," he said, his voice only half-joking.

"Monkeys, go play upstairs. Quietly, please. Dinner will be ready in an hour," Ophelia instructed.

Marco and Esme giggled conspiratorially before turning on their heels and trotting back up the stairs.

Once their footsteps faded, Ophelia sighed, rubbing her temples. *Why does dinner always creep up on me? It's not like I don't have to handle it every single night.* She moved to the refrigerator, pulling out tomatoes, an onion, a red bell pepper, garlic, and mushrooms and set them on the cutting board.

"How about *pollo alla cacciatora*[3]?" she called out, starting to chop vegetables. If it were just her, she would've become a vegetarian years ago, but when she'd suggested it to Gianluca once, he had balked.

"Sounds great," he replied. "Hey, so I had an idea for your big birthday coming up."

---

2 Hey, kids.

3 Chicken cacciatore

"Forty. Bloody hell," Ophelia paused, knife in midair. "I really must book myself in for Botox."

"You're beautiful," Gianluca replied. "And I think we should get a villa in Ibiza for Ascension weekend in May. Invite whoever you want, and I'll organize everything."

Ophelia set down the knife, her eyes widening as a smile spread across her face. "What a brilliant idea. Yes, let's do it. It'll be such fun. Oh, we must invite Luis and Jack. It wouldn't be Ibiza without them."

Gianluca nodded from his perch on the couch. "A long weekend might be tough for Luis given how demanding his work schedule is, but I'm sure Jack will get on a plane for this. He's not one to miss a good party. Plus, he adores you."

A fond smile tugged at her lips. The four of them had met in Ibiza during the first summer of Ophelia and Gianluca's relationship. Luis worked as a technology sales executive, constantly traveling for work, while Jack embraced life as a house husband in New York, managing their busy social life. Those carefree summer days felt like a lifetime ago.

"And if we like Matt's new girl, we can invite them too," Ophelia added, bringing herself back to the present. "That's six. We should optimize for anglophones, I suppose. Hmmm. Maybe Kristin and Charlie could round out the group. Eight seems like a good number, yes?"

"Have I ever met Charlie?" Gianluca asked, scrunching his nose. "Seems like a random choice, no? But eight sounds perfect. I was thinking maybe Raffaele and Sofia?"

Pulling spices from the rack, Ophelia replied, "Their baby's too young to leave for a weekend, and Raffaele's English isn't great. Besides, you met Kristin that one time at Al Piave last year, so let's bring her and Charlie. I've met him a few times when I've been back in London. I think you'll get along great with him. He brews his own beer."

"How about Viviana? She's always up for a getaway, and her English is excellent," Gianluca suggested, scratching his beard.

Ophelia uncorked a bottle of pinot grigio and splashed some into the pan before pouring herself a glass. "She's single. This is a couples' weekend. She'd be bored. Kristin and Charlie are perfect. Also, five minutes ago, you said I could invite whoever I wanted."

Gianluca drained his beer and headed to the refrigerator for another. "I did say that."

"Well then, it's settled. I'll send the invites this week," she grinned.

"I can take care of it," Gianluca replied.

Ophelia shook her head while starting to chop vegetables. "You don't have contact info for half of these people. You find the villa; I'll send the invites. *Grazie.* I mean it, it's a wonderful idea. And I'll make a dinner reservation for that second weekend in March when Matt and his girl are here."

Gianluca picked up a slice of tomato from the cutting board and popped it into his mouth, lifting his beer in a toast. "My wife—event planner extraordinaire."

Ophelia clinked her glass against his bottle and took a sip. "Bring on Spring."

CHAPTER 2

Matt, Paris

Matt lifted his champagne glass, tapping it lightly against Austen's. With his free hand, he reached for hers across the table, interlacing their fingers. Her hands were tiny compared to his, but somehow, they fit together perfectly.

"Cheers to a fantastic first month together," he said, looking into Austen's cat-like green eyes. He'd chosen L'Escudella, a bistro in Paris's seventh arrondissement for the occasion. The soft light from the restaurant's artfully arranged filament lightbulbs seemed to make her eyes sparkle even more than usual.

Austen smiled back her all-American grin—big, toothy, and sincere. "You remembered our one-month anniversary. That's so cheesy, and I absolutely love it. Give me all the cheese. And all the champagne," she beamed.

He lifted her hand to his lips. "All the cheese and all the champagne shall be yours," he said, pressing a slow kiss to the back of her hand before turning it and brushing his lips against the inside of her wrist. He knew it was one of her flash points—one kiss there and the effect always rippled straight through her. Goosebumps rose on her arm, her eyes darkened, and he felt his blood rushing south. They hadn't even gotten their food yet. He shifted in his seat, trying to stay composed, and flipped his thoughts to Italy.

"Out of curiosity, how do you feel about prosecco and parmesan?"

"I never discriminate when it comes to the origin of bubbles or cheese," she declared. "Actually, I just discovered a new favorite cheese from this little Italian grocery down the street from my place. It's called *scamorza*—ever had it?"

"Afraid my tastebuds haven't had the pleasure," he admitted.

"It's cow's milk cheese, and I swear the cows were probably blessed by the Pope himself because it's totally divine."

Matt chuckled. "You probably shouldn't swear about the Pope. But, how about I take you to Rome for a weekend and you can introduce me to this holy cheese. And I'll introduce you to the Pope."

Austen nearly choked on her champagne and pulled her hand away to cover her mouth as she swallowed. "You want to take me to Rome? To meet the Pope?"

"Very much so on the former," he smiled. "One of my oldest friends—who is not the Pope; I was kidding about that part—lives there, and I want you to meet her. Her name's Ophelia. She's British, a bit bonkers but in the best way, and she's married to an Italian doctor named Gianluca. They've got two kids, one of which is my goddaughter."

A playful smile crept across Austen's face. "You're a godfather—in Italy? Are you secretly in the mafia and this is your way of breaking the news to me?"

Matt laughed, though inwardly, he noted her hesitation. She didn't fully trust him yet. He suspected it had something to do with her past relationships. He had heard fragments of her "before-him" stories—enough to know her romantic adventures hadn't always been straightforward, but he was determined to win her complete trust. It wasn't always easy with the non-disclosure agreement he'd signed for his job—he couldn't always tell her where he was going when he accompanied Omar, and he knew trust had to be earned. But he never lied to her. The truth was always easier to remember.

"Your imagination is wild and wonderful," he said. "But no. Just responsible for being a good role model to one adorable eight-year-old named Esme."

Austen's eyes widened in feigned shock. "You're secretly Catholic and were totally serious about not swearing about the Pope, aren't you?"

"Still atheist." He offered her a reassuring smile. "I'm just very close with Ophelia and Gianluca. I'm overdue for a visit, and I want to take you to Rome."

When the waiter arrived with their food, Austen sat back and tucked her long red hair behind her ears. "You've mentioned Ophelia before. Hard to forget a name like that. Remind me how you know her?"

Matt carefully considered his response as he refilled their glasses of *Monthelie*. He didn't think Austen was the jealous type, but he knew it was better to be upfront. Ophelia would probably mention their past eventually, and he didn't want it to seem like he was hiding anything.

"We met in college. I spent a semester studying in London. I was twenty. Back then, she was an uber fan of Amy Winehouse. Never left the house without that crazy eyeliner that was Amy's trademark look. Luckily, that was just a phase." He hesitated, then went for honesty. "I'll just come right out and tell you that we were each other's first love, but it was a short love story. I had to go back to Jozi at the end of the semester."

Austen cut into her tarragon chicken, not meeting his eyes. "Geographically inconvenient, to be sure. Johannesburg to London is no short hop. So now you're the godfather to your first love's kid? That's soap opera-ish."

Matt waited for her to look at him, needing her to see the sincerity in his eyes. "I assure you it's not. I know how it sounds but it was over twenty years ago. It was puppy love. Is that even real love? And she's been happily married for over a decade. I went to their wedding."

"Puppy love is absolutely real love. Maybe even the purest of them all," Austen said, one side of her mouth pulling downward into a half pout.

Matt noticed it immediately. It was one of her tells. She always did that when she was worried about something.

"How did Gianluca feel about you being invited to their wedding?" she asked.

"He isn't the jealous type, but regardless, there was no need for jealousy from his side at any point, nor is there a need from your side now. It's ancient history. And when I told Ophelia about you earlier, she was genuinely happy for me. For us."

Austen seemed to relax at that, her lips returning to their normal position. "What exactly did you tell her about me? About us?"

A naughty smile crept across Matt's face as he chewed slowly. He waited a few beats then leaned in toward her and whispered, "I told her about that thing you do to me with your tongue running up my—"

Austen's eyes widened as her hand shot across the table and her thumb and forefinger pinched his lips closed. "You did not."

He shook his head, locking his eyes onto hers, making sure they said what his lips could not, under her tight but gentle hold.

When she let go, he grinned. "Of course I didn't. I just like watching you get worked up. "I told her a very brief and socially appropriate version of our story. She's excited to meet you."

"A romantic trip to Rome as our first getaway together. To meet your ex-girlfriend. What could possibly go wrong?" Austen shrugged, one palm rising upward with her eyebrows.

"Trust me. Meeting Ophelia will be a lot less intense than meeting my sister. Vivienne has a sense of 'stranger danger' that is typical of small children. She's suspicious of everyone. Consider Ophelia a warmup act."

Despite only dating for a month, Matt already knew he wanted to introduce her to his family. Ophelia was family to him, and this trip would be the perfect first step. A weekend away together was an important milestone in any new relationship.

"Okay yes, of course. I'd love to go to Rome with you. We'll drink Chianti Classico, and it'll be magnifico. Plus, you'll definitely score points with Chiara for picking Italy."

Matt let out a silent breath of relief. *That went well. Once they meet, Austen will know she's got nothing to worry about,* he thought.

"You know Chiara calls you Frank Farmer, right?" Austen asked.

He raised an eyebrow. "Who's Frank Farmer?"

"Kevin Costner's character in *The Bodyguard.*"

Matt rolled his eyes. "I should've known that one. It'd be less obscure if she just called me Kevin. Or you know, Matt would work too."

"I had a Kevin in my past. And as I'm sure you know, the French think the name 'Kevin' is ridiculous thanks to *Home Alone*. Chiara is being kind calling you Frank Farmer."

"Remind me to thank her for her extreme kindness next time I see her."

"Teasing is a sign of affection," Austen quipped. "She likes you."

"I like her too. I like all your friends. But Chiara is particularly spunky," he smiled. "So, I was thinking we could do Rome in the second weekend in March, after you wrap up François's big speech in Geneva. I thought you could pop straight down from that and I could meet you there on the Friday night."

Austen's gaze softened. Matt could tell she was thinking but couldn't read the thoughts he saw clearly racing through her mind.

"I find it strangely reassuring that you know my travel schedule for next month by heart," she admitted, taking a sip of her wine.

He leaned back in his chair and crossed his arms. "I listen when you talk."

Austen's eyes dropped to the table, and he saw both corners of her mouth turn up into a quiet but unmistakable smile. Her quiet smile was his favorite because it was never performative. It only came out when she was happily lost in thought. Inevitably, making her smile brought on his own. He'd found himself smiling more often in this past month with her than he had in the past year. He was a goner.

"How about you? How's work going?" she asked, looking back up at him. "It's been almost two months since you've been working for Omar. Are you two building a good rapport?"

Matt straightened the napkin in his lap. "I'm not hearing any complaints. He doesn't want any surprises, so it's my job to make sure there aren't any and be as invisible as possible in the process."

Austen's brows furrowed as she studied his face. "You, sir, are larger than life. How could you possibly be invisible?"

"Wearing sunglasses and black suits every day helps," he quipped. "Also, I think your interest in me and his come from wildly different places, thank God."

She rolled her eyes playfully. "I get that's your job—to operate behind the scenes. But you should know that you've got main character energy oozing out of your pores. 'Leading man' might as well be scrawled all over that gorgeous face of yours." She traced a circle in the air around his face with her index finger.

"I prefer a supporting role. Less pressure," he declared.

Austen raised her hands defensively. "No pressure from me."

"I didn't mean you. I'm still thinking about Rome. Ophelia and Gianluca will be all about getting to know you while we're there, so I'll get to fade into the background and just enjoy it," Matt explained with a smile. "I'm really looking forward to being in Rome with you, and maybe we should start thinking about all the bank holidays in May too. We could plan another weekend somewhere else for just the two of us?"

Austen clenched her jaw. "Look at us making vacation plans."

Matt eyed her suspiciously. Austen had been single for several years before they got together, and every once in a while, he saw her unease with coupledom creep in. He found her to be utterly fearless in so many other aspects of her life, but over the last few weeks, he'd seen her independent streak flare up—usually when he mentioned plans more than a week or two in advance. He hoped it was more about old habits than real doubts.

"Uh oh. Is this advanced planning of 'couple stuff' making you twitchy?"

Her eyes traveled upward toward the ceiling—a sure sign she was thinking—and then returned to meet his confidently. "Not at all. I can't wait to travel with you, Mister Richmond."

"Mister Richmond? Are you traveling somewhere with my father?" he joked, trying to keep things light.

All that confidence drained from her face. "I'm so not ready to meet your parents," she replied, with mild panic in her voice.

"No parents yet. Just my first love," he said, and then instantly regretted the reference. He didn't want her to think of Ophelia in those terms. Their relationship had been over for decades.

"Right. Just that," she breathed, her voice getting squeaky. "Did you lose your virginity to this girl? I mean, that would be a great opener. 'Nice to meet you, girl-who-took-my-boyfriend's-virginity.'"

Matt shook his head softly. "I was twenty when we met, so no. She wasn't my first. Remember when I said you had nothing to worry about? That applies to every single woman from my past. When I close the door on a romance, it stays closed."

Austen took a deep breath. "Yes, I remember. And I trust you."

She'd never said that before, and Matt filed it away in his mind as a solid win. When they got back to her apartment later that night, he very intentionally, slowly, and tenderly made love to her. He wanted her to feel safe in his touch, to know that she could trust him completely. Until then, they'd been having sex, and quite a lot of it, but this time felt different. As he drifted off to sleep with her head on his chest, arms wrapped around her, he knew something had shifted between them. And he liked the direction they were heading.

CHAPTER 3

Austen, Paris

The following weekend, Austen met her friends Chiara, Daphne and Isobel for dinner at Marco Polo, their favorite red-velvet draped Italian restaurant in the heart of Paris's cobblestoned Saint-Germain neighborhood.

"Sylvie rolled onto her stomach the other day for the first time, and I swear she may as well have cured cancer for how excited Jean-Marc and I were," Daphne cracked, twirling *cacio e pepe* onto her fork. "I swear, babies make you stupider. I'd never have believed I could get so excited about something so inane before she was born."

"It's not inane, and you're not stupid," Austen corrected, scooping scattered tomatoes back onto her piece of bruschetta. "You're a mom. And that's an important milestone."

"You girls don't give a shit about babies' developmental milestones. Please, somebody tell me something juicy," Daphne pleaded. "Love her to pieces, but I'm desperate to talk about anything else tonight. And thank you again for dragging me out of the house."

"Old married lady here," Isobel said, pointing to herself. "I have no juice. Only wine. Which I suppose is technically grape juice."

Austen wiped her mouth with a napkin. "That depends on how you define 'juice.' Aren't you and Luc planning a fabulous trip to Fiji? I'd wager they have delicious juice there."

Isobel smiled broadly. "Yes, fine. Luc is taking me to Fiji for our first wedding anniversary in June. He has to be in Singapore for some deal with the firm, so we're just going to pop over after his work stuff is done. Given this utterly dismal weather we're having, I admit I cannot wait to be on a beach basking in the sunshine."

"Your juice is going to have so much rum in it," Daphne said wistfully. "Can you please fit me in your luggage?"

Isobel smiled and rubbed circles into Daphne's back, shaking her head. "No honey. Sorry. I love you—but not that much."

Daphne playfully punched Isobel's arm, and everyone laughed.

"What about you, Austen? Where's the next trip?" Chiara asked, twisting her brown hair up into a ponytail.

"For work, it's New York next week, but more interestingly, Matt is taking me to Rome next month for our first weekend getaway," Austen said with a smile, before her expression quickly shifted into a frown. "He wants me to meet his ex-girlfriend who lives there. Ophelia. Is that weird?"

The question had been spinning around in her mind since Matt's invitation, and she'd been anxiously awaiting her friends' input. Over the years, they'd never let her down when she needed honest, objective opinions to balance out her hopes and fears.

Daphne raised her hands into a T-shape. "Time out. Going to need more info here. Your first weekend away together is to go hang with his ex-girlfriend?"

Austen pointed at Daphne with her fork and screwed up her face. "His first love, more precisely. They dated briefly at university, and now he's godfather to one of her kids."

"So, this Ophelia is married?" Isobel asked.

"And Italian?" Chiara inquired, looking confused. "Ophelia doesn't sound Italian."

"Yes, married. Italian husband. She's a Brit," Austen explained.

"One of my people," Isobel smiled, putting her hand over her heart. "But I will absolutely hate her if you want me to. Just say the word."

Austen counted herself incredibly lucky to have friends like these—women who offered unconditional support and love in the face of any challenge. As expats living far from their blood relatives, they had become family to each other.

"He assures me their romance is ancient history, and she's now one of his best friends, so he wants us to meet," Austen continued. "I guess it's sweet?"

Daphne nodded. "He wouldn't be pushing you two together if there was any room for drama. Just roll with it. And use it as an opportunity to get some dirt from her on him, if there is any in that squeaky-clean-seeming guy's past."

From what Matt had shared in their first month together, his past seemed remarkably free of red flags, which made Austen nervous. In her experience, anything that seemed too good to be true usually was, so she was proceeding with caution, emotionally speaking. She wanted to trust him—wanted to fall headlong into love with this man who truly seemed to be everything she'd been waiting for—but fear held her back.

Isobel waved her hand in front of Austen's face. "Hello? Earth to Austen. I can see your wheels turning. Stop overthinking. It's the enemy of joy," she declared. "Your boyfriend is sweeping you away to Rome for the weekend. It's fabulous."

"I agree. It's sweet, and I'm sure this Ophelia won't be a threat. And Frank Farmer gets extra points for taking you to Italy," Chiara added.

"I told him you'd say that. And I told him about the Frank Farmer thing too," Austen laughed, then grew serious, smoothing out the tablecloth with her fingertips. "He also mentioned maybe going away for one of the holiday weekends in May, which feels so far away, doesn't it?"

"May is basically tomorrow," Daphne replied, wiping up olive oil with a stray piece of focaccia. "You just think it sounds far away because you haven't dated anyone longer than five minutes since Brad, so planning for a holiday months away scares you."

Austen threw her hands up in wonder. "How do you know me so well?"

Daphne shrugged, looking smug. "I just do."

"I think it's great that he's planning for things months in advance," Isobel said. "It means he's serious about you, which we knew since he's already done the rounds and met all of us. Things are going well, aren't they?"

"Yes, he's wonderful. I'm excited. But I'm waiting for the other shoe to drop. With me, it usually does," Austen lamented.

Chiara pointed at Austen with her wine glass. "Sounds like your 'excitement' about this trip might be anxiety in disguise. Also—sidebar—stop associating shoes with anxiety. Shoes are happiness."

Austen didn't consider herself anxious, but Chiara's comment struck a chord. It had been years since she'd been in a solid relationship. She realized she hadn't fully relaxed around Matt yet.

"Oh my God, I'm Cindafuckin'rella," Austen exclaimed. "She obviously left that glass slipper behind while fleeing in a rush of anxiety."

Daphne cocked her head to the side. "I think I missed something. How did this turn into a Disney princess story?"

"Roll with me for a second," Austen pleaded. "Matt and I have been together for a month, and most of the time it's wonderful. I'm Cinderella, twirling and whistling through a forest with little cartoon animals happily frolicking at my feet. But sometimes, he looks at me so intensely that I want to bolt—leaving the proverbial glass slipper in my wake."

Chiara harumphed. "I maintain that you need to disassociate shoes from your anxiety, but in all seriousness, what makes you want to bolt?"

Austen paused and lifted her eyes to the ceiling, as if an answer might be hovering there. "Has no one else noticed that those twirling Disney princesses are always singing alone? Serious question: was Cinderella happy because things with her prince were going great, or was it because she finally had some time to herself or with her adorable forest friends?"

"You can have your me time and your friend time and be with him," Isobel pointed out. "You have to be intentional to get the balance right, but if anyone can make it work, it's you, my friend."

"I've gotten used to life on my own terms," Austen confessed. "Being part of a couple means compromise, and that freaks me out. I don't want my world to revolve around him."

Daphne rolled her eyes. "Did he ask for that?"

Pouting, Austen admitted he had not.

"It's only been a month. Give it time," Chiara said. "Enjoy the honeymoon phase. Wear the damn glass slippers. Go to Rome. And deal with the red flags if they show up or someone turns into a pumpkin."

"Good plan," Austen nodded. "What about you gals? Any news?"

"I've joined a climbing gym near my office," Chiara announced, sitting up straighter in her chair. "Figured it's a great place to meet men, and those harnesses make my ass look incredible. Very lifting."

"Sounds like a brilliant plan." Daphne laughed. "Somebody around here should be sporty."

Austen raised her pointer finger. "I read the other day on Instagram—the definitive source for all health information—that opening a bottle of wine activates fourteen muscles. Fitness is my passion."

"You're hopeless," Daphne sighed, raising her glass to toast.

PART TWO

MARCH

Invitations

CHAPTER 4

Austen, Rome

Despite the long work week in Geneva and the fact that it was almost dinner time, Austen felt energized as she made her way through Fiumicino Airport. Rome was one of her favorite cities, and Matt was quickly becoming one of her favorite people. She wasn't even that worried about meeting his first love. In the weeks since he'd suggested the trip, he'd shared enough stories to reassure her that their history was truly ancient—just like the city itself.

She picked up her phone to call Chiara, who answered on the first ring. "*Ciao cara*[4], happy Friday," Chiara sang into the phone.

"Ciao back, *bella*[5]. I just landed in *Roma*, so had to call to say *buongiorno*[6] since I'm on your home turf," Austen explained with a smile.

"*Ah siiii*," Chiara squealed. "The first big weekend getaway to meet the ex. Good luck and call me immediately when you're back in Paris to tell me all about it. Promise?"

"I promise. What are you doing this weekend?" Austen asked as she made her way through baggage claim.

---

4 Hi dear

5 beautiful

6 Hello

"Shopping, as usual. And I'm going dancing with Isobel tomorrow night at some new club in the Marais that'll almost inevitably be full of twenty-year-olds, which we love. You'll be missed," she exclaimed.

"That's my girl. Don't do anything I wouldn't do," Austen said.

"I think that leaves me a fairly wide berth," she giggled. "Ciao ciao ciao. Have fun and we'll talk soon."

Austen tucked her phone into her pocket as she blew through the arrival doors into the cool air of an early spring evening, balancing her laptop bag on top of her trusty silver Tumi carry-on. The sky was painted in hues of pink, orange, yellow and cobalt as she scanned the waiting cars. Her eyes soon fell on Matt's muscular frame, leaning casually against a black rental Audi Q5, wearing a black sport coat and his signature Ray-Ban aviators—just like the day they met on the tarmac in Dakar.

Good God that man is sexy as hell, she thought, admiring his square jaw and beautiful olive skin as she made her way across the street. As she approached, he raised a small whiteboard with her name on it, looking perfectly stone faced.

"Hello Ms. Keller," he said in an oddly professional voice, extending a hand. "I'm Matt. I've got you in this car with me today."

She wiped the grin from her face and shook his hand, quickly realizing he was recreating their first meeting. The Ray-Bans were clearly intentional, but the whiteboard was a new touch.

"Please, call me Austen," she replied in the same businesslike tone, just as she had back then. She shook his hand firmly and then launched her body into his, wrapping her arms around his neck, and kissing him hard. He smelled like sandalwood and nutmeg, and she reveled in the feel of his arms around her as she pressed him against the car and ground her hips into his.

Pulling apart to catch her breath, she whispered, "I wanted to do that from the very first moment we met."

"Would've been pretty awkward back then, but it's the only way I ever want to be greeted by you at an airport from now on," he smiled, releasing her and opening her car door. "*Benvenuti a Roma,*[7] my dear. Shall we? Pasta and wine await."

"Why thank you, sir." She said with a playful nod, planting one more kiss on his lips for good measure. "Let's not keep the pasta, wine—or your friends—waiting."

As she climbed into the car, he smacked her ass lightly with the whiteboard. She glided into her seat, letting the slit in her charcoal gray pencil skirt reveal just enough leg to catch his attention. She gave him her most sultry look and bit her lower lip. His eyes rolled into the back of his head, and he growled lightly as he closed the door.

It's going to be a sexy weekend, she thought.

Matt's bodyguard training made him a master of defensive driving—a blessing on Rome's chaotic streets that were always teeming with scooters weaving haphazardly between cars. Austen took advantage of the smooth ride to touch up her makeup in the visor mirror, determined not to look shiny or smudged when meeting Matt's ex-girlfriend.

"How was Geneva?" he asked, stroking her back as she leaned toward the mirror.

"The speech went well, but a journalist cornered François with questions about a price-gouging scandal involving one of our partners. It's all over the news there. It has nothing to do with us, and I'd prepped him well, so he handled it fine. The journo was like a dog with a bone though, so I had to very politely remove François from the situation. Once the camera was off, I gave the guy a rather stern talking to, but you know, it's all in a day's work." She snapped her lipstick shut and smiled at Matt.

"That's my girl. Managing the situation like a boss," he said, squeezing her thigh.

As she admired the beauty of the tree-lined Viale di Trastevere,

---

[7] Welcome to Rome

Austen entwined her fingers with his. "Never let 'em see you sweat, right?"

"That's right. You sure you're not too tired to meet Ophelia and Gianluca for dinner? Ophelia said we could meet them tomorrow if you prefer."

"No, I'm good," she confirmed, running her thumb along his hand. "I'm looking forward to meeting them. And I'm starving."

Thirty minutes later, Matt led her into Rimessa Roscioli, a cozy restaurant where the walls were lined with bottles of wine, boxes of pasta and various jars of oils, olives, and preserved lemons. Mouth-watering smells of roasted tomatoes, fresh basil, garlicy pesto, and freshly baked bread invaded her senses. She watched as Matt scanned the room and quickly spotted his friends who were already getting up from the long wooden table at the back of the room, ready to greet them.

Austen eyed Ophelia curiously as they approached. She was petite with black, shoulder-length, board straight hair with bangs, and wore a simple but elegant black polka dot dress. Her skin had the typical translucent pallor of the English. She smiled warmly at Austen, not Matt, which she took as a good sign.

Ophelia clasped both of Austen's hands, rising on her tiptoes and leaning in for the Italian-style kiss on both cheeks. Austen knew from her work travels that the Italians always started the hello kisses on the right cheek, whereas the French always go left. Getting it wrong can cause awkward near-kiss-on-the-mouth collisions, which she was pleased to have avoided.

"Austen, I've heard not nearly enough about you. I'm so glad you're here this weekend so I don't have to rely on him for details," Ophelia said, her brown eyes sparkling as she dipped her head in Matt's direction.

"It's great to meet you too. I look forward to hearing all your most embarrassing stories about this man in his youth," Austen replied, giving Matt a teasing smile.

Ophelia cackled as she reached for Matt and air kissed him on both cheeks. "I like her," she said into his ear, winking at Austen over his shoulder.

Matt shook Gianluca's hand, greeting him in Italian. Gianluca, tall and fit with salt-and-pepper hair, smiled as he kissed Austen's cheeks. "Good to meet you, Austen," he said. "We ordered a bottle of Barolo to welcome you to *Roma* properly, with a toast to *la dolce vita*[8]."

Matt pulled out a chair for her, and she knew he picked that spot for her so he could sit facing the door. She'd learned that his professional training put him on edge if he couldn't properly surveil a room. This reflex of his made her feel exceedingly safe.

Gianluca poured the wine, and she smiled. "*Grazie mille*[9]. I think we're going to get along famously."

Wine glasses were filled, and pleasantries were exchanged about their respective flights into Rome and whether they'd had any trouble finding the restaurant or parking. Matt assured them it had all been smooth sailing as Austen read the menu and tried to recall her very basic restaurant Italian vocabulary. *Vino rosso*[10], the one phrase she never forgot, was already ordered, and her stomach was rumbling.

Soon, the get-to-know-each-other games began.

"Matt told me about how you met three times in three countries before you got together. What a remarkable story," Ophelia said.

"Yes, it seems fate had plans for us." Austen replied, brushing Matt's arm. "How did you two meet?" she asked, gesturing between Ophelia and Gianluca.

"I almost ran her over with my Vespa," Gianluca smirked, smoothing his beard with one hand.

Ophelia confirmed with a nod. "I was on a girls' holiday in Rome for the weekend when I was twenty-five, and he nearly ran me down

---

8 The sweet life

9 Thanks very much

10 Red wine

just outside of Piazza Navona. I like to say that he swept me off my feet, although technically, the Vespa did that. It was the definition of a meet-cute from some American-made romcom set in Italy."

Gianluca placed his hand on the back of Ophelia's neck and picked up where she left off. "I was thirty-three, with much less gray in my hair, and already working in the emergency room at Policlinico, which is Rome's biggest public hospital where I still work today. Luckily, the encounter was a near-miss, and no ER visit was required. I was able to treat on-site."

The couple's easy rhythm told Austen they had shared the story countless times, and she felt the love between them in its retelling.

"His bedside manner—curbside manner in this case—was excellent. I was hooked immediately. That was fifteen years ago. Then we dated long distance between here and London for three years before we got married, and I moved over," Ophelia shared, leaning into her husband.

"You never lived in the same city before you got married?" Austen asked, surprised.

Ophelia's eyes bugged out as if even she still couldn't believe it. "Huge risk. I know. But I was young, stupid. Okay, well, I suppose I wasn't that stupid because here we are fifteen years later with two kids and still going strong. I guess I just knew."

"The heart wants what the heart wants," Gianluca nodded casually.

Matt smiled, looking at Austen with affection. "Sometimes you just know."

Austen smiled back at him, feeling her pulse quicken. Matt's looks, so full of meaning, always sent her heart racing, but she still couldn't tell if it was the result of anxiety or love. She pushed down her fears, determined to be fully present and get to know his friends.

"Speaking of things you just know," Ophelia interjected, "we're organizing a villa in Ibiza for my fortieth birthday for Ascension weekend in May, and I just know that I want you two to come. Say you will."

Austen glanced at Matt to gauge his reaction. He was smiling brightly at Ophelia.

"I have to check with Omar, but assuming I can clear it with him, I'd love to come," he replied before turning to Austen. "What do you say?"

He hadn't hesitated. Yet for her, the fears she'd pushed down moments earlier popped violently back to the surface, forcing her into a game of mental whack-a-mole. "I love Ibiza. Sounds amazing," she replied with imposed calm.

Ophelia jumped in quickly. "Yes, I really hope you two will join. It's going to be marvelous. I've invited two other couples. The first is Luis and Jack who live in New York. We met them years ago in Ibiza through some other friends we've since lost touch with."

"We've never been to Ibiza without them, oddly," Gianluca added, turning to Austen. "And they're both American, so you'll have some of your fellow countrymen there."

"And the other couple is Kristin and Charlie, who live in London. She's also one of your lot—an American in her early thirties, I think. Insanely fit—I'd kill for her body," Ophelia groaned, rolling her eyes, but not unkindly.

Gianluca scratched his beard and turned to Ophelia. "Did they confirm?"

She nodded quickly at him and continued. "Charlie's British, a banker of some sort. They've been together for maybe five years? But not married. Kristin and I became friends while working together over the last three years. Did Matt tell you I work in event marketing for Eni?"

"The energy company, yes. I was well briefed on you two as well," Austen confirmed.

Ophelia sucked in a breath. "Renewables, yes. Very hot area—no energy-slash-heat pun intended. I manage all customer events, and Kristin leads my marketing agency team in London, so she comes to Rome for most of our events. She's a delight."

"And you've met her guy?" Matt asked.

"I've met him twice when I've been back in London. He's got a young, floppy Hugh Grant vibe, but blond. He's from some impossibly posh family, although he's very down to earth. Gianluca hasn't met him yet."

"Sounds like a fun crew," Matt chimed in. "I've never been to Ibiza, but I've certainly heard stories."

Ophelia grabbed Matt's arm, looking shocked. "How is it possible that you've never been to Ibiza, Richie?"

"Well, Fie," he said, emphasizing the nickname, "I've spent the better part of the last few years bouncing around Africa. Strangely, none of my corporate security clients seemed to need me in Ibiza."

"Richie and Fie?" Austen asked, with a playful smile, looking back and forth between them.

"We Brits adore a nickname. Richie for Richmond. Everyone called him that at uni," Ophelia explained.

Matt shook his head. "Absolutely no one called me that at uni except for her. So, she had to have a nickname too, and she preferred 'Fie' over 'Mad Dog.'"

"Mad Dog?" Austen tilted her head to the side.

"My last name is Maddox," Ophelia explained.

"Ah, well, yes, I think Fie was definitely the better choice," Austen laughed.

"Indeed," Gianluca muttered. "Anyway, we're going a bit early in the season—and most of us are old—so it won't be the crazy club scene that probably comes to mind when you think of Ibiza. More like tapas, cava sangria and lizarding in the sun."

"And a whole lot of SPF 50 to protect my pale English skin. Because we really know how to party," Ophelia cracked.

"Sounds like heaven. I could do with some heat after this crazy, long winter," Austen said. "My legs are practically translucent—like Nicole Kidman pale."

A waitress appeared with their appetizers, and Matt took advantage of the distraction to lean over to whisper in Austen's ear, "I can't wait to get those legs of yours wrapped around me in our hotel room later, Nicole. I have some rather detailed ideas about generating heat."

The comment alone lit all her nerve endings on fire. She subtly slid her hand up his thigh under the table, whispering back, "You always have the best ideas. Can we go now?"

Matt smiled, giving her his best bedroom eyes before returning to the conversation with Ophelia and Gianluca.

"Tomorrow, Austen and I are going to play tourist for a bit, but can we come by the flat at some point so I can see the kids?" Matt asked.

"Yes, you must. Esme was furious that we got to see you tonight while she was stuck at home with the nanny. She can't wait to see you. Marco, too."

"I'm working tomorrow, so I'm afraid I'll miss you," Gianluca said.

"No problem," Matt replied. "Someone's gotta save lives and all that."

Gianluca gave a lopsided smile. "Might as well be me."

Ophelia looked at her husband with pride and then returned her attention to Matt. "In the afternoon, we'll be either at home or at Villa Borghese, which is nearby. Just let me know, and I'll do my best to ensure the monkeys are at least moderately presentable."

Ophelia's mention of monkeys made Austen think of the three wise, Japanese monkeys—speak no evil, hear no evil, see no evil—a symbol of living a virtuous life. She couldn't help but think of all the decidedly less virtuous things she and Matt would likely get up to later that night, once they were alone.

CHAPTER 5

Gianluca, Rome

Gianluca groaned quietly when his alarm went off at six o'clock the next morning. He was due in the ER by seven, so he needed to hustle. A hot shower and a double espresso were his only thoughts as he dragged himself into the bathroom. But once the hot water blasted him back to his senses, his thoughts turned to Kristin, and his blood began to boil.

What the fuck is she thinking coming to Ibiza? he wondered. *Blond temptation in a goddamn string bikini, walking around all weekend while I'm hosting Ophelia's birthday. Christ. I'm going to wring her fucking neck.*

The image of Kristin in a bikini with his hands around her throat got him hard, and he decided the quickest way to empty his head—both heads—was to jerk off in the shower. *This woman is going to be the end of me,* he thought as he turned off the water.

Toweling off, he tried to think practically. It was Saturday, so he wouldn't text her. They had a rule to never text on weekends when they were more likely to be with their partners. But this situation warranted an exception. He had to talk her out of this impending disaster—and fast. As penance for his sins with Kristin, he wanted Ophelia's birthday weekend to be perfect.

When he went downstairs, Ophelia handed him a steaming double espresso. He kissed her on the forehead, threw it back in two scorching gulps, shrugged on his jacket as her tea kettle started to whistle, and made for the door as she turned her back to grab a mug. He couldn't force small talk this morning. The combination of guilt and stress over the upcoming birthday weekend was too much.

"Ciao, see you tonight," he called over his shoulder, shutting the door as quickly as he could.

When he got to the hospital, he slid on his white coat and sat down at his desk, opening his email. He grimaced and tugged at his shirt collar, feeling like his tie was a noose. He quickly fired a message off to Kristin, having decided on the commute that an email was a safer bet for a Saturday than a text. The subject line was simply "Ibiza," and the body consisted of two short sentences: "Ophelia told me you and Charlie confirmed. Can you call me today before 17h to discuss plans?"

He wanted to write, "What the actual fuck are you thinking? That we're all going to become some happy quad?" But he knew better than to incriminate himself in writing. Charlie could see the email. It needed to be neutral while still conveying urgency.

He'd juggled his relationships with both women for just over a year now, carefully catching one as he gently released the other, back and forth. It was a balancing act that required dexterity, intelligence, and extreme emotional compartmentalization—all of which he was adept in as the head of an emergency room. His wife and mistress each filled a different need, both of which felt crucial to his happiness. He was a good juggler, but everyone had their limits, and he wasn't about to have this birthday weekend endanger his precious balls. *I'd like to keep both of my balls exactly as they are. Thank you very much.*

At two in the afternoon, his phone buzzed. "K" lit up the screen. It was a slow afternoon in the ER, so he quickly walked to an empty on-call room and locked the door.

"Kristin, what the fuck are you trying to do?" he growled.

"I miss you too, Gianluca," she cooed.

"I'm not in the mood for games."

She sighed. "She called and asked what Charlie and I were doing for Ascension weekend. I had no idea what Ascension even was since it's not a holiday in the UK, so I told her we weren't doing anything and that we desperately needed a holiday, which we do. Then she told me about Ibiza. I got caught. I didn't know how to get out of it after that."

"And you didn't think to tell me about this fucking debacle? I had to hear about it from her over dinner last night," he hissed, banging his head lightly against the door. *I'm always wiggling out of situations I don't want to be in. Why can't you?*

"Yes, I should've told you. I'm sorry. I can't believe she even wants me there in the first place. You know how guilty I feel when she's nice to me. I try really hard not to be friendly with her, but she's constantly mistaking my professionalism for friendship. I was trying to find a way to fix it," she whined back.

Ophelia didn't have many close friends. Inviting Kristin to the birthday weekend proved that Ophelia considered her more than just a colleague. It made Gianluca feel even more guilty about the affair. He hated that both he and Kristin were deceiving her so mightily.

"There has to be. Ophelia likes you because you're smart and agreeable, but Jesus, I need you to be significantly less agreeable here—and significantly smarter. This cannot happen," Gianluca insisted. "Blame Charlie. Say he can't get the time off or that he made other plans without telling you, so you have to back out."

Kristin hesitated. "I kind of already told Charlie about it, and he's excited to go."

Gianluca yanked his stethoscope from around his neck, tossing it onto the nearby bunk bed. "Do you want to get caught?"

"I don't know what I want," Kristin snapped back. "I love you, Gianluca. I love Charlie, too. And if I could, I'd really like Ophelia too but loving you has made that impossible."

Gianluca pounded his fist on a wall, then slumped against it, breathing heavily. Every time she told him she loved him, he felt the endorphins and oxytocin course through his veins, pushing him deeper into this mess. He craved her loud, insistent version of love, but it threatened the fragile balance of his life.

"A villa weekend in Ibiza for my wife's fortieth birthday is not the time or the place to figure your shit out, *amore mio*[11]."

"It's our shit, love. You're in this too," she pointed out.

"Don't I know it," he sighed. "Listen, the trip is two months away. We'll figure out an excuse to get you out of it. You're not coming. It's not an option."

"Of course. It would be totally uncomfortable for us both. We'll figure it out," Kristin agreed. "In the meantime, I found out yesterday that I'll be in Rome the second week of April for meetings with Eni. I'll text you the dates."

"Okay." Gianluca pushed the threat of the Ibiza weekend into the back of his mind in favor of the more immediate opportunity to be with her, on his terms. "Good. I miss your mouth."

"I miss you too and not just your mouth. I can't stop thinking about last time. I had to wear a turtleneck for a week to hide your fingerprints," she snickered. "You know I bruise like a peach."

Gianluca's mind drifted back to their last night together, when she'd practically begged him to choke her during sex. If he hadn't recently treated a patient in the ER after a "fun" night gone wrong,

---

11 My love

he wouldn't have even known that was a thing. Kristin, sixteen years his junior, always pushed him to interesting places in bed. Choking her had gone against every instinct he had as a doctor, but he'd done it anyway. When they were in bed together, he was putty in her hands. He did anything she asked. She got off on it, so he had too.

"I may have had an imaginary go at your throat again in the shower this morning," Gianluca admitted, feeling the heat rise in his body again. "It started as punishment, but even in my imagination, you have a way of making everything sexy as fuck. I'm getting hard again just thinking about it."

"That's right, Doctor D'Angelo. And don't you fucking forget it. I'll be thinking about your rock hard—Shit." Her voice dropped. "I've gotta go. Charlie and Miles just got home. I love you."

Gianluca pocketed his phone with a frustrated sigh, his groin still tight with arousal. He considered jerking off again, there in the on-call room, but was interrupted by the sudden buzzing of his pager. Duty called.

CHAPTER 6

Matt, Rome

Sunlight streamed into the hotel room through a gap between the curtains, bathing Austen's side of the bed in warm light.

"*Buongiorno.* Can I order breakfast, *per favore*[12]?" Matt said into the phone, leaning shirtless against the padded headboard.

Austen smiled up at him, her red hair fanned out across the crisp white hotel pillows—a tangled mess from their pre-breakfast activities.

"One cappuccino, one espresso, the fresh pastry basket, and a fruit plate. Yes, that's it. Room 209. *Grazie mille.*"

He hung up and slid back under the sheets, remembering another hotel they'd stayed at together—but not together—years earlier. "You probably don't remember, but there's an interesting coincidence here. Your room number at that hotel in Senegal was also 209."

Austen's eyes widened. "How on earth do you remember the room number?"

"I spent several excruciating minutes staring at that door, trying to decide whether to knock. I'll never forget that room number. It's burned into my brain," he revealed. "I came so close to knocking."

Matt had felt an undeniable pull toward Austen since that first day in Senegal, and the first few months of their relationship had lived up to all his fantasies. He was in the bliss of new-relationship-having-loads-of-sex mode. They hadn't even been awake for an hour, and he was almost ready for round two.

"And here we are, same room number in a different country," she grinned, walking her red-manicured fingers down his bare, muscular torso.

Propping himself up on a forearm, he slowly peeled the sheet away from her body and let his eyes and his fingertips roam her skin. "Thirty minutes until room service. Plenty of time to play out the fantasy of what would've happened if I'd knocked that night."

Austen hooked a leg around him, pulling him hungrily to her. "Show me," she whispered into his mouth.

It was nearly eleven by the time they stepped out of Albergo Lunetta into the spring day. The sky was cobalt blue—Matt couldn't recall ever seeing a gray day in Rome. The dome of one of the city's many churches peeked through the rooftops, filling Matt with a sense of reverence—though more for Austen than anything holy. He hung back a step to admire her in her short, flowy, white dress. Her shoes, while not practical, were decidedly on point.

"Those are some sexy gladiator sandals you've got there."

"Thank you for noticing. When in Rome, right?" she teased, pointing her toe for effect.

"You are, hands down, the sexiest gladiator I've ever seen," he confirmed, opening her car door. Once she was inside, he reached in and buckled her seatbelt before stealing another kiss. She tasted like mint toothpaste and smelled like lemons and ginger. Her scent enveloped him as hungrily as she did, and he breathed her in deeply.

As he walked around to the driver's side, he glanced at the street sign, Piazza del Paradiso, and grinned to himself. In this little slice of paradise, he almost forgot to scan his surroundings for threats.

"Where are we headed?" she asked as he climbed in.

"The Trevi Fountain. Important order of business on every trip to Rome, to toss in a coin and make a wish to ensure your return. I've never been to Rome without doing it, so the legend appears to be working for me. We're not going to break the streak today," he said, putting on his Ray-Bans and easing the car into drive.

He'd Googled the fountain's legend beforehand to impress Austen. He learned a second coin in the fountain was said to bring love, while a third guaranteed a marriage—or divorce, depending on your relationship status. It was meant to represent hope for a significant change in your love life. He and Austen had a thing with threes.

"Then lunch at a place Ophelia recommended nearby, and we'll meet her and the kids at Villa Borghese around three-thirty. Sound good?"

Austen laced her fingers into his and relaxed into her seat. "Sounds perfect."

"You're perfect," he replied, squeezing her hand.

"No one is perfect."

Her reply was hasty, defensive. He still hadn't gotten past her protective wall. *I wish your heart had never been broken,* he thought. But then she drew his hand to her lips and kissed it.

"But I sure am glad I've got you fooled," she whispered into his knuckles.

He kept his eyes on the road. The smile in her voice was audible, and that was enough.

When they arrived at the fountain, it was as crowded as ever. The sun reflected off the limestone walls of the Palazzo Poli and the aquamarine water of the fountain, making for a postcard-perfect scene. The beauty of it drew tourists in droves, which set off all his professional, protective instincts. Matt took Austen's hand and led her through the crowd, scanning for exit routes and potential threats. He glanced over his shoulder at her and saw only contentment on her face.

At the fountain's edge, he handed her a euro coin and kept two in his own palm. They both turned their backs to the water, smiled at each other and tossed their coins over their shoulders.

"I'm totally the girl who would miss. Did mine make it in?" she asked, searching the ground.

"Toss another in, just to be sure," Matt said, handing her another coin. *Maybe you'll find love in Rome,* he thought. *With me,* he thought more specifically, to avoid any confusion in this wishing business.

She tossed the coin dramatically over her shoulder.

"That one definitely made it in. I watched it," he assured her, leaning in for a kiss.

"Good. I'd hate for this to be my last trip to Rome. Smile," she instructed, lifting her phone high to get a good angle for a selfie. "We must immortalize our first weekend away together."

Matt wrapped one arm around her waist and kissed her cheek for the photo. *May it be the first of many,* he thought. As she clicked, he casually flung a third coin behind them, straight into the water.

After some sinfully delicious pizza and bottle of velvety *Valpolicella*, they made their way to Villa Borghese and found Ophelia sitting cross-legged on a bench on the side of the playground, watching her kids buzz around.

Esme spotted them first. "Uncle Matt," she squealed, running toward him with her brown curls bouncing.

Matt waved at Ophelia with one hand as he hugged Esme with the other. He knelt keeping one hand on her back and turned to Austen.

"Princess Esme, may I introduce you to my girlfriend, Austen."

"Hello, Austen," Esme said shyly.

"Hi there, Princess Esme." Austen replied, curtsying. "I've never met a princess before."

Esme was charmed. She smiled at Matt and then back at Austen.

"I like your red hair."

"Well, thank you very much. I like your curls. They're awesome."

"Hiya Fie," Matt stood and kissed Ophelia on the cheek. As she and Austen greeted each other, he turned to scan the playground, looking for Marco. He spotted him happily swinging on the monkey bars, oblivious to the fact that his sneakered foot was about to smack another kid in the head. Clack.

The other kid, who looked a few years older, grabbed Marco's ankles, yanking him down. Matt saw it happen in slow motion—the dust cloud rising around Marco as he hit the ground with a thud, landing on his back and elbows. Matt was already in motion, headed that way as the kid started pounding on Marco. He closed the distance between them in seconds and firmly but gently pried the kid off Marco, pinning his arms to his sides as the lanky boy continued to try to swing.

Seconds later, the kid's mom appeared, snatching her son from Matt's arms.

Matt turned to Marco, who was groaning on the ground. "Hey little man. You all right? Anything hurt?"

"Hi Matt," Marco said weakly, rolling onto his side with a small groan. "I'm okay."

Ophelia flopped down beside him, frantically pushing Marco's brown hair from his lightly freckled face, checking for injuries.

Matt spotted a few scrapes, likely from the fall, but nothing serious. As he scanned the scene, his eyes landed on Esme, wide-eyed and clutching Austen's legs. He walked over and scooped her into his arms, resting her on his hip. "You okay, kiddo?"

She nodded hesitantly and gripped his shirt collar tightly as he carried her back over toward Marco and Ophelia, so she could see everyone was fine.

"Who knew Italian playgrounds were like Thunderdome?" Matt joked to Ophelia. "I didn't think I'd be on duty this weekend."

Ophelia sighed, brushing dirt off Marco's clothes. "He's bleeding. I need to take him home and get him cleaned up so it doesn't get infected. We're just across the street, and Gianluca has every medical thing imaginable stashed in the bathroom cabinets."

"I don't want to go," Esme whined, still perched in Matt's arms.

"It'll just take a minute, monkey, and then we can all come back," Ophelia offered.

"But I don't wanna," she insisted.

Matt patted her back. "Go. Better safe than sorry. We can stay here with Esme while you get Marco sorted. It's not a problem."

Ophelia exhaled and her shoulders dropped several inches. "You don't mind?"

"Not at all."

"I can come help you with Marco, if you want," Austen offered, turning to Ophelia. "Looks like Esme will be in good hands here."

"That's lovely, cheers," Ophelia replied warmly.

Matt watched the exchange, recognizing Austen's effort to connect with Ophelia, and gave her a grateful wink. The smile she returned was one he hadn't seen before—reserved but somehow lighting up her entire face. *She's never seen me with a kid in my arms. That's probably it*, he thought. *Although she's never mentioned wanting kids, so who knows. Who cares. I love this woman.*

"Matt, sure you're okay alone with her for a bit?" Ophelia asked again, snapping him out of his thoughts.

"We'll be fine. Go ahead," he assured her, gently setting Esme down on the ground but keeping one hand on top of her head. "I can handle my goddaughter."

Ophelia mouthed "thank you" at him and wrapped an arm around Marco's narrow shoulders, leading him away.

Austen gave a small wave to Esme, blew Matt a kiss, and followed Ophelia toward the flat.

Matt moved toward the nearest bench, guiding Esme with the hand on her head. "Come here, sweet girl. Tell me how you've been. What's interesting in your world?"

Esme's eyes went wide as she settled in next to him. "My friend Serena got a puppy. It's white and so cute. I asked Mummy and Papà if we could get one, but they said no."

His heart squeezed for her. She looked so dejected, her gaze falling to her lap.

"Well, puppies are a lot of responsibility. You've got to give them so much love," Matt consoled. "Maybe when you're a bit older, they'll reconsider."

"I think I could be really good at loving a puppy," she insisted, still looking down.

Matt reached out and rubbed small circles on her back. "I'm sure you'd be amazing at it. I bet if we put you in a room full of puppies, every single one of them would want to be loved by you."

She looked up hopefully at him, her brown curls falling away from her face. He watched as a small smile spread across her lips, her mind probably imagining that puppy-filled room. Her innocence warmed him. But then very quickly, her smile faded.

"Can I tell you a secret, Uncle Matt?"

"You can tell me anything."

Esme scooted closer to him on the bench, looking concerned. "I think maybe Mummy doesn't want a puppy because she doesn't like to love."

Matt was officially out of his godfather depth. *An imminent threat to physical safety I can handle. Existential questions about love from an eight-year-old, not so much.* He tilted his head, studying her carefully. "What makes you say that, Esme?"

She whispered, "Mummy never says she loves me, or Marco, or Papà... or even her favorite flowers. Papà says it all the time, but Mummy never does."

Matt's mind raced. *Is that true? Have Ophelia and I ever said "I love you" platonically in all these years of friendship? We must've said it when we were together, back in the day.* He couldn't recall, but that didn't seem strange. It had been twenty years since they were romantic. *Do friends even say "I love you" to one another?*

"Sweetheart, your mom loves you, and Marco, and your dad so much," Matt assured her.

Esme pointed to her head. "I've been thinking maybe how much you can love is tied to your hair color."

"Hair color?" he asked, trying to keep his expression serious so as not to discourage her. "How might that work?"

She pulled at her curls. "You see, my hair is light brown, and yours is darker brown like Marco's, and I think we're all pretty good at love. Papà and our *Nonni's*[13] hair is gray, and they love super good. Serena's is blonde, and her puppy's is white, and the puppy is the lovie-est of them all. So, maybe the lighter your hair, the better you are at love."

Matt saw where she was headed. "So, you think that because your mom's hair is black, she doesn't like love?"

"Maybe. Maybe her black hair means her heart is darker, so it's harder for her to love us."

Matt gently tugged her curls. "That's an interesting idea, and I can see you've clearly thought a lot about it. You're so smart, but I think your theory might be a little flawed."

"What does 'flawed' mean?" she asked.

"It means that it might not be right. I know for an absolute fact that your mom loves you so much. She's told me a million times,"

---

13 Grandparents

he said, the white lie sliding easily from his lips to calm Esme's innocent heart.

Of course, Ophelia loved her kids and Gianluca—it was obvious to him. But the more he thought about it, the more he wondered if Esme was right—perhaps Ophelia never used the word "love."

CHAPTER 7

Ophelia, Rome

Marco looked over his shoulder skeptically at Austen, lips pursed. "So, you're Uncle Matt's new girlfriend? What happened to Aunt Eve? She was nice."

Austen glanced between him and Ophelia, visibly stunned by the question.

Ophelia stepped in quickly, trying to smooth over the awkwardness. "Monkey, I told you. Uncle Matt and Aunt Eve broke up a while ago. Sometimes adults decide that they're not meant for one another, even if they're both really nice people, which of course Eve was. But now Matt's met Austen, who gets to be our new friend. Isn't that great?"

Marco gave her a cautious side eye as they continued up the stairs into the flat. "I guess so."

"What did you like about Eve?" Austen asked him, seemingly intrigued.

Cheeky, Ophelia thought, surprised by the boldness of the question. *Pumping a ten-year-old for information on the ex.*

"She always had candy," Marco replied earnestly.

Austen nodded, and Ophelia caught the hint of amusement in her eyes despite her attempt at seriousness. "Hard to argue with that. What's not to like about a lady who always has candy?"

Marco smiled, seemingly satisfied with her answer. Then, as if sensing the need to shift focus, Austen turned to Ophelia. "How can I help?"

"Let's all go upstairs to our bathroom. Gianluca's got a medical kit stashed up there."

As they made their way toward the stairs, Ophelia felt a wave of self-consciousness. She hadn't planned for guests, and the house was messier than she would've liked, but there was nothing to do about it now. *What must Austen think of this chaos?* she wondered, glancing at the colorful clutter of children's toys, books and knick-knacks strewn around their living space.

"Your flat is gorgeous," Austen said as if reading her mind, her voice warm. "I love all the art. So much color and life everywhere."

Ophelia shook her head, brushing off the compliment. "You're very sweet. But it looks like a storm blew through here. Tidy has never been my strong suit, and it's only gotten worse with two kids running rampant."

"It's lovely," Austen insisted. "And such a great location, so close to the park."

Ophelia smiled. "Marco was a year old, and we were already expecting Esme when we bought it. I grew up in Bedford, about an hour north of London. It's full of parks and green spaces, and I just breathe easier with my toes in the grass. The proximity to the park was what made me fall in love with the flat."

In the master bathroom, she hoisted Marco onto the counter. "My goodness, you're getting big. I can barely lift you anymore," she exaggerated with a grin. She pulled the medical kit from under the sink, turned on the faucet, and unzipped the case. "Austen, will you please grab a washcloth from that cabinet?"

Austen handed over the cloth, and Ophelia quickly cleaned and disinfected the small scrapes on Marco's elbows and forearms.

"Do we need plasters?" she asked Marco while rinsing out the soapy washcloth.

He inspected his arms, turning them over before nodding solemnly.

Austen sifted through the medical kit and pulled out a few plasters. "Looks like we've got spaceships, pirates—oh, and Anna and Elsa from *Frozen*?"

"Pirates," Marco confirmed without hesitation. "The *Frozen* ones are Esme's."

Ophelia took the pirate plasters from Austen's outstretched hand and applied them to Marco's scrapes. "Fancy a cuppa before we head back to the park?" she asked, tossing the plaster wrappings into the bin.

"I'd love that," Austen replied.

"Righto. I think you'll live, monkey," Ophelia said, kissing his head before lifting him off the counter. "Go play in your room for a bit, okay?"

"Thanks, Mum," he mumbled before darting off.

"Let's head to the kitchen," she added, leading the way downstairs. She was grateful for the chance to be alone with Austen for a moment. It was sweet of her to leave Matt behind and offer to help. *I like her. She's got a good heart,* Ophelia thought as she set the kettle to boil while Austen perched on a bar stool.

"So, how's the weekend been with Matt? Your first one away together, right?"

She knew the answer but wanted to ease into conversation naturally.

"It's been great," Austen replied, tucking her hair behind her ears. "It's nice to get out of town with someone. You see them in a different light when you're both out of your usual routine."

Pouring loose jasmine tea into an infuser, Ophelia's mind wandered back to the one mini-break she and Matt had taken to

Brighton when they'd dated. *It feels like ten lifetimes ago,* she mused, seeing his younger face flash before her eyes—so carefree as they explored the pier, laughing and eating fish and chips out of newspaper.

Becoming a mum had made her much more regimented, out of necessity. Kids need a schedule. She'd watched life harden Matt too, in ways that made her wonder about the things he'd seen in his military days. Eve had never seemed to soften him. *He seems different with Austen—better matched*, she thought.

"So, what have you learned about him this weekend?" Ophelia asked, genuinely curious.

Austen paused, contemplating her answer. "It's hard to say. We've only been dating a few months, so we're still getting to know each other. He seems happy here."

Ophelia studied her. "Does he not seem happy in Paris?" she asked, brow furrowing as concern crept into her voice.

"No, he does," Austen assured her. "Maybe he's just more relaxed around you and Gianluca. He doesn't have many friends in Paris besides me, I guess. It's nice to see him around people who've known him so long."

Ophelia poured the tea, steam curling from the mismatched mugs. "Old friends make your heart feel like it's home. As do new loves. He seems very at home with you," she observed.

"Do you think so?" Austen asked, her tone open.

"I do—more so than when he was with Eve," Ophelia said, lowering her voice with a wink. "You asked Marco about her earlier. Between us girls, I'm happy to tell you anything you want to know about her."

Austen shook her head, blowing on her tea. "I didn't mean to pry. I'm just not great at talking to kids. Marco brought her up, and I ran with it."

Ophelia patted her arm. "I wasn't judging. It's natural to be curious about an ex. I liked Eve and she did always carry candy, which was quite odd for a grown woman, truth be told. But seeing Matt with you… it reminds me of the old Matt. He seems lighter, quicker to smile. I like that for him. For you both."

A broad smile spread across Austen's face. "Thanks for saying that. I like it for us too. He's a good man."

"One of the best," Ophelia agreed. "I'm genuinely pleased you two found each other—and three times, no less. Good things come in threes. I always wanted a third kid, but Gianluca was dead set on two, so I let it go. Do you have siblings?"

"Only child," Austen said.

"Me too. I always thought it would be fun to have a big family. What about you? Haven't wanted or haven't gotten around to having kids?"

"Both," Austen said, haltingly. "Definitely didn't want any with my ex-husband. I've always wondered if I'd feel differently if the right person came along, but I'm forty-two now, so I think that ship has sailed."

"Matt would be a great dad, I think. And women have babies in their forties all the time now," Ophelia exclaimed.

Austen choked a little on her tea, her face flushing as she quickly gulped it down. "Look at the time. We should probably get back to Matt and Esme."

Ophelia blinked, startled. "Christ, you're right. I got carried away talking and totally forgot we left them in the park." She scrambled to gather her things. "Marco," she shouted up the stairs, "Did you hide my phone again?"

CHAPTER 8

Austen, Rome

Bright yellow mimosa bloomed in gardens all over the city, releasing a sweet, powdery fragrance into the air. Austen had first noticed the scent earlier that day when she'd been walking back to the park with Ophelia, and it lingered as she and Matt wandered the curving, ancient streets of Rome hand-in-hand on their way to dinner.

"Ophelia and I had a nice chat earlier. She's very sweet," Austen said.

Matt squeezed her hand. "She is. You're both super important to me, so it means a lot that you get along."

Austen listened to the sound of their shoes clicking against the cobblestones, replaying some of the earlier conversation in her mind. "She told me she thinks you seem 'lighter' with me than she remembers you being with Eve. I found it interesting, because adulting so often makes life heavier."

"What do you mean by heavier?" Matt asked, wrapping a protective arm around her shoulders.

"Well, for example in college, I backpacked through Europe for a summer—including a stop here in Rome—with my then-boyfriend David," she started.

"I hate him," he grimaced.

"It's cute that you're jealous of someone I was with twenty-plus years before we ever met." Austen draped her arm around his waist and leaned in to kiss his neck, just below his chiseled jawline. "Anyway, we were perpetually lost and having the craziest adventures, never knowing who we might meet or where the day would take us. It was just light, easy. I don't think I've ever lived that spontaneously, before or since."

"Spontaneity is my personal, professional nightmare," Matt declared. "And I can see how that could come across as 'heavy.' If I haven't scouted the place in advance I never feel at ease. Although, I'll agree with Ophelia that traveling with you is somehow easier on my psyche than it was with Eve. I worry about you less."

"It's not like we're in Mogadishu," Austen teased. "We're in Rome. What's the worst that could happen?"

Matt stopped dead in his tracks and pulled her toward him, wrapping his arms around her waist. His jaw clenched. "Don't ask that question. No matter where we are. I've seen too much. My brain in worst-case-planning mode is a dark place."

"Okay, I won't. I'm sorry." She cupped his face in her hands, pressing a tender kiss to his lips. When she saw the tension ease in his eyes, she took his hand again, continuing their walk. "I think I got my first glimpse of you in action mode today. You were there one second, crouched down with Esme, and the next thing I knew, you were pulling some kid off Marco ten feet away. You were like Edward from *Twilight*—in one place one second and another the next."

Matt looked at her quizzically. "Edward who?"

"Never mind," she laughed. "You were very commanding and in control. It was kinda sexy."

Rolling his eyes playfully, he said, "If you think watching me break up a playground brawl between a couple of scrawny kids is sexy, you should see me in a real fight."

As they crossed the bridge over the Tiber toward Trastevere, Austen noticed two priests walking in the opposite direction approaching to Matt's left, and she subtly nodded her head toward them, urging him to look.

His grip on her hand tightened instinctively as he quickly surveilled the crowd. "What's the matter?" he asked, voice on alert.

Austen giggled. "Nothing, I just didn't want you talking about sexy things and street fights in front of the priests. God forbid. Literally. Rome must have the highest priest per capita ratio in the world. There's practically one on every street corner."

Matt looked back over his shoulder at the retreating priests and chuckled as he rubbed his fingertips across his forehead, smoothing away his worry lines. "If I weren't an atheist, I'd thank you for protecting my immortal soul. Good looking out."

"My pleasure. But back to the subject, I don't think I'd enjoy seeing you in a real fight. Have you been in many?"

"Corporate security work is surprisingly low on fistfights, you'll be glad to know," he replied, wrapping an arm back around her. He pressed a kiss on her temple. "My specialty is preventing or diffusing conflict, not getting into it. Don't you know by now that I'm a lover, not a fighter?"

"And a particularly skilled one at that," she winked.

They soon arrived at their dinner spot—a gorgeous restaurant called Pianostrada on Via della Luce. The warm glow of vintage chandeliers bathed the space in light, and an open kitchen sat at the center, lined with brown leather bar stools. Mirrors and fairy lights added a touch of magic to the room, with fresh flowers scattered throughout.

A host with a handlebar mustache led them to two stools at the bar, giving them a perfect view of the busy yet spotless kitchen. Austen leaned in, whispering to Matt, "That guy was straight out of central casting. What a 'stache."

"Fan of the mustache?" Matt asked, stroking his own clean-shaven upper lip. "I could grow one."

Austen swatted his hand playfully. "Don't you dare. Mustaches make everyone look like a child molester. Handlebar guy might be an exception because he's an Italian restaurateur, but no one else can pull it off."

"That's a pretty strong opinion you've got there," he teased, opening the wine menu.

She shrugged with a coy smile. "Don't you know by now that I'm a woman with strong opinions?"

"Oh, I've noticed. It's one of the many things I love about you."

He loves many things about me, she repeated to herself. Her insides felt warm and gooey, and she felt like cartoon hearts had just replaced her eyeballs. *I love many things about him too.*

"Speaking of love—" he began, but the sudden ding of a bell from the kitchen line interrupted him.

Her breath caught and her eyes widened, cartoon hearts dropping into the abyss. The heat from the kitchen suddenly felt oppressive. *What is he about to say?*

Sensing her reaction, Matt raised his hands, palms facing her. "Woah, don't panic. It's about Esme and Ophelia."

"I wasn't panicked," she lied.

Their waiter arrived, and while Matt ordered a bottle of *Montepulciano* and focaccia with burrata, prosciutto and basil, Austen ran her fingers over her clammy palms. Reaching for her napkin, she wiped her hands down her thighs as she placed it in her lap. *I totally panicked. Must chill.*

Matt, thankfully, ignored her obvious lie and continued. "Okay. So, while you and Ophelia got Marco cleaned up, Esme said something strange to me."

"What?" she asked, pushing her hair back over her shoulders and trying desperately to play it cool.

"She said she wasn't sure if Ophelia—" he made air quotes, "'liked to love.' She told me Ophelia never says the word 'love,' so she's worried her mom doesn't love her or anyone or anything at all."

Austen felt stricken, her stomach clenching. "That's so sad. She doesn't think her mom loves her?"

"Her little face was so concerned. My heart broke for her. But I told her that, of course, her mom loves her very much. I just hope she believed me."

Austen's heart swelled at the image of Matt comforting Esme. She wrapped her hand around the back of his neck, tracing her fingers through his hair. "I'm sure you did. You seem to have a way with kids." *Ophelia is right—Matt would be a great dad,* she thought, despite herself.

"It really got me thinking. Esme may be right. I remember Ophelia telling me her dad never said he loved her when she was a kid."

"What about her mom?" Austen asked.

Matt rubbed his temple as if trying to pull out the memory. "Ophelia's mom was killed in a car accident only a few months after she was born. Her dad raised her alone. She said he never dated again."

Austen's hands flew to her mouth. "Oh God. She mentioned she was an only child, but I had no idea. That's tragic. Did she ever say 'I love you' to you when you were together?"

Matt shook his head. "I've been trying to remember that too, and I'm not sure. It was so long ago. I know we were each other's first love, but I don't have any memory of either of us ever saying the words. I was probably too immature to say it, even if I felt it."

Why am I doing this to myself? Austen thought, unable to stop her next question. "How many women have you been in love with?"

Matt smiled and looked sideways down the bar, clearly contemplating his answer. He was silent for a while before looking back straight at her with his gorgeous light blue eyes and responding, "Three—Ophelia, Eve, and you."

Austen stared back at him, feeling her face drop. She'd not been expecting that.

The waiter returned with their wine, and they remained in awkward silence while he poured each of them a glass. Austen could feel the blood pounding in her ears, her thoughts racing.

Once the waiter left, Matt took a deep breath. "Given your low-grade panic a few minutes ago when I mentioned the word 'love' in passing, I have no idea why I just told you that, but it's the truth. I love you." His gaze held hers for a few more seconds, but when she said nothing, he turned away, jaw clenched and focused on the line cooks who buzzed around the kitchen, stirring sauces and swirling linguini into perfectly presented towers.

Austen sipped her wine nervously, her mind buzzing like a swarm of agitated bees. When he finally looked back, she asked, almost in a whisper, "How do you know?"

"I just do." His smile was tight. "But it's okay if you're not there or not ready to say it or whatever."

Her mind flashed back to a few weeks earlier at her apartment. Matt had cooked dinner and while she loaded the dishwasher, he took out the trash without her asking. She'd watched him leave and thought to herself, *Good God, I love this man.*

But then she'd checked herself—hard. *No one has taken a bag of trash out for me in years, and while I'm stupidly happy that he's doing that for me, taking out the trash doesn't equal love. Does it?*

That night, lying beside him, she recalled Victor Hugo's quote about how "great acts of love are done by those who are habitually performing small acts of kindness." She had wondered at what moment those small acts became love.

The simple truth was that she was scared.

After her marriage ended, and after falling for Kevin and then Sam, both of whom broke her heart, she'd built walls around herself. Now, here Matt was, telling her he loved her.

Part of her wanted to tear those walls down and scream "I love you too." But she didn't trust herself to fully understand the distinction between being in love and simply appreciating that someone finally wanted to take care of her. She didn't want to get it wrong.

"I'm too much in my own head," she finally said, tapping her forehead. "I'm sorry."

Matt smiled sadly, reaching for the focaccia. "It's fine. Forget I said it."

Well, that's impossible, she thought, feeling mortified. She bit into her focaccia and used the few moments of silence to think of a way to change the topic.

"Are you going to tell Ophelia about what Esme said?"

Matt took a sip of wine. "I think I have to. She'd want to know. Right?"

"One hundred percent."

"Yah. I'll call her when we get back to Paris. Oh, and I cleared the Ibiza weekend with Omar over email today, so if you're sure you're up for it, I can confirm that with her too?"

"Also, one hundred percent," Austen replied, trying to sound enthusiastic. She didn't want to hesitate after her reaction to his unexpected declaration of love. "This weekend has been marvelous. Thank you for bringing me and introducing me to your friends. I'm very glad to know that you're an excellent travel companion—not that I doubted it."

I may be caught up in my own head about what's going on in my heart, but I don't want to lose you. The problem isn't you, Matt. It's me.

PART THREE

APRIL

Deception

CHAPTER 9

Gianluca, Rome

Gianluca felt lips on his neck, then his earlobe being lightly sucked as a hand stroked down his chest toward his already hard groin. He awoke slowly, reveling in the sensation of her mouth and hands on him. Kristin was in town for an event with Eni, which she managed for Ophelia. She'd been here for three nights, and he'd spent every one of them in her hotel room, lying to Ophelia about covering night shifts at the hospital for a doctor who didn't even exist. He knew he was a bastard, but whenever Kristin was in town, he couldn't pull himself away. This was their last morning together for this trip, and they'd only fallen asleep a few hours ago. They always prioritized sex over sleep.

"God, I love waking up to you." He pulled her body on top of his and buried his face in her long blond hair.

"What do you love about it?" she cooed into his ear, guiding him inside her. She lifted onto her knees, giving him a perfect view of her naked body, and started to move. "Tell me every wonderfully filthy thought running through your head."

He groaned, grabbing onto her hips, pushing himself inside her to the hilt as she rocked against him. The sensation deprived him of speech. Gianluca was convinced there was no better way to wake up, even if he'd only been asleep for four hours. His years as an ER doctor had trained him for sleep deprivation, but he hadn't realized how much that training might benefit his personal life until Kristin came along.

After their particularly athletic morning sex, they showered together, savoring the time before her imminent departure. She had one more night in town, but Ophelia had proposed the two of them go out to dinner to celebrate another successful customer event. Kristin felt obligated to go despite his repeated suggestions that she make an excuse and cancel.

"She's my client, Gianluca," Kristin insisted. "I can't really say no."

"You can. Get creative. You'll be getting creative about getting out of Ibiza next month, so get creative about getting out of dinner tonight too. Say you're feeling unwell. Anything," he pleaded. "I hate the idea of you two alone over a bottle of Chianti."

Kristin brushed the tangles out of her wet hair and frowned. "You don't trust me?"

Gianluca pulled their towel-wrapped bodies together and kissed her hard. She dropped the brush and encircled him with her arms. When he came up for air, he said, "I trust you. But you've already spent almost a full week with her and kept everything totally professional, and I know it's not easy to keep up that charade."

And I can barely breathe every time I know you two are together, he thought. *It'd be so easy for you to slip up and ruin everything.*

She ran her fingers through his salt and pepper hair. "I think I'm better at compartmentalizing than you are, my love. I just don't think about you when I'm with her. I'm here to do a job, and I'm great at doing it. The job has nothing to do with you."

"Fine, but the woman does, and you're playing with fire."

We both are.

"How many times do I have to tell you that we shouldn't talk about Ophelia? Do you hear me bringing up Charlie? No, you don't," she nagged, tossing the towel aside and sliding into her lingerie.

Gianluca never gave a single thought to Kristin's boyfriend. He'd never met the man and never planned to, so why should he? In his mind, Kristin existed only for him. To be fair, he rarely even thought about Kristin when she was back in London. He had enough going on with Ophelia, the kids, his own aging parents, and his work to keep his mind busy. He was better at compartmentalizing than Kristin thought.

He pretended to pout. "Okay, fine. Go to your dinner. Be professional."

"You know I'd rather spend the night with you, but I think we'd be pushing our luck to get away with a fourth night in a row," she conceded as she began drying her hair. "And you did say you're on daddy duty tonight, Daddy."

Gianluca knew "daddy issues" when he saw them. He had to guess Kristin's hadn't been good to her, though he'd never dared to ask. He liked to keep things light and sexy with her—deep conversations were avoided at all costs.

His thoughts drifted back to his own kids who were with Stefania, their nanny, whose patience had been tapped out this week between Ophelia's work schedule and his philandering. He had to be home tonight to take over. He hadn't seen the kids in days, and the guilt made his chest tighten. *God forbid Esme turns out like Kristin in adulthood because I've been too absent.* Gianluca loved his kids, but childcare was a responsibility he rarely had to shoulder alone. Ophelia was always there. She was a saint. And he was a sinner.

Dealing with them while my wife is having dinner with my mistress is a fitting re-entry into my "normal" life—whatever "normal" means, he thought. *I mean, isn't everyone having an affair these days?*

Gianluca knew that wasn't true, but he always worked hard to justify his behavior. He left the bathroom and reluctantly pulled on his slacks and shirt, watching Kristin preen in the mirror—the paper-thin, lacy pink lingerie covered the bare minimum of her perfect body.

"I miss you already," he said from his perch on the bed as he tied his shoes. He meant her body, but he cared about her enough to let her think he meant more. He knew she was in love with him. She told him all the time, and although he did nothing to discourage it, he knew he wasn't in love with her.

Predictably, she walked over to him slowly so he could take in the full view, then draped herself over him, straddling his thighs. He grabbed her ass and pulled her body tight against his, as their foreheads touched.

"We'll find another time soon," she promised, her hands tracing his shoulders.

He flipped her onto her back, kissed her, then stood up, letting his eyes roam her body as he slowly backed toward the door.

"*A presto, amore mio.*[14]"

"My love" was the closest he ever came to saying "I love you" to Kristin. *Tesoro* which meant "darling" was his term of endearment for Ophelia, given her discomfort with the word "love." But Kristin lapped up any version of it, and each time he said it, the smile that spread across her face fueled his addiction. She was all dirty talk, orgasms and dopamine, and every time he walked away, he knew he'd come running back for more.

Later that evening, after a full day's work at the hospital, a car horn blasted him fully awake. *I should not be driving,* he thought. He was so sleep-deprived he could barely see straight, and the stress of Ophelia and Kristin's dinner gnawed at him.

As that nightmare scenario danced through his tired brain, his phone buzzed.

---

14 See you soon, my love.

K: In about 5 minutes, I am going to fake illness/exhaustion and cancel on O.

I can't stand the thought of not spending my last night in town with you.

Are you already home? Can you not be?

    Gianluca snapped awake. All the exhaustion that had been weighing him down moments earlier vanished in a rush of adrenaline and testosterone. His mind raced, evaluating his options. *The kids can wait one more night. What harm can it really do?* He hit the record button to send her a voice note. "I'm in the car and turning around now. I'll make up some excuse with the nanny and meet you at the hotel. You'll be punished for this."

K: Yes. I'm a very bad girl. See u there.
I fucking ♥ you.

    As he made a U-turn at the light, he hated how much he loved reading those words.
    "Dial Stefania," he said to his dashboard. The sound of the ringtone echoed through his car until she picked up.
    "Ciao Stefania. *Mi dispiace*[15] but all hell just broke loose at the hospital. I was on my way home, but I'm turning back around. Can you stay until Ophelia gets home?"
    He heard her sigh through the line. "She mentioned she had a work dinner tonight. Sorry, Gianluca. I can stay a bit longer but not past nine o'clock."
    Shit. The dinner's off, but I'm not supposed to know that yet. Navigating a delicate web of lies was especially challenging when

---

15 I'm sorry

one was being led by the head in their pants rather than the one on their shoulders.

"I'll call her to see if she can cancel or at least make it a short one," Gianluca said, already spinning up the lie in his head. "Not past nine o'clock. Understood. Really sorry, Stefania."

"*Va bene*[16]. I'll get some spaghetti going for the kids," Stefania conceded, sighing again.

"*Grazie mille*," he said to no one. Stefania had already hung up.

He took a deep breath and again spoke to the dashboard. "Dial Ophelia."

She answered after two rings. "*Ciao*. I was just about to call you."

"*Ciao, tesoro*. I know you have your work dinner tonight, and I was on my way home, but the hospital just called me back in. Apparently things got crazy right after I left," he said, intentionally adding some stress to his voice. "I called Stefania, and she can stay a bit longer but not past nine. I'm so sorry to ask, but is there any way you can make your dinner a short one tonight?"

Her voice came through his car speakers, clear as a bell. "My dinner was cancelled, and I'll be on my way home shortly. It's not a problem."

Gianluca exaggerated his relief. "Ah *perfetto*[17]. I mean, I'm sorry it was canceled. I know you were looking forward to it."

Ophelia sighed. "Clearly, it's all for the best. Hope you can get out of there soon. See you when I see you."

When he knocked on Kristin's hotel room door twenty minutes later, he felt like a horny, misbehaving teenager. The feeling brought him back to when he *was* that horny teenager, sneaking around with his then-girlfriend, Vittoria, whose deeply Catholic parents would have killed them both had they been caught in the act. He had crawled out of her bedroom window more than a few times when

---

16 All right

17 Perfect

they heard her parents keys in the door. Those escapades in his formative years had left him with an appetite for danger-infused sex, which had followed him well into his twenties. By the time he met Ophelia, he thought he'd gotten it out of his system. But Kristin brought him right back to the thrill of living on the edge.

She opened the door in nothing but lingerie—a fire-engine-red lace concoction he immediately wanted to tear off. Gianluca tossed her over his shoulder, slammed the door closed, spanked her ass hard for throwing tonight's plans up in the air, and threw her roughly on the bed.

"You're terrible," he said, pulling off his tie and kicking off his shoes.

"I know. What are you going to do about it?" She smiled up at him sultrily, slowly tracing her index finger from her sternum down to her navel.

"I'm going to do my best to fuck some sense into you," he snarled, pulling her roughly by the ankles toward him.

"That's what I was hoping," she purred, reaching up for him.

CHAPTER 10

Ophelia, Rome

Ophelia had been looking forward to her girls' night out with Kristin. She hadn't managed to form a close circle of girlfriends in Rome, something she blamed on not being a native Italian speaker. She'd latched onto Kristin as a fellow expat, anglophone and colleague, and over time, they'd become friends after bonding over their shared daddy issues. Kristin's father had abandoned her family when she was ten in favor of creating a new one with a much younger woman. Ophelia's father, though physically present, had been emotionally absent ever since her mum died. She wasn't sure which was worse.

Regardless, tonight, she felt quite relieved when Kristin cancelled their dinner. Ophelia couldn't shake the mum guilt, especially after Matt told her about his conversation with Esme. She wanted to be home with her kids. *It would've been better if Gianluca wasn't stuck at work again, but time with just the kids and me will be good*, she thought.

As she drove home, her mind wandered to all the major and minor moments in her children's lives—birthdays, first days of school, Christmases, summer holidays, school plays, musical performances, and everything in between. The in between moments were the most special. Their faces would light up over utterly trivial things, like trying a new flavor of gelato or hearing their favorite song on the radio. She loved her kids with her whole heart but saying it out loud always felt impossible.

Gianluca was never afraid to tell them they were loved. Ophelia did what she could to make sure they felt it, even if she didn't say the words. She'd always quietly hoped that would be enough, but poor Esme clearly needed more concrete proof. Maybe Marco did too but hadn't said anything.

It's probably time to go back into therapy. I'm inflicting my damage on them, Ophelia thought, biting her thumbnail. *I need to learn how to communicate so these kids don't grow up like me, unable to say what's in their hearts.*

Her thoughts turned to the early days with Gianluca, back when this issue first reared its ugly head. She was twenty-six, breezing into Rome every few weeks, their time together limited and ravenous. She remembered one Friday night arriving from London, letting herself into his apartment, and waiting for him stark naked on the couch, his stethoscope hanging from her neck.

She'd never forgotten how his pupils dilated, his lips parted, and his breath caught in his throat when he saw her. The power she felt at that moment had been intoxicating. He'd taken her on the couch, and her release was the strongest she'd ever had. Later, as they lay entwined on the living room rug, basking in the afterglow, he pushed her hair from her face and whispered the words for the first time.

"I love you."

The post-orgasmic calm vanished. Every muscle in her body tensed, and she rolled onto her stomach, turning her head away from him. Her pulse raced, and she willed herself to disappear through the floorboards.

"Why are you hiding from me?" he asked, stroking her bare back with his fingertips. "What happened to that fearless woman who was stark naked in my stethoscope thirty minutes ago?"

Ophelia slowly rolled over to face him, her hands tucked in tight fists beneath her chin. "I don't want to hide. I want this. All of it."

"Good," he nodded, kissing her nose. "Because I really do love you. You make me feel seen, and you make me want to be a better man."

Ophelia squeezed her eyes closed momentarily and then took a deep breath. "Thank you," she whispered.

Gianluca frowned and rolled onto his back, running his palms over his forehead. "I must admit that 'thank you' wasn't what I was hoping for."

She knew it wasn't enough. She also knew she loved him, but she was thoroughly incapable of saying it. She'd never uttered those words to anyone, though at the time, she didn't understand why.

"I feel the same way," she finally said. It was the best she could offer.

His head turned, a smile creeping across his face. "You love me?"

She nodded, feeling her muscles relax. *Maybe he doesn't need to hear the actual words.* Just because she couldn't say them didn't mean they weren't true.

In the years since, her inability to say "I love you" had come up often. She knew it bothered him, but thanks to the therapy she had done before their wedding, they both understood why she couldn't. The reason was both dreadfully simple and horribly complex—the word "love" had disappeared with her mum.

After her mother's tragic death, her father had become a hollow shell of a man with nothing left to give to her or to anyone else. Ophelia had no memory of him ever saying he loved her, so the words simply never became part of her vocabulary.

Once the kids were born, the issue became more painful. Every time Gianluca told Marco or Esme that he loved them, Ophelia felt inadequate—as a wife and as a mother. He assured her they could feel her love—that it was enough. But maybe it wasn't. Certainly not with Esme, it seemed. *What about Marco? What about Gianluca?*

The memory of that stethoscope escapade reminded her how long it had been since she felt genuinely sexy. These days, all her effort went to the kids—none to herself and the bare minimum to her marriage.

Her therapist had once said that to give love to others, you first had to love yourself. Ophelia had spent so little time thinking about her own needs. *I'm a mother first, a wife second, and who can really keep three things straight anyway?* she thought, another wave of exhaustion washing over her.

She stepped through her wisteria-framed front door, the smell of bolognese and both her children greeting her. She hugged them tightly.

"Mum, we started studying world capitals in class today. Do you know what the capital of Burkina Faso is?" Marco asked, excitedly.

Ophelia scrunched up her nose. "Afraid not. Please enlighten me, my little geography genius."

"Ouagadougou," he shouted, jumping up and down, clearly delighted by the rhythmic quality of the name. "Ouagadougou. Ouagadougou. Ouagadougou."

"That's a very fun name," Ophelia acknowledged warmly, as Marco continued his chant, jumping in circles.

"Stop saying Ouagadougou," Esme whined, pulling Ophelia by the hand toward the kitchen. "Mum, Stefania is making spaghetti, and I'm starving."

"Me too, monkey. We'll eat ASAP," she said, as they turned the corner into the kitchen. "*Grazie*, Stefania. I can take it from here. You can go. Sorry we kept you late."

Stefania was already untying her apron. "*Va bene, grazie. Buona serata*[18]."

Ophelia slipped on Stefania's apron and stirred the pasta sauce, licking the spoon. It needed more basil. As she reached for the refrigerator door, her phone buzzed.

---

18 Have a nice evening.

"Monkeys, this is Uncle Jack calling from New York. Run upstairs and play for a bit," Ophelia instructed. "I'll shout as soon as dinner is ready."

The children scurried off, and Ophelia answered the call.

"Well, if it isn't Jack Scott," she smiled into her mobile, propping it against the paper towel rack while she started to chop basil.

Jack grinned back from the FaceTime screen. "Hey, darlin'. How's Rome? Whatcha cookin'?"

She held up the basil and the knife. "Spaghetti sauce. How is it possible that you get more handsome every time I see you?"

"God, I adore talking to you. Don't stop. Tell me more," Jack said, leaning into his phone and batting his eyelashes dramatically.

Ophelia laughed, feeling some of her energy return. "Rome's better now that I'm talking to you. How's New York? How's Luis?"

"Luis is traveling, as usual—probably drinking champagne in some tedious first-class lounge right now. And that's why I'm calling. Unfortunately, he won't make it to Ibiza. Some work trip to Japan came up, and he can't get out of it."

Ophelia frowned, pressing the point of the knife into the cutting board. "Rats. Well, we knew that was a possibility. Assuming you don't want a roommate, I guess we'll just be seven for the weekend."

"I've got an eighth to propose if you're open to randoms," Jack replied, his voice full of mischief.

"How random are we talking?" she asked, cocking her head to one side. "With you, one can never be too sure."

"Random for you, but not for me. It's my friend Rosalie. She's French, lives in Paris, and is an *artiste*. We met when she studied in New York, and we've been friends ever since. She's a creative genius with desert-dry wit, and just broke up with her latest terrible boyfriend, so she could use a weekend away."

Ophelia considered this as she chopped basil into thin strips. "She'd be the only single. It's otherwise all couples and you. Does she know that? Not exactly fertile get-over-a-breakup ground."

Jack nodded. "I told her. She's up for it if you don't mind a gatecrasher. I promise you'll get on like a house on fire. I've traveled with her a ton over the years. Not high maintenance at all. And she's connected to the Ibiza art scene, so she might have some cool suggestions."

"Why not?" Ophelia said, blowing her fringe out of her eyes. "The more, the merrier. Put us in touch, and I'll get her all the info. Although Luis will be missed."

"Thanks, Lady O! You're the best," Jack sang. "And Luis is truly sorry he can't make it. See you soon."

In truth, Ophelia wasn't thrilled about a random woman crashing her birthday, but she was even less thrilled about causing drama. As always, she let it slide. Dumping the basil into the sauce pot, she resolved to keep the peace. *If my friends are happy, I'll be happy too,* she thought.

PART FOUR

MAY

Pre-Flight

CHAPTER 11

Austen, Paris

Austen walked into her bedroom, carrying a small stack of bikinis and beach coverups she'd just pulled out of storage. She hadn't yet needed to rotate her summer wardrobe back into her tiny Parisian closet. "Are you folding my delicates or being a perv?"

Matt was sitting on her bed beside the laundry basket, a pair of her black lacy underwear dangling from his fingers.

"If they were dirty and around my head, I'd be a perv," he quipped. "But as it is, I'm being a fantastic boyfriend and folding your delicates to help you pack for our trip. You're aware our plane leaves in four hours, right?"

He had shown up the night before, already packed and ready to go. His suitcase was stashed neatly in the corner of her room. She'd meant to pack earlier, but they'd gotten distracted by food and sex. Clothes were now strewn chaotically all over her bed as she hurried to pack for Ophelia's birthday weekend.

"You're folding my delicates," she repeated, a smile tugging at her lips.

There he goes again with those small acts of kindness. First the trash, then helping me hang my new art. The groceries last week. And now my underwear. He might be the perfect man, she thought.

"Speaking of delicates," Matt said, now twirling the underwear on his finger, "I got Ophelia this lace table runner for her birthday. I'm going to tell her it's from both of us, just so you know."

Austen looked at him quizzically and snatched the undies from his hand. "I wondered where you were going when you said, 'Ophelia and lace' and were elbow-deep in my underwear, so a table runner was the best possible outcome there. Why a lace table runner? It's a very specific gift."

"She mentioned Esme cut up a lace table runner that used to belong to her mom. She doesn't have much from her. Her dad threw out most of her mom's things after she died. Ophelia's family is from Bedford, which is known for lacemaking. Did you know lace, like wine, has regional specialties and traditions in craftsmanship?"

"I did not," Austen said, shaking her head, genuinely impressed.

"The things you learn on a Google rabbit hole. Long story short, I found an antiques dealer who located something from that region that might be from the right era," he concluded, looking satisfied.

Her insides slowly turned into goo. It didn't matter that the gift wasn't for her. This act of loving kindness showed her yet again the kind of man Matt was. *That Victor Hugo was right, and I'll be damned. I love this man,* she realized.

Matt held up her skimpiest thong. "Bring these. Your ass looks incredible in them."

He tossed them toward her, and she caught them with one hand. "Does it now?"

"Your ass always looks incredible—even in these," he teased, holding up her most worn-out cotton underwear, which she purposefully never wore when he was around.

"You've never seen my ass in those," she pointed out, grabbing them from his hand and tossing them over her shoulder. "And you never will."

With a grin, Matt pulled her down onto the bed, rolling on top of her. "You could wear a potato sack with your hair in a wad on top of your head, no makeup, and you'd still be the most beautiful woman in the room."

Austen ran her hands down the length of his muscular back. "You're the kindest, most wonderful man I've ever met, and I'm so in love with you."

The words tumbled out before she could stop them, surprising her. It had taken four months of internal negotiation to believe things were as good as they seemed. But right there in her bedroom, lying beside a pile of neatly folded underwear, she became a believer.

Matt pulled back slightly, his blue eyes sparkling. "Well, it's about damn time. I love you too, Austen Keller."

She kissed him as intensely as she ever had—joy, love, heat and hunger all pulsing in her blood in the most delicious dance. When they finally came up for air, she flipped on top of him, breathless. "How much time did you say we had before our flight?"

"Plenty," he said, pulling her shirt up over her head.

CHAPTER 12

Gianluca, Rome

Gianluca tugged on his T-shirt and tossed his toiletries into the suitcase, zipping it closed with a deep sigh. He rested his hands on the bag, head hanging low as he took a few long, calming breaths. Between work, planning Ophelia's birthday weekend, and looking after his parents, he'd been stretched to his limit. His phone was overflowing with missed calls, unread texts, and unanswered emails, but all he wanted to do was switch it off the moment they took off for Ibiza—and leave it off for the weekend. Ophelia deserved a perfect birthday, and he needed the break more than ever.

He dragged himself toward the stairs, calling down the hallway. "Marco! Esme! We're leaving in five minutes for *Nonni's*."

"Thank your parents for me," Ophelia said from the foot of the stairs, handing him a canvas bag filled with the kids' favorite snacks. "I packed a few things so they don't have to go shopping."

"They're Italian grandparents. You don't need to worry about the kids going hungry," Gianluca said with a smile, slinging the bag over his shoulder.

Ophelia shook her head. "I know, but I don't want them feeling put out. Just thank them for me, okay?"

"Yes, dear. I'll be back in an hour, and then we'll head to the airport. You're all packed?" he asked, already knowing the answer.

"I will be," she assured him with a nod, just as Marco and Esme clattered down the stairs. She wrapped them both in her arms and kissed the tops of their heads. "You two monkeys behave for your *Nonni*. Say '*per favore*' and '*grazie*,' and don't turn their flat upside down. Got it?"

"Yes, Mummy," they chimed together.

"Have fun at your birthday party," Marco added, giving her an extra squeeze. "Make sure you eat lots of cake."

"Thank you, my little monkey," Ophelia beamed. "For you, I promise I'll eat all the cake."

"For me too," Esme squealed. "And bring us back presents."

"Presents? Whose birthday is it?" Gianluca teased, palming both kids' heads and gently steering them toward the door. "*Andiamo*[19], you two. Your mamma and I have a plane to catch."

"Bye Mummy," the kids shouted as Gianluca corralled them out.

While driving across Rome to his parents' flat, his phone rang. It was Kristin. It had been almost two weeks since they last talked. They'd agreed that she would cancel her Ibiza trip at the last minute, feigning illness to both Charlie and Ophelia. She normally only called at agreed upon times when he knew he'd be alone, so the spontaneous call unsettled him. A furtive glance at the kids through his rearview mirror confirmed that he couldn't answer, so he sent her to voicemail. At a stoplight, he fired off a text.

> Gianluca: Kids in the car. Will call you back after I drop them at my parents'.

K: We need to talk!

---

19 Let's go.

He tightened his grip on the wheel, worry gnawing at him. When they arrived at the flat, his mother greeted the children at the door, warmly as ever, wearing the green-and-white gingham apron she always wore when she was cooking.

"*Ciao, amori di Nonna*,[20]" she said, pinching their small cheeks.

The kids raced toward the back garden while Gianluca started carrying their bags to the spare bedroom. His father met him in the hallway, uncharacteristically silent. He looked older and grayer than usual—more frail in his black slacks and white tank top. With a small nod, he took the tiny suitcases and shuffled back down the hall.

Gianluca turned to his mother, handing her the tote of snacks. "These are from Ophelia, who sends her deepest thanks for watching them this weekend." He tilted his head toward his father. "Is he okay?"

Her expression darkened as she looked in the direction he'd headed. "He saw Doctor Conti yesterday," she said, lowering her voice. "His stomach has been bothering him, and he's been losing some weight. Conti found some kind of mass and wants to do a biopsy next week."

Gianluca's gut twisted, his vision blurring as the full weight of his father's frailty hit him. "Why didn't you tell me? Did he say anything else?"

She shook her head gently, rubbing his arm. "No. We just have to wait and see. Your Papà's tough. Don't tell Ophelia. We don't want to spoil her birthday."

Just then, his father reappeared, and Gianluca hugged him tightly. When they separated, he placed his hands on his father's shoulders, taking in his tired face—the deep creases, the wrinkles, the age spots. "Papà, if you're sick you talk to me. I'll call Conti's office today to make sure the biopsy results are expedited."

---

20 Hi, Grandma's loves.

"We don't know if I'm sick. But okay fine. *Grazie*," his father said, patting his chest. "For now, go celebrate your wife's birthday."

"You're sure you're up for taking care of the kids this weekend?" Gianluca asked, concern coursing through him.

His mother hooked her arm through his, steering him toward the door. "We've got it under control. Go. Enjoy the weekend. We'll call one of your brothers if we need help."

"I love you both very much," Gianluca said, his voice cracking. He hugged them tightly and then reluctantly let go. Clearing his throat, he called toward the back garden. "Ciao Marco. Ciao Esme. Be good for your *Nonni*."

He zombie-walked back to his car, every step heavy with childhood memories. His father was omnipresent in each one. Everything Gianluca believed and valued about family and unconditional love had been born in that flat. Tears pricked his eyes. Wiping them away, he climbed into his car and pulled up Doctor Conti's office number, leaving an urgent message with the receptionist before even putting the key in the ignition.

The drive home was a blur. *What if it's cancer?* He couldn't imagine a world without his father in it. He was a giant among men—the patriarch of the expansive D'Angelo family which included his three younger brothers, their spouses, and a combined ten grandchildren. Though Gianluca faced death nearly every day in the ER, he'd never allowed himself to think about his own parents' mortality. The idea of losing his father was unbearable.

He was so lost in his own frenetic thoughts as he returned home that he forgot entirely about returning Kristin's call. It was the faint sound of a suitcase being dragged down the upstairs hallway in his own flat which first broke through his mental fog.

Ophelia smiled at him from the landing. "Everything go okay with the drop off?"

"Fine," Gianluca nodded, meeting her halfway up the stairs and carrying her bag down.

She patted his back in thanks. "Want to eat something before we go?"

Shaking his head, he forced a smile and stroked her cheek. "Are you excited about the weekend?"

Her arms encircled his waist in a short but firm hug. "Very. Thanks again for the brilliant suggestion," she beamed up at him. "I can't wait to see everyone and have my toes in the sea."

Gianluca let his fingers linger at her sides, dropping his gaze toward his shoes.

She tilted his face upward, her brows furrowed. "What's wrong?"

"Just tired. Nothing some sunshine and sangria won't fix," he lied.

Looking unconvinced, she slowly released him and then walked toward the kitchen, talking over her shoulder. "Okay. I'm going to nibble on something before we go."

Gianluca watched her walk away, feeling a heavy knot of anxiety in his chest and the absence of her too-short embrace. He ached for the comfort she'd readily offer him if she knew what he was going through, but he was determined not to let anything darken her birthday weekend.

PART FIVE

MAY

Before She Knew

CHAPTER 13

Ophelia, Ibiza

Ophelia and Jack stood outside the Ibiza airport, basking in the warm Spanish sunshine that glinted off Jack's bald head. She glanced at the arrivals door, bouncing lightly on the balls of her feet. A light breeze stirred the hem of her black caftan, tickling her legs.

"Jack, does Gianluca seem distracted to you?" she asked, her gaze flicking to his face.

He shrugged. "We've been together for, what, an hour? Hard to say. Is he?"

"He was quiet on the flight. Maybe it was just the turbulence." She bit her lip and sighed. "Keep an eye on him for me? You read people so well."

Jack tipped an imaginary hat and winked. "At your service, milady. Driver, spy, drink-fetcher—whatever you need."

She nudged his arm affectionately. Across the lanes of traffic, she spotted Matt and Austen making their way over with their luggage. "There they are," she said, waving energetically. Austen's white linen pants and turquoise peasant blouse fluttered as she walked, while Matt cut a commanding figure in khakis and a white button-down, his sleeves rolled up to his forearms.

"Happy birthday, Fie!" Matt scooped her up in a bear hug, spinning her in a circle before setting her back on the ground. "Let the games begin."

Ophelia wiped her sweaty palms against her thighs. "Was your flight a nightmare? Ours was pure chaos—utter hell in a flying tube. I'm already dreading the return trip."

"Not at all," Austen replied, greeting her with a kiss on each cheek. "It was easy breezy. Happy birthday. We're really excited to be here. The temperature is perfect."

Ophelia gestured to Jack with a flourish. "Matt, Austen—this is the Fabulous Jack Scott of the New York Scotts."

"That's my legal name—The Fabulous Jack Scott. But you may simply call me Fabulous Jack. No need for formality while cavorting on an island. Oh, there she is!" Jack suddenly darted off, shout-singing a hello toward his friend.

Matt chuckled. "You weren't kidding about him, Fie. He's quite the character."

"You've barely scratched the surface," she teased, following Jack's gaze. "That's Rosalie. She was on your flight from Paris. I've never met her, but we're about to."

Ophelia watched as Jack greeted Rosalie, slinging what looked like an antique carpet bag over his shoulder. Rosalie, with her long, wavy brown hair, bright red lips, and flowing white cotton dress, looked every bit the bohemian artist, with colorful bangles on her wrists and designer combat boots.

"Rosalie, this is Ophelia—the birthday girl," Jack announced as they reconvened by the car.

Ophelia leaned in to kiss Rosalie's cheeks, nearly brushing lips in the process. "Oops, sorry! Living in Italy too long. Italians always start on the right."

Rosalie waved it off with a swipe of her immaculately manicured hand. Her lipstick perfectly matched her fingernails. "It's nothing. Thank you for letting me crash your party," she said, in a thick French accent.

"Matt, Austen—meet Rosalie," Ophelia continued. Everyone exchanged cheek kisses, all leaning correctly to the left.

Once they'd squeezed all the luggage and bodies into the car, Jack steered them away from the airport and toward the villa.

"Fabulous Jack, how did you and Rosalie meet?" Austen asked from the backseat.

Jack glanced in the rearview mirror. "Rosalie, this goddess who hasn't aged a day in twenty years, was living in New York studying art at Parsons. I was pretending to study literature at NYU, and we met in some dank bar which neither of us would be caught dead in today."

Rosalie's voice floated forward from the backseat. "Every French girl dreams of having a gay best friend in New York, so I made him mine. I called him a few weeks ago after I broke up with Bernard—the latest in my remarkably long string of horrible Parisian boyfriends—and Jack insisted I join this weekend since Luis had to work."

Ophelia caught Austen's sympathetic smile as she replied. "I've had my fair share of horrible Frenchmen. Happy to swap horror stories if you need the comic relief."

Matt's voice rose in protest. "All right, ladies. No need to knock the French."

"Not you. You, I love," Austen declared.

Ophelia smiled out the window. *They're in love.* She'd witnessed the early signs in Rome—their stolen glances and shared quiet smiles—when they were still cautiously falling for each other. *They made it.*

"Are you still making art?" Matt asked Rosalie.

"I paint when I can, but it doesn't pay the bills. For that, I manage an art gallery in the Marais—mostly modern, with a focus on expressionism."

"I really enjoy modern art," Ophelia said, turning toward the backseat. "Our flat in Rome is filled with it. I love big, bold color explosions on a canvas, and no one does that better than the modernists."

"And yet you always wear black," Jack teased, eyes still on the road. "Curious."

It was true. Her wardrobe had faded entirely to black over the years. Whether it was age, living in Rome, or having messy kids who smudged everything, her once-colorful sartorial pallet had dulled. But her love for bold art had never waned.

Austen broke the brief silence that followed. "I'm ashamed to admit I'm not very knowledgeable about modern art. I mean, I can appreciate a Pollock or a Warhol, but when it's a toilet seat hanging on a wall, I don't get it."

Rosalie chuckled. "No one wants to see a toilet seat on a wall. Sometimes, it *is* bullshit."

"Thank you," Austen sighed in relief. "Now I can say I met a gallerist in Ibiza who agreed with me on the bullshit factor. I feel validated."

"Some. Some of it is bullshit," Rosalie corrected with a smile. "But a lot of it isn't. I'll let you know when we have an exhibit that's not-bullshit-but-could-be, and you can come see for yourself."

"Sounds like a plan," Austen replied. "I love that about Paris—meeting people who expand your world. I've known you for ten minutes and already feel smarter. Ending each day a little less stupid than I started is a life goal of mine."

Jack laughed heartily. "That's a solid goal. I like her," he said to Ophelia, thumbing toward Austen in the backseat.

"Me too," Matt agreed.

Rosalie deadpanned. "Let me guess—four months together?"

"Well spotted," Matt said, sounding impressed.

"*Oui.* You two reek of new love. It's revolting," Rosalie teased.

Jack's laughter filled the car as he smacked the steering wheel.

"Ignore her. She's French and currently hates men. And love. And anything resembling a relationship."

"I don't hate men or love," Rosalie corrected. "I'm bored of men and think life would be entirely more satisfying if we didn't insist on putting romantic love at the top of the hierarchy. But I'm not here to rain on anybody's love parade."

I see why Jack likes her, Ophelia thought. *No shortage of interesting opinions. She'll keep things entertaining this weekend.*

As they turned off the main road onto the narrow, rocky path leading to the villa, Ophelia announced, "This is our street. Almost there."

"We're using the term 'street' very loosely here, people. It's what I imagine driving across the surface of the moon might feel like, with more dust and gravity, which doesn't work in our favor on these craters," Jack cracked. "But what you'll find at the end will make all these bumps worthwhile, guaranteed. The villa is glorious."

CHAPTER 14

Gianluca, Ibiza

Gianluca sat in the back garden, staring out at the Mediterranean, his fingers mindlessly and rapidly tapping against his leg. Neither the peaceful sea view nor the Spanish sunshine had soothed his anxiety. The crunch of Jack's tires on the gravel outside the villa announced their return, jolting him to his feet.

Earlier, he'd popped out to the grocery store, stocking up on snacks and drinks. He'd prepared a large pitcher of cava sangria but, lost in his thoughts, had forgotten to prepare the snacks. Cursing himself, he slipped into his flip-flops and hurried to greet everyone.

"*Bienvenidos a*[21] Can Blanco," Gianluca called out, forcing a smile as he held open the thick olive wood door. "That's the name of the villa—Can Blanco. The White House. Austen and Jack, a little nod to your homeland, right here in Spain."

"Gianluca, do not even *think* about getting me started on the nightmare that is American politics," Jack shouted, throwing up a hand to stop him. "Austen, girl, you made the right choice fleeing the country when you did. It's an absolute shit show back there."

"All the more reason to be delighted to be here instead," Austen said, raising her voice. "*Viva España.*"

---

21 Welcome to

"Hey, man, nice to see you," Matt said, shaking Gianluca's hand.

Gianluca greeted Austen and Rosalie with perfunctory cheek kisses. "Jack, why don't you show Rosalie to her room, and I'll show Matt and Austen to theirs?"

"*Perfetto, gracias*[22]," Ophelia chimed in, mixing her Italian and Spanish. "Oh, by the way, I just saw a text from Kristin from earlier."

Gianluca jerked his head around at the mention of Kristin's name. *Fuck. I never called her back. Oh well. This'll be her cancellation anyway.*

"She said she and Charlie rented a car at the airport, so we don't need to pick them up. They should be here by seven at the latest," Ophelia added, kissing his cheek and walking away.

His heart sank into his stomach. *Fuckfuckfuckfuckfuck.* He glanced at Matt and Austen, waiting with their bags.

"Right. Follow me," he said, trying to appear nonchalant while his pulse pounded in his ears. He showed them to their room, gesturing for them to enter. His mind was racing, and it showed.

"You all right, man? You look a little pale," Matt said, placing a hand on his shoulder.

"I'm fine, just hungry," Gianluca replied dismissively. "You two get settled, and we'll see you downstairs."

He veered toward his and Ophelia's bedroom, relieved to find it empty. He needed a moment to regroup.

What the fuck is Kristin thinking? Why didn't I call her back? How on earth are we going to pull this off? His head throbbed as he checked his watch. He locked himself in the bathroom and sank onto the cold tile, putting his head between his knees. Ninety minutes until his life risked total implosion. *I'm fucked,* he thought.

His first instinct was to invent an emergency at the hospital and catch the next flight back to Rome. Ophelia would hate him

---

22 Perfect, thanks

for it, but it would be temporary. If everything exploded with Kristin this weekend, it would be far worse.

Surely, Kristin's not coming here to torch both of our relationships at once. She's not that crazy. Right? The idea that he might not know terrified him even more. *Get it together. You're excellent under pressure. You're a God of the ER. You've kept this secret for over a year. You can do this.* He pushed himself up off the floor, flushed the toilet just in case, and splashed cold water on his face before heading back downstairs.

Gianluca found everyone gathered around the outdoor dining table beneath a wooden pergola, pink bougainvillea dripping from its edges. Chorizo, Manchego, chips, and sangria were laid out. The party had begun without him.

He poured himself a glass of sangria. "How is it?" he asked, raising the pitcher.

"It's perfect. Thank you," Ophelia beamed, the love in her eyes nearly breaking him.

"Tastes like vacation," Austen added, raising her glass toward the Mediterranean. "And this view. Heaven."

Feels like hell to me, Gianluca thought as he scanned the garden, staring at the red, iron-laden dirt that covered the so-called White Isle.

Austen's ice clinked against her glass, the sound reverberating like shattering glass in Gianluca's mind—his dread about his father's health now intertwined with the fear of Kristin's imminent arrival. He felt like he might collapse under the weight of it all.

Pushing himself into the present, he brushed a bead of sweat from his brow and raised his glass. "To the birthday girl," he toasted, his hand trembling lightly.

Glasses clinked around the table. "To the birthday girl," they all cheered.

CHAPTER 15

Matt, Ibiza

He definitely seems on edge. Something is up with him, Matt thought, watching as Gianluca settled into the seat across from him. He glanced around the table, assessing the group. Ophelia sat at the head with Austen to her right and Rosalie to her left. He was beside Austen, with Jack on his left. The villa's grounds were securely fenced in. Threat levels were low. Sitting outdoors, having drinks in a private villa in Ibiza was far from his usual professional setting, but old habits die hard.

His heart warmed as he observed how easily Ophelia and Austen connected. They were chatting happily next to him, though he wasn't listening. He read their body language—it was open, relaxed—and could tell they were becoming friends.

And Austen had finally said she loved him. He'd been confident for at least a month that she did. Every time he caught her watching him when she thought he wasn't looking, he could see it in her eyes. Reading people was one of his strengths, and Austen had become his favorite book. Early in their relationship, she'd been scared, but now, she felt safer. He'd worked hard to get her to that point, ensuring she had no reason to doubt. And today, it all paid off when she said those three little words for the first time.

He was mad about her. He'd never met anyone with her combination of book smarts, street smarts, beauty, sex appeal, and humor. His previous girlfriend, Eve, had been too innocent. She lacked the street smarts Austen had, so with Eve, he always felt like he had to be "on," professionally speaking. He was constantly watching, assessing, waiting for something to go wrong. He thought of himself as a pessimistic realist. But with Austen, things were different. She was scrappy and capable. He still felt protective, but he didn't always expect the worst. She made him believe good things were possible.

Ophelia looked happy, too, though Matt often wondered if she was pretending. He'd known her for years and always thought of her as a chameleon. She had an uncanny ability to mold herself into whatever or whoever was right for a given situation. Some might call her generous, always tuned into the needs of others, but Matt suspected she often didn't acknowledge her own needs—or even know them. He'd noticed it even more since she became a mother. Matt wasn't a father, but he understood that kind of self-sacrifice was common for parents.

Today, she was in hostess mode, making sure her guests had everything they needed and listening attentively to the conversations around the table. But every so often, he noticed her smile falter, and her eyes glaze over, like her mind had drifted somewhere far away. He wondered where it went.

Jack and Rosalie seemed lost in their own world, catching up on life.

"How long's it been since you two last saw each other?" Matt asked.

Rosalie looked at Jack for confirmation. "Eight months? I was in New York for a gallery opening last September."

"Yep. Luis and I tagged along, pretending we knew all about the snooty art. Honestly, does anyone go to those things for anything besides the free champagne and gratuitous gawking at all the beautiful, artsy people?" Jack quipped.

"People with culture do," Rosalie replied, rolling her eyes. "I cannot take you anywhere, Jack."

Suddenly, a chime rang from inside the house. Everyone looked at each other in confusion.

"It's the buzzer for the gate," Gianluca explained.

Ophelia glanced at her watch, biting on a fingernail. "It's too early for Kristin and Charlie."

Gianluca stood, spreading his arms wide in a grand gesture. "That'd be the cook. Dinner will be served at nine."

Ophelia's eyes widened, and a smile slowly spread across her face. "What did you do?"

He kissed the top of her head before heading toward the front door. "It's your birthday," he called over his shoulder.

"Well, that's a fun surprise," Austen said. "What a lovely husband you have, birthday girl."

The smile on Ophelia's face was pure sunshine as she nodded in agreement. *Maybe it was the surprise that had Gianluca on edge,* Matt thought.

"Well, I'll be damned. This is my kind of weekend," Jack declared exuberantly. "I love nothing more than a private chef in a private villa. Classy as always, darlin'. So glad we're friends, so I don't have to slum it and actually cook something myself."

Matt got up, squeezing Austen's shoulder. "I'll go see if they need help unloading."

As he walked toward the villa, he overheard Austen say, "He's assessing the potential threat from the cook. He works in security. Can't help himself."

Better safe than sorry. He smiled quietly as he made his way to where Gianluca and the cook, Carlos, were unloading boxes from a van. Gianluca introduced them, and when Matt shook Carlos's hand, he took note of the man's solid handshake and muscular build. They'd probably be equals in a physical fight. "Need any help?"

"*Muchas gracias*, very kind," Carlos replied, handing Matt a box of produce.

The three men carried boxes into the villa's pristine white kitchen, where Carlos began unpacking. Matt mentally noted where the knives were stored and checked for a fire extinguisher. He didn't see one but assumed it would be under the sink. Instinct. "What's for dinner?" he asked.

Carlos explained the menu with pride. "We'll start with gazpacho, followed by a few tapas—*patatas bravas*, garlic shrimp, Spanish omelet, Padron peppers, and, of course, Ibérico ham. The main course will be grilled seabass and a vegetarian paella. For dessert, *tarta de Santiago* and fresh fruit."

Gianluca nodded absently, checking his watch, then his phone. "Sounds good."

"Sounds excellent, Carlos, thank you," Matt said, trying to compensate for Gianluca's lack of enthusiasm. "We'll leave you to it. Just ask if you need help with anything."

Matt watched Gianluca closely as they headed back outside. *So, it's not the surprise that's got him on edge.* Just before they reached the door to the porch, Matt placed a hand on Gianluca's shoulder, stopping him. "What's going on? You seem off."

Gianluca shook off Matt's grip with a pinched smile. "Nothing. Everything's fine."

Matt's suspicions lingered, but he tried to push them aside. He didn't want to be on edge, even though his instincts told him he should be. As they rejoined the group, Matt resisted the urge to run his hand down Austen's back. She had suggested they not be too visibly affectionate this weekend out of consideration for Rosalie, who'd commented on how they "reeked of love." Austen had been the lone single at countless couple-filled events in her single years so was sensitive to Rosalie's feelings. Matt found the suggestion thoughtful, but he also found the idea of resisting each other during the day titillating. It inevitably meant fantastic sex at night. He happily accepted the challenge.

He tuned back into the conversation as Austen asked Rosalie, "In the car, you said something about how life might be more satisfying if romantic love wasn't so important. That intrigued me. Can you elaborate?"

Matt immediately focused, trying to understand Austen's curiosity.

Rosalie tucked her legs under her on the bench, sighing deeply. "You know the saying, 'It takes a village'?"

Austen nodded. "Sure. It's an African proverb, popularized by Hillary Clinton."

"*Oui*. It's about raising children and how you're not supposed to have to meet all your kids' needs alone. But I think it applies more broadly," Rosalie said, pursing her bright red lips. "My idiot ex-boyfriend was great at lifting heavy objects and giving me orgasms, but he couldn't meet my emotional needs."

Amusement flickered across Austen's face. "Lifting heavy objects and orgasms are important work."

Matt waited for her to look his way, and when she did, they exchanged a silent smile. I'm good at both, he conveyed with his eyes. You definitely are, hers replied. He felt the look all the way to his core.

Oblivious to their exchange, Rosalie continued, "Of course they're important. But I stayed with him longer than I should have because my friends filled in the gaps in his emotional intelligence."

Ophelia leaned in, clearly curious. "So, why'd you break up? If it's not too personal, I mean."

"It's fine. I left him because he was stuck in the twentieth century—expecting me to cook, clean, and do all the other household shit," Rosalie groaned. "I like taking care of people, but at some point, I realized he was taking me for granted, and that, I couldn't accept."

Matt noticed Ophelia glance briefly at Gianluca, recognition flashing across her face, before returning her gaze to Rosalie and silently nodding her understanding.

Austen stirred the fruit in her sangria with a metal straw. "But if he'd helped out more with the housework, you would've stayed even though he didn't meet your emotional needs?"

Rosalie popped a piece of Manchego into her mouth, chewed thoughtfully then swallowed. "My retirement fantasy is to live in a villa like this one in the South of France with friends who all take care of each other. A kind of sustained platonic love amongst friends feels more realistic to me."

"Platonic love sounds all cozy and fluffy, but I need sex," Jack interjected emphatically.

"And you get that from Luis, which is great," Rosalie replied. "But is there something you don't get from him that a friend could provide to make your life richer?"

Scratching his head, Jack looked stumped. "Like what?"

Matt was glad Jack asked so he didn't have to.

Rosalie shook her head, exasperated. "Every year after your birthday, you call me frustrated because Luis didn't plan it exactly how you wanted. What if you stopped expecting him to and let a friend handle the planning?"

Austen's finger shot up. "My friend Liz gives her husband an Excel sheet ahead of her birthday, listing a series of highly specific, acceptable options for plans. He gets to pick, so she still gets a surprise, and it's always a good one."

"Liz sounds exceptionally practical," Jack said. "I can dig it."

"Yes, but it's wildly unromantic," Austen argued. "Isn't it special when someone knows you so well, they can surprise you with a perfect gift—and maybe it's something you didn't even know you wanted?"

Matt shook his head. "In my experience, people are bad at reading minds. And we've all had to pretend we liked a gift we hated."

Rosalie grinned at Austen. "That spreadsheet is genius. We should stop expecting our partners to be everything all at once and recognize their strengths and weaknesses—and surround ourselves with people who help us live our best lives. How many fewer divorces might there be if we could all live with our friends and just date our spouses on the weekends?"

"It's an idea," Ophelia laughed. "However perhaps one better suited to couples without children."

Heads nodded around the table.

Austen leaned into Matt, smiling. "Your birthday's in two months. I'd like a spreadsheet with your wishes, please."

Matt rolled his eyes and looked at Ophelia. "Save me."

There were few things Matt hated more than being the center of attention. In his job, if people noticed him, it meant something had gone wrong. Even as a kid, he hated wearing a birthday hat and having everyone sing to him. Fading into the background suited him perfectly.

"Matt hates birthdays," Ophelia chimed in. "No spreadsheet needed. Just pretend it's a normal day."

"What? Why do you hate birthdays?" Austen sounded crushed. "I love birthdays. I celebrate my whole birthday week. Sometimes the whole month. How can you not like birthdays?"

"He doesn't like being the center of attention," Ophelia explained. "And he's modest enough to believe, despite all that hunky-ness, that he can pass through life without drawing absolutely everyone's gaze."

Jack raised a hand, blocking Gianluca from view. "Your husband is sitting right there," he stage-whispered to Ophelia.

Gianluca smiled blandly. "Sure, if muscles and tattoos are your thing, he's all right."

Matt buried his face in his hands. "That's enough of that."

The gate buzzer sounded again.

"That'll be Kristin and Charlie," Ophelia announced, jumping up. "The gang's all here."

CHAPTER 16

Ophelia, Ibiza

Ophelia buzzed the gate open for Kristin and Charlie's car and bounced out onto the front steps to greet them. She glanced around, frowning slightly, when she noticed that Gianluca had disappeared. She waved as they parked and climbed out.

"Welcome to Ibiza, friends. How was the trip?"

Kristin's blonde hair fluttered in the breeze as she walked up the steps, her eyes shadowed with heavy bags beneath. Ophelia had never seen her looking so knackered.

"Uneventful—the best kind," Kristin replied, giving Ophelia a weak hug.

"Happy birthday, Ophelia," Charlie chimed in, hoisting their bags up the steps. "Beautiful place you've got here. Thanks so much for inviting us. I can't tell you how much we've been looking forward to this."

"Come in," Ophelia said, gesturing toward the entrance and looking around for Gianluca once more. *He should be here to help carry the bags up. Where on earth did he go?*

"Is Gianluca cooking? Smells like heaven. I'm starving," Kristin said as soon as she walked through the door.

"That's a certain *señor* named Carlos," Ophelia explained, still searching for her husband. "Our chef for the night. It was a surprise from my lovely husband. Let me go find him, and he can help you with your bags."

"If you just point the way, I can take them up myself. It's no trouble," Charlie offered graciously.

Ophelia sighed, waving her hand. "All right. Follow me. I've put you two in the room next to ours." She led them upstairs and then murmured another apology as she left them to freshen up.

She made her way outside and dropped back into her chair at the head of the table. "Kristin and Charlie are getting settled, but they'll be down shortly. Dinner smells incredible—especially since I'm not the one cooking it. Hope everyone's hungry."

"More sangria?" Matt offered, lifting the pitcher.

"Yes, please." She leaned forward eagerly, holding out her glass for a refill and looking over her shoulder toward the house. "Where did Gianluca run off to?"

"I think maybe to the loo?" Matt guessed.

Moments later, Charlie appeared, and Ophelia introduced everyone around the table.

"Nice to meet you all. I'm Charlie Fisher. Kristin should be down any minute. Mind if I sit here?"

Matt gestured to the empty spot beside him. "This spot's been waiting for you. Sangria?"

Charlie nodded and smiled as he took a glass. "The name's Charlie. Not 'Sangria'—at least not yet. It might be soon enough. Cheers. And keep it coming."

Polite laughter rippled around the table.

"What a beautiful place," Charlie remarked, taking in the villa and the stunning view. "It's so nice to escape the gray of London. I'm in desperate need of some vitamin D—and whatever vitamins are in this sangria." He took a long sip.

Ophelia couldn't help but chuckle quietly at his entirely gray ensemble—a light gray T-shirt and slightly darker gray shorts. "You brought the gray with you, I see," she teased, gesturing to his outfit.

"Blimey, I guess I did." Charlie glanced down and laughed. "Left all my sunshine yellow clothes at home. Well, they say to dress for the job you want, so apparently, I want to be a London weatherman. Really must get some new ambitions. And new clothes."

He went around the table, asking Matt, Austen, Jack, and Rosalie the standard questions—how they knew Ophelia, where they lived, and what they did for work. Ophelia listened quietly as her guests shared the condensed, dinner-party versions of their lives.

He'd made it through the whole group by the time Kristin finally joined. She'd changed into a teal-colored mini dress, but if anything, she looked even more worn than when they'd arrived. Ophelia's worry deepened. *Is she coming down with something?*

"Everyone, this is Kristin Wilson. That chair is yours," Ophelia said, pointing to the empty seat at the tail of the table. "I'm so happy everyone is finally here."

"Hi, all. Lovely to meet you," Kristin murmured as she dropped into the chair.

"You just missed everyone's life stories. Sorry, love. I should have waited for you before I started lobbing questions," Charlie said with a sheepish smile, taking it on himself to repeat everyone's names and hometowns for her benefit.

"What about you two?" Jack asked, looking between Charlie and Kristin. "Tell us everything."

Charlie gestured toward Kristin with an open palm. "Ladies first."

"No, you start," she countered softly, shaking her head and fidgeting with her necklace. "Can someone please pass the water?"

Matt handed over the bottle and then raised the sangria pitcher. "Some of this too?"

Kristin shook her head again. "Just water for now, thanks. Airplanes dry me out. I need to hydrate. Charlie, go ahead."

Ophelia's brows furrowed. Kristin wasn't one to turn down alcohol. *What's going on with her?*

"Charlie Fisher, at your service. I work at Barclay's in wealth management. Born and raised in London. Met Kristin five years ago. I've got a son, Miles, who's fourteen. And apparently, I secretly want to be a weatherman."

"A weatherman?" Kristin echoed, tilting her head sideways.

"Joke. Ophelia was giving me grief about my outfit."

"I wasn't," Ophelia protested, laughing softly. "Gray is a great color on you."

Gianluca finally reappeared, shaking Charlie's hand and greeting Kristin with a kiss on each cheek before dropping back into his seat. "Here we all are," he declared, refilling his glass from the nearly empty pitcher.

He looked as gray as Charlie's shirt. Ophelia caught his eye and mouthed, *You okay?*

He nodded quickly, then stood up, holding the empty pitcher. "More sangria coming right up."

Ophelia's eyes flicked to Jack, who gave her a curious look. *He sees it too,* she thought. *Something's definitely off with Gianluca.*

"What about you, Kristin Wilson?" Jack asked, smoothly covering for Ophelia's distraction.

Kristin's gaze snapped back from Gianluca's retreating figure. She cleared her throat and took a sip of water. "I'm originally from Chicago but have lived in the UK since uni. I work for an events marketing firm, and Ophelia is one of my clients. We've been working together for three years, so I'm in Rome about once a month."

"Kristin's a powerhouse," Ophelia declared. "I couldn't do my job without her. And she's also very fun at parties. Around her, I feel like I need to up my old boring married lady game."

"Well, that's just nonsense," Kristin interjected. "You're hosting a fabulous birthday weekend in Ibiza. Old boring people don't do that."

"The forties are the best," Austen added. "You're definitely not old."

"Thank you, Austen!" Jack clapped. "For fuck's sake. I'm forty and married, too. Don't you dare call us old, Lady O. I've still got oh-so-much game."

"That's true, Fabulous Jack," Ophelia said with a grin. "Luis is a very lucky man."

"As is Gianluca," Jack returned, with a gracious nod. "It's not for nothing I call you Lady O. You earned that nickname in that first villa we stayed in with the way too thin walls."

"That was a thoroughly unnecessary story," Ophelia blushed, her smile slipping as her gaze drifted back to Gianluca. *That feels like so many lifetimes ago,* she thought.

The last year, their intimacy had dwindled to almost nothing. They had sex maybe once every three months, though not for her lack of trying. Ophelia's sex drive had surged in recent years, but Gianluca was always so tired after his hospital shifts, and she wouldn't dare badger him.

It wasn't their first dry spell. The first had lasted a full year after Esme was born, but once their daughter started sleeping through the night, they'd found their way back to each other. That had been easier to explain—they were both exhausted.

This time, she couldn't pinpoint an obvious cause. After fifteen years together, twelve of them married, and two kids, keeping romance alive wasn't easy. Still, she'd never summoned the courage to bring it up. Instead, she'd bought new lingerie for this trip, hoping to end the dry spell without having the awkward conversation. It was time, for both their sakes.

Kristin stood abruptly, snapping Ophelia out of her thoughts. "Excuse me. So sorry. My tummy is feeling a bit rumbly," Kristin said, excusing herself and slinking away toward the house.

Gosh, she must be feeling rough, Ophelia thought, pity welling up for her.

CHAPTER 17

Gianluca, Ibiza

Gianluca was headed toward the patio door with a fresh pitcher of sangria when Kristin marched through it, giving him a clear "follow me—now" message with her eyes and a slight jerk of her head. He watched as she moved toward the stairs and then turned to Carlos.

"Would you mind taking this out to the table?"

Carlos nodded. "No problem, *señor.*"

Gianluca stole a glance through the large plate glass windows toward the table outside. The guests were laughing, looking sufficiently absorbed, so he quickly turned on his heels and followed Kristin upstairs. Hers and Charlie's room was inconveniently located next to his and Ophelia's. When they arrived, and Ophelia told him where she wanted to put everyone, he agreed without blinking since Kristin and Charlie weren't coming. If he had thought for two seconds that they would, he would have come up with a reason to put their room as far away as possible. But now it was too late. Everyone was here and settled.

Her door was cracked open, and he slipped inside without knocking. When they locked eyes, he put a finger over his lips and caught her wrist, leading her into the en suite bathroom. He turned on the water, hoping to drown out their voices.

"Talk fast," he said, closing the door. "What the fuck are you doing here?"

"I'm pregnant," Kristin said, a desperate look in her eyes as she lurched toward him.

He raised a hand to stop her, the ground falling out from under his feet. Time slowed to a crawl.

"Is it mine?" The words slipped from his mouth.

She shook her head and shrugged one shoulder. "I don't know."

Gianluca was speechless. Every muscle in his body went numb, and his vision blurred—his world narrowing in on itself. He thought his stress levels couldn't get any higher, but she had just proven him wrong. Kristin's hand reached toward his chest, but he recoiled, steadying himself against the bathroom counter. Her hand dropped. Both times Ophelia had told him she was pregnant, he had felt joy.

This was a far cry from joy.

This felt like terror.

"I'm going crazy. I texted you a million times, but you never fucking answered, and I really needed to talk to you about this, so I came," she continued. "I haven't told Charlie. I'm about a month along, so based on my last trip to Rome, it could be yours. But it could also be his. Gianluca, tell me what to do."

Get rid of it, he thought. But he couldn't bring himself to say the words aloud.

"It's Ophelia's birthday, for fuck's sake," Gianluca spat. "I can't believe you got on that fucking plane. Jesus Christ. I need to think. And we need to get downstairs. We'll talk about this later. Go. I'll follow in a few minutes."

She reached for him again, wrapping her hands around his neck and pressing her body into his. "I know it's so awkward, but I needed you," she whimpered.

Gianluca's hands rose involuntarily to her waist. He stared into her hazel eyes, noticing the dark circles beneath them. He could feel her breath on his lips, only inches away. But looking at her now, he felt nothing but fear.

"Get out of here," he sighed, gently pushing her hips away. "Right now."

She hesitated, slowly letting her hands trail down his chest before turning toward the door. Gianluca faced the mirror, watching her reflection as she put a hand on the doorknob and paused.

"I love you," she said, still facing the door. Then she slipped out.

He turned off the water and stared at his reflection. His face was creased with stress.

I'm never going to survive this weekend, he thought. Dread crept into every cell of his body, making him feel like he might be sick.

When the wave passed, he snuck out of Kristin and Charlie's room and went into his own to gather his thoughts. He had asked Kristin if she wanted kids on the first night they met, but it had never come up since. And they were careful. Usually. Gianluca tried to remember if they had been as careful as they should have been on her last visit. He wasn't sure.

I'm an absolute fucking idiot, he thought. *I'm going to lose everything.*

CHAPTER 18

Austen, Ibiza

The tapas were dwindling, bite by scrumptious bite, and a light Mediterranean breeze carried the scents of pine and sea salt through the air. Fairy lights strung through the pergola's latticework had come on as the sun dropped toward the sea, and the whole evening felt enchanted. Austen had eaten more than her fair share of Padron peppers and was eyeing the last *patata brava* when Ophelia asked, "What did you do for your fortieth?"

Her memory raced back to the South of France and the trip with Liz and Milena. "Ten days on the Côte d'Azur with my two besties from university. We ate all the seafood, drank all the wine, and swam in the sea. It was incredible," she recalled. "And then I sent a love bomb to this guy via email who proceeded to shatter my heart into a million tiny pieces. That part was less fun."

Ophelia placed a hand on Austen's forearm. "It sounded great right up until the bomb."

"Why are you two talking about bombs?" Matt asked, leaning into the conversation.

Ophelia laughed softly. "You know how mums can always hear their babies cry even from the other side of the street? I think Matt is like that with the word 'bomb.' He has radar ears, tuned into anything that sounds like a threat."

"He's so protective. It's adorable," Austen added, shifting her attention to Matt. "It was a love bomb that didn't detonate the way I'd hoped at the time—a happy accident that ultimately led me to you."

Matt smiled warmly. "That's the first bomb-related story I've ever enjoyed."

"Everything happens for a reason," Ophelia said, looking earnestly between Austen and Matt. "I really believe that. I'm genuinely chuffed you two found each other."

Austen smiled. "Me too. I'm a big believer in fate."

Rosalie, who'd been quietly listening, turned toward the others at the table. "Who here believes everything is predestined, determined by fate? Austen and Ophelia are fatalists. I'm undecided."

"Everything is totally random," Charlie said with certainty. "At least it seems that way in my life."

"Explain please," Austen said, flattening her palms on the table.

"I mentioned my son, Miles. Now, don't get me wrong. I love him, but he was the product of a one-night stand when I was twenty-two," Charlie explained, pointing a finger idly. "I met his mum in a bar. We hooked up, and then there was Miles. But she could have just as easily gone home with some other bloke that night, and there would be no Miles."

"But she didn't go home with someone else. She went home with you," Austen replied, raising an eyebrow. "You were fated to be Miles's dad."

"And you're a really good dad," Kristin added reassuringly from down the table.

Charlie sighed and shook his head. "People think that fate always creates happy things. I resented the shit out of Emma, his mum, for years for keeping him. We had no relationship at all for the first eight years of his life because I was an immature wanker. Miles didn't deserve that."

"Better late than never," Kristin said, clearly trying to bolster him.

"What changed after eight years, if it's not too indiscreet of a question?" Rosalie asked, topping up her sangria from the sweating pitcher.

"There was some father-son event at his school that I wasn't there for, and it broke Emma's heart. She insisted that we start meeting once a month so we could get to know one another," Charlie recounted. "Once that started, I realized that I wanted to have a relationship with him. But I can't say any of it was fate. I think there are loads of different paths our lives could take, and we could be just as happy on any of them."

"Or just as fucking miserable," Jack cracked. "Sorry to all the breeders here, but kids just seem to suck all the life out of people. Luis and I have these friends in New York—another gay couple—who adopted a kid about a year ago, and we haven't seen them once since. I'm sure they'll be moving to New Jersey or Connecticut or some other suburban hellhole any day now. No two men were 'fated' to have a kid together, and now I've got to wonder if they're not wishing they'd paid more attention to fate."

"Jack, please. No one regrets having a child," Ophelia interjected. "I mean, yes, kids are a lot of work, and that first year or two can certainly be tough, but it's all worth it. Right, Gianluca?"

Gianluca looked up, seemingly startled by his own name. He paused a few beats too long, then said, "Some people do regret having kids. They just don't admit it."

The table fell silent.

Ophelia's eyes widened. "But not you, Gianluca. Obviously not you."

"No, of course not me," Gianluca replied, looking at Ophelia earnestly. "Our children are wonderful. But that's mostly because of you. You're a fantastic mother."

Matt raised his glass, clearly attempting to lighten the mood. "She is a great mom. To Ophelia, the birthday girl."

Everyone fumbled for their glasses to join Matt's toast, except for Kristin, who pushed back from the table.

"Excuse me. Afraid I need the loo again."

"You okay, love?" Charlie asked, his voice low, concerned.

Kristin nodded quickly and walked away.

Austen studied Charlie as his eyes tracked his girlfriend's hasty retreat, his comment about the "multiple paths" life could take bouncing around in her head. Hers could have gone in countless directions over the past few years, given the unforeseen twists and unexpected outcomes of her romantic choices. Most of those could be summed up by a single line: *Well, that didn't fucking go as planned.* And yet in that moment, with Matt at her side, she felt genuinely grateful for where those choices had led her.

She took a breath, letting the words form before she spoke. "Charlie, you said a minute ago that there are loads of different paths and that maybe we'd be just as happy on any of them, and I think you're right. I guess I just believe that the reasons we end up in one place or another in life aren't random."

She looked around the table, her voice softening. "I think fate has a way of steering our direction. But happiness… that's a choice we make along the way."

Ophelia stood. "Beautifully said, Austen. I, for one, am truly happy to have all of you here with me for my birthday. Thank you all for coming, and thanks to my darling Gianluca for organizing dinner tonight. I think the main course should be almost ready, so I'm just going to pop inside to check."

"I'm going to follow Kristin's lead and run to the loo," Rosalie said, walking away.

With Ophelia and Rosalie both away from the table, Austen reached for Matt, placing her hand high on his thigh under the table. She leaned in to whisper into his ear.

"Keeping my hands off you is torture. I can't wait until we're alone later. I plan to make you very happy."

He nuzzled his face into her neck. "I think fate has some good things cooking for you tonight as well, my love."

It was the first time he'd called her "my love," and her body flooded with desire. "Oh yah?" she cooed, tracing her fingertips along his leg. "You have ideas cooking?"

Matt fixed his hooded eyes on her. "Anticipation is one of the lost pleasures of adulthood. It's like a drug." His hand moved slowly up the base of her neck, under her hair. "I feel like a teenager right now, utterly high on it, dying to have my hands and my mouth all over you."

Austen gripped the edges of the bench, forcing herself to breathe. She felt his breath on her neck as he pulled away reluctantly when Ophelia opened the back door.

"Sea bass and paella are on their way out. I hope everyone's still hungry," Ophelia announced.

"Starving," Austen whispered so only Matt could hear.

"I'm going to have to move to the other end of this table to put some distance between us so you'll behave yourself," he said with a wink.

CHAPTER 19

Gianluca, Ibiza

Gianluca couldn't believe the subject of whether to have kids had come up at the dinner table. He was in hell. The night he and Kristin met, she'd mentioned that Charlie's son was the product of his "misspent youth." The phrase had stuck with him because, as the oldest of four sons, Gianluca never had that luxury. His parents expected him to help raise his younger brothers and set the example by following the traditional path: university, then marriage, then children. He'd always craved their approval, living his life to ensure he had it while occasionally resenting them for his inability to rebel. Kristin had been his first true rebellion, and right now, none of that thrill seemed worth it.

The group's conversation flowed around him, but Gianluca wasn't following. His gaze wandered to Charlie, sitting across the table on Matt's right. Until today, Charlie hadn't existed for him. But there he was—pale, blond, and goofy—everything Gianluca wasn't. If this baby was his, it would certainly be blond. *Please, God, let it be his.*

The thought of Charlie fucking Kristin made his stomach turn. He'd never been a jealous man, and he knew he had no claim on her, but seeing her boyfriend in the flesh brought up feelings he didn't recognize. His emotions were all over the map. Sensing a headache coming on, he pressed a thumb slowly across one temple and let his eyes wander the table.

He noticed Austen and Matt pawing at each other at the far end, and his jealousy flared in a new direction—envy. Their relationship, in its early, passionate phase, seemed so simple. Early love or lust—it didn't matter which—was intoxicating. In the first three years of their relationship, Ophelia commuted between Rome and London, and their desire for one another built into a passionate crash of bodies every time she visited. *How times have changed,* he mused.

Gianluca's thoughts were interrupted by Jack's hand firmly gripping his shoulder.

"Did you know that this guy," Jack said, pointing at Charlie, "brews beer in his garage? In my experience, all hoppy endings start with a good beer. Or five."

Charlie laughed, slapping Jack on the back. "Look at you with the beer puns. Nice one, mate."

Curious about Charlie, Gianluca joined the conversation. "What kind of beer do you brew?"

"Mostly bitter," Charlie replied with a goofy smile. "It's my go-to down at the pub, so I wanted to give it a try, make my own."

"I'm a Peroni guy back home," Gianluca said, raising his bottle of Cerveza Isleña, a popular beer brewed on the island. "But I always say, 'go local' when traveling."

"This is good stuff," Charlie agreed, raising his own bottle in a toast. "But bitter's the way to go in the UK."

You'd be more than bitter if you had half an idea of what's going on around here, Gianluca thought as he clinked bottles with Charlie and Jack. The memory of a night with Kristin in Rome flashed before him. They'd shared a particularly nice bottle of *Valpolicella* in their underwear in her hotel room, and she'd passingly disparaged Charlie's love for beer while extolling the virtues of his taste in wine. She had "accidentally" spilled a few drops of wine down her cleavage. He had happily licked her clean.

The parallels between the beginnings of his relationships with Ophelia and Kristin suddenly became clear. He couldn't believe he'd never seen it before. Both began with visits that were too short, leaving them hungry for more sex, more discovery. *Absence makes the heart grow fonder. Whoever said that was spot on.* The thrill of the unknown kept him coming back to Kristin. He and Ophelia had lost that years ago, replaced by comfort and familiarity.

For the first time, he wondered what perceived gap he filled for Kristin in her relationship with Charlie. There had to be something. But he couldn't imagine her ever losing the heat in a relationship—not with the way she dressed, not with the way she exuded sex. The sun sank lower, casting a fiery glow across the horizon behind Kristin's now empty seat. Kristin somehow felt like fire personified. But Ophelia had been fire once, too.

Ophelia. She was back outside now. *She's still so beautiful,* Gianluca thought. He looked inside the villa and saw Kristin lingering in the hallway just off the kitchen. She gave another subtle jerk of her head, signaling for him to come to her. Gianluca shook his head, turning his attention back to the table as Carlos began serving paella onto colorful, ceramic plates.

"This is a vegetarian paella. Made with bell peppers, tomatoes, onions, artichokes, asparagus, mushrooms, and saffron rice," Carlos said. "It's paired with an *Albariño*—a crisp, citrusy Spanish white wine that I hope you'll love. Enjoy."

As soon as Carlos went inside, Jack said dryly, "Mushrooms are the devil's food. I'll be picking them out with a pitchfork. Who wants mine?"

Charlie offered his plate to Jack who scraped the offending fungi away. Jack's devil and pitchfork imagery sent Gianluca's guilty mind deeper into turmoil. He felt nauseous, but he forced some paella down, knowing he needed it to absorb some of the alcohol.

Kristin returned, her expression steely. She looked like she'd finally decided to just power through the night. Ever since she'd arrived, she'd looked like she could burst into tears at any second, but now she looked resigned and somehow, calm.

Gianluca allowed himself a small moment of relief. *We'll take this weekend one hour at a time and try to avoid all hell breaking loose.*

His heart softened slightly. *She must've been feeling so desperate to come here, to face all of this in person.* He wanted to offer her a look or a touch of solidarity, to silently convey, "We can get through this. Just hold it together." If Jack hadn't been sitting between them, he would've touched her under the table. But Jack was there, and perhaps that was for the best. Yet, the more he tried not to look at her, the more he wanted to. He angled himself away from Kristin and toward Ophelia, pretending to engage in the conversation happening around him. He fidgeted with his cutlery, hearing nothing but the buzzing static of his own tortured thoughts.

Matt's voice eventually cut through asking, "Hey Kristin, do you want to swap seats with me? You look bored over there with the guys. No offense, Jack and Charlie."

Kristin's face brightened, and she stood, collecting her plate. "You sure you don't mind? I don't want to split you and Austen up."

Matt winked at Austen before saying to Kristin, "I know where she lives. Don't worry. I'll find her later."

They switched seats, and Charlie helped relocate their drinks. Kristin was now sitting directly across from Gianluca.

She immediately leaned into the conversation with the women, but before he could count to three, under the table, her foot slid up his leg, setting his skin on fire. He caught her eye momentarily, and they exchanged a brief, hungry look before he turned away.

Fire. Something about this woman makes me want to bathe in the flames. I'm fucked.

CHAPTER 20

Matt, Ibiza

From his new seat at the end of the table, Matt had a clear view of all the guests and the door to the house. He liked being able to see everyone and everything. By the time dessert was served, he'd decided Carlos was harmless but definitely had his eye on Rosalie. Each time he brought out a new course, his gaze lingered on her.

His mind drifted back to the first time he met Austen in Senegal. She had climbed into the back seat of the SUV, and he'd caught her looking at him repeatedly in the mirrors mounted on the dashboard. Even back then, he thought her green eyes could lure a man to his death, like a siren's call. Eyes could say so much without a single word.

Matt was enjoying the wine like everyone else, so he knew his usual sharp sense of observation might be slightly dulled. Still, he couldn't shake the uneasy feeling that Kristin's eyes fell on Gianluca too often and too intensely. He'd been watching them both for a while and with each round of tapas and every newly opened bottle of wine, his suspicions grew.

As Carlos explained the dessert course, Matt let his napkin casually drop to the floor. Leaning down to retrieve it, he caught a glimpse of Gianluca pulling his leg away from Kristin's bare foot.

Her other foot was still in its sandal, but this one dangled suspiciously in the space between them.

Does Kristin have unusually long legs? That would be one explanation. Or had her foot been on Gianluca's leg? Surely, neither of them would be that stupid—not at Ophelia's birthday, for heaven's sake.

His mission for the next few days suddenly became clear: find out if Gianluca was cheating on Ophelia with Kristin. The thought made Matt's jaw clench. He glanced at Ophelia, her face warmly lit by the candles as she laughed with Austen and Rosalie. Kristin sat quietly, seemingly disengaged.

How would Ophelia handle this if it were true? No. Don't go there. He pushed the thought away. *He's innocent until proven guilty.*

Matt tried to join in the conversation with Charlie, Jack, and Gianluca, but his mind kept drifting back to Ophelia, mentally gaming out different scenarios for how the weekend might unfold. He prided himself on his ability to predict the unpredictable, but he had a sinking feeling this might be beyond even him.

Trying to get ahead of the game in his mind, Matt asked Gianluca, "What's on the docket for tomorrow?"

"Good question," he declared, clinking his wine glass lightly with a knife as he stood.

All heads turned toward him, but Matt continued to observe. He saw Kristin pull back in her seat to sit up straight. *Pulling her foot away from him?*

"Matt just asked about the plan for tomorrow, so before everyone is too drunk to remember, here it is," Gianluca announced. "Sleep in as long as you want. Carlos will be back in the morning, and breakfast will be set up from eight-thirty until ten. Come down whenever you want."

"Three cheers for vacation and personal chefs," Jack said raising his glass festively, sloshing a few drops onto the table.

Gianluca grinned and continued, "We'll lounge by the pool until one-thirty, then head to Aiyanna—a nice restaurant by the sea—for lunch at two. Bring your bathing suits if you want to swim after. Dinner is at Sunset Ashram at eight forty-five, just in time for the sunset."

Ophelia leaned back, swirling her wine in the glass, her smile serene. "*Grazie,* Gianluca," she said, slightly slurring the words.

The others chimed in with their thanks, but Matt noticed Gianluca's gaze linger on Kristin for a moment too long.

Why would he plan a birthday party for Ophelia and invite his mistress? Unless Ophelia chose the guests and thinks Kristin is her friend. God, I hope I'm wrong.

"When is your actual birthday, Ophelia?" Rosalie asked.

"Tomorrow," Ophelia confirmed with dramatically raised eyebrows. "The big four-oh. As in oh-my-God, I'm old."

Gianluca raised a hand in mock objection. "Don't forget how many people around this table are older than you. Be careful who you insult there, birthday girl."

Ophelia raised her hands defensively but kept a smile on her face. "My sincere apologies. Especially to you, Gianluca, since you're the oldest in the group. No need to mention anyone else's age, but of course, Kristin and Charlie are mere babes, still in their thirties."

"Me too," Rosalie chimed in.

"Just barely forty," Jack exclaimed, pointing to himself. "Forty and fabulous, just like Lady O."

"Well, given tomorrow's the big day, I'm going to call it a night and save my energy," Rosalie announced. "Lovely to meet you all. Very much looking forward to the rest of the weekend."

Jack jumped up, moving to take her seat next to Ophelia. "I need more time with the birthday girl. Sleep tight, Rosie," he called, blowing exaggerated air kisses as she waved and headed inside.

Sliding into Jack's vacant seat, Matt positioned himself next to Gianluca, who was in mid-conversation with Austen about his work at the hospital.

"What's your weirdest ER rescue story?" she asked him. "Strangest thing you ever pulled out of someone, for example. We're all done eating, right?"

Gianluca let out a pained laugh. "Last week, I removed a stiletto heel from a man's neck. His wife caught him cheating and used her Prada slingback to express her displeasure."

Matt immediately looked at Kristin for a reaction and saw her eyebrows raised meaningfully at Gianluca. *I think she and I are both wondering the same thing. Why tell that story if you're currently cheating on your wife?*

Austen leaned toward Matt. "Didn't you have a story about almost getting whacked with a stiletto?"

"Unfortunately, yes. I was on a security detail in Ivory Coast, sitting in an SUV waiting for my guy to come out, and some 'ladies of the night' tried to talk to me," Matt explained. "I tried to politely get rid of them, but they were rather insistent, so I had to get a bit more forceful in my request that they move on, and one of them took off her shoe and tried to hit me with it. Luckily, I was faster."

Ophelia laughed and shook her head. "What about you, Jack? Has every man at this table been involved in a stiletto incident?"

"Well, there was that one night at drag bingo," Jack mused, with a crooked smile.

"Drag bingo? Is that a thing?" Ophelia asked.

"Oh, it's a thing. But I'm just kidding. No stilettos for me. Although now I'm feeling tragically left out," Jack cracked. "And speaking of tragedies, I now realize I'm the only single at a table full of couples, so I think I shall retire and go call my husband before I pass out."

Ophelia blew him a kiss. "Sweet dreams, Fabulous Jack. We'll have loads of time tomorrow to catch up. Say hello to Luis for me and that we're sorry he's not here."

"Will do, Lady O. Thanks for a great first night, all," Jack said as he staggered inside. "*Hasta mañana*[23]."

"And then there were six," Charlie said. "Although I'm going to make it five. Long week at work, and I'm knackered."

"I'm going to stay for a bit," Kristin said to him. "I'll be up later."

Charlie kissed her on the top of the head. "Okay, love. Goodnight, all."

Matt surveyed the remaining revelers—Ophelia, Austen, Gianluca, and Kristin. Austen shot him a subtle "let's go upstairs" nod and wink, which he desperately wanted to follow, but he was hesitant to leave Ophelia, Gianluca, and Kristin alone. He shook his head regretfully and hated seeing her small but playful pout.

I'll explain everything to her later. Or should I? Two sets of eyes are better than one to get to the bottom of this, but maybe it'd be better to be discreet and keep my suspicions to myself. I need to push on this a bit.

"Gianluca, why don't you scoot down next to your lovely wife," Matt suggested.

Matt watched as Gianluca's eyes darted between Ophelia, the empty spot beside her, and Kristin.

"You take it, Matt. I get way more time with Ophelia than you do," he gestured toward the seat.

Reluctantly, Matt switched places and settled between husband and wife.

"It's been a beautiful first night, Ophelia. Thanks again for having us," Austen said. "Did the evening turn out as you'd hoped?"

Ophelia raised her glass. "All I wanted was to be surrounded by good friends and for you all to have a wonderful time, so if you're happy, I'm happy."

"It's your weekend. Let's focus on you," Matt said, pointing at her with his beer bottle. "Any hopes or dreams for your fortieth year?"

---

23 See you tomorrow.

Ophelia leaned forward, resting her chin on her hand. "I haven't really thought about it. But tonight, sitting with the ladies, I realize I've missed the gift of female friendships. No offense, Matt."

"None taken."

"I don't have as many girlfriends as I'd like. I suppose I've been so focused on the kids these past few years. So, maybe my plan will be to nurture my female friendships."

"I think that's a wonderful plan. I hope I can be part of it," Austen replied.

If he hadn't been so focused on Kristin's conspicuous silence and avoidance of eye contact with anyone left at the table, he would have loved Austen's warm and generous reply.

"I'm going to pop to the loo," Ophelia said, standing up and draining the contents of her wine glass.

As she walked away, Matt felt Austen's foot crawl up his own calf. Normally, the contact would have thrilled him, but given his suspicions about Kristin and Gianluca, it only heightened his discomfort. He now had proof that it was possible to play footsie without any sign of movement above the table.

CHAPTER 21

Gianluca, Ibiza

As the night wound down, Gianluca felt more wound up than ever. Kristin's foot brushing against his leg under the table had him feeling equal parts aroused and conflicted. Dread had been pooling in his gut for hours. Being with her this weekend was impossible. He wouldn't even consider sneaking away for sex, but they needed to talk—about the baby and how to keep the peace this weekend so his entire life didn't implode.

Three more days. I just have to keep this nightmare in check for three days. He knew that physical distance would be key to survival.

He rose from the table and began collecting empty bottles for recycling. Normally, he would've left that for Carlos, but he needed to clear his head and put as much space between him and Kristin as possible. With several empty bottles in a cardboard box, he walked into the kitchen and found Ophelia slightly staggering.

She lunged toward him, cupping his face in both hands and planting a dramatic kiss on his lips. She tasted like wine.

"What was that for?" he asked, trying to keep his thoughts off Kristin while balancing the box of bottles.

"For organizing Carlos. For taking care of me. For asking your parents to watch Marco and Esme. For being your incredible self," she replied, pushing her fingers through his hair. "*Grazie.*"

Gianluca's palms started to sweat, and the box in his arms became even more unwieldy. He exaggerated the motion of adjusting its weight to slip out of her grasp—and away from his guilt.

"*Prego.* No one deserves it more than you. Let me go put these down and make sure everything is sorted for tomorrow with Carlos."

Ophelia kissed him again, holding his face as her eyes, slightly unfocused, filled with gratitude. His heart ached as he twisted away from her hold and walked outside.

After depositing the bottles in the recycling bin, he stood in the darkness for a moment, his hands on his hips and his head tilted up toward the sky. He took sixty seconds to breathe, sending up a silent prayer. He could still feel Kristin's foot pressed into his shin and Ophelia's lips pressed against his. *Fuck my life,* he thought.

When he returned to the kitchen, Carlos was packing up. "*Gracias*, Carlos. Everything was perfect tonight," Gianluca said, forcing a smile. *Other than my pregnant mistress being here with my wife,* he thought as he poured himself a shot of *hierbas*[24] from the bottle he'd purchased this morning. He tossed it back, letting the aromatic digestif burn its way down his throat.

Carlos nodded and shook his hand. "I'll be back in the morning to get everything ready for breakfast. Eight-thirty, yes?"

Gianluca nodded and then noticed Kristin in his peripheral vision, lurking near the door leading from the kitchen into the rest of the house.

"Sorry to interrupt," she said. "Gianluca, can you show me where the beach towels are? I want to do yoga by the pool in the morning and then go for a swim, and I'll probably be up before anyone. I'm an early riser."

"Of course," Gianluca said, heat exploding up his neck. "Carlos, thanks again. See you tomorrow, or rather, in a few hours. Drive safe and sleep fast."

---

24 an aniseed-flavored liqueur made from herbs native to Ibiza

Gianluca took a deep breath and followed Kristin toward the front of the house. It was clear she was leading him as far away from the group as possible, and she seemed to know exactly where they were headed. His skin burned from fear, survival instinct and arousal. He wanted her. The house was dark. She led him toward the small powder room near the front door and dragged him inside by the wrist, locking the door.

"You're crazy. We can't," he insisted, backing up to the wall and holding up one hand.

She grabbed his outstretched hand and pressed it into her breast. "Shut up and kiss me," she whispered into his mouth, sliding her other hand under his shirt and around his back as she leaned her hips into his.

The *hierbas* buzzed in his brain and her familiar lavender scent invaded his senses, triggering him to comply hungrily. His mouth crashed into hers as he picked her up by the hips and put her on the small counter. Her legs wrapped tightly around his waist, removing any space between them as the hemline of her dress was pushed high up her toned thighs. Their tongues and breathing entangled like they needed each other to survive, and her hands pushed hungrily into his hair as he hardened against her. He grabbed her ass tightly to press their bodies together, and she responded with a sinful moan into his mouth.

"I'm absolutely aching for you. Take me. Right now," she begged, reaching for the button on his shorts.

He grabbed her by both wrists to stop her, jolting suddenly backward into reality. "We cannot fuck in the bathroom at my wife's birthday party. Christ, it's like you want to get caught," he whispered harshly at her. "We can't do this. They're thirty steps away."

"I love you. I'll never make it for three days being so close to you and not being able to have you," she breathed, grabbing hold of his shirt.

"You absolutely will. I'm sorry. I shouldn't have let you bring us in here. We'll go for a walk or something tomorrow so we can talk, but we've got to keep our distance," he insisted, pushing her hands away and stepping backward until his back met the wall. Only inches separated them.

Her thighs were spread wide, and he could see her wetness through her gauzy pink panties. Everything in his body wanted to fuck her senseless right there on the counter, but he forced his eyes upward and shut them tightly, for once thinking with his brain.

"That's the last time I'm going to touch you this weekend," he said, his voice low.

Gianluca unlocked the door and slipped out, leaving her inside. He hurried toward the stairs, running his hands through his hair, hoping not to run into anyone as guilt washed over him in waves. He rushed upstairs, stripped off his clothes, and jumped into a freezing cold shower.

The icy water hit the back of his neck, sending shivers down his spine. *Fuck. I'm an idiot for letting this go on as long as it has. The baby has to be Charlie's. Even if it's not, she can pretend it is. I can't let this destroy my marriage or my family. I don't want to be this man.*

With that resolution, he turned the hot water on full blast and in penance, forced himself to stand under it until it almost burned his skin. He dried off quickly and pulled on boxers and a T-shirt. Ophelia walked in just as he started brushing his teeth.

"I was outside waiting for you," she said, sounding annoyed.

Gianluca glanced at her through the mirror, hoping she couldn't see the guilt in his eyes. "I didn't see you. Sorry. I settled up with Carlos and came up to shower. I'm beat."

She wrapped her arms around him from behind, kissing his shoulders and sliding her hands under his T-shirt—just as Kristin had earlier. His heart clenched with guilt. He slipped out of her embrace, retreating to the bedroom, where he quickly turned off the light and climbed into bed. He lay on his side with his back to the bathroom door, uncomfortably aware that behind the wall in front of him, Kristin was likely lying in her own bed. He heard Ophelia turn the water on and tried to steady his breathing, despite the tornado of emotions swirling in his chest.

The bathroom light spilled into the room when Ophelia re-entered. "This birthday girl is in her birthday suit and would very much like to get lucky tonight," she said, her voice playful.

The image of Kristin behind the wall in front of him and Ophelia standing naked behind him made his dick twitch, but he didn't dare move. He clenched his eyes shut, his mind warring with his body. *Kristin would hear everything. I can't do it. It'd be like cheating on both of them at the same time.*

"Gianluca?" Her whispered voice echoed in his ears.

Feigning sleep was his only escape from the impossibility of the situation. He stayed motionless, listening as Ophelia sighed, put on her pajamas, and climbed into bed. She kissed his shoulder before rolling away with another sigh. Only when he heard her breathing slow did he turn onto his back, staring at the ceiling. He let the self-loathing consume him, wondering what fresh hell awaited him tomorrow.

CHAPTER 22
Matt, Ibiza

Matt was an early riser. Austen was not. When he opened his eyes, he gently brushed a few strands of hair away from her sleeping face, slid out of bed, and left her to dream. He loved the quiet solitude of early mornings, especially knowing it was only Friday—they had the whole weekend ahead. Carlos hadn't arrived yet to set up breakfast, but Matt found some coffee in the kitchen. Steaming mug in hand, he wandered outside and reclined on a pool lounger, just as the sun began casting the horizon in pale, warm light.

Listening to the birds chirping and the cicadas humming, he sipped his coffee, replaying last night's highlights with Austen in his mind. He'd been right about the sex being spectacular after a day of resisting each other. Yet despite those good memories and the peaceful morning, his thoughts drifted back to his suspicions about Gianluca and Kristin. The whole situation bothered him greatly, and he was determined to get to the bottom of it.

Fifteen minutes later, he heard a female voice say, "Good morning." Turning, he saw Kristin, dressed in red spandex, holding a yoga mat.

"I was going to do some yoga by the pool. Do you mind?" she asked.

"Be my guest," Matt said, standing up and heading for the house. "I'll leave you to it."

"I didn't mean to run you off," she called.

Matt looked over his shoulder. "Not at all. Going to refill my coffee and take some up to Austen. See you in a bit." He didn't want to be alone with her and his suspicions while she was in downward dog.

He set two mugs on the bedside table and fanned the aroma of coffee toward Austen's still sleeping face. Her nose twitched in recognition, and he let his fingers brush lightly down her arm, further stirring her.

"Is that coffee?" she asked sleepily, opening one eye as a smile curled onto her lips.

"Good morning, sunshine. *Café con leche*,[25] just like you like it."

The thin strap of her forest green silk sleep tank slipped off her shoulder as she sat up, reaching for the mug. "You're my hero. What time is it?"

Matt kissed her shoulder as he dragged the strap back up. "Almost seven-thirty."

Frowning, she replied. "We're on vacation. Not that I don't appreciate the coffee, but why are you wearing so many clothes at this hour?" She planted kisses down the side of his neck, careful not to spill the coffee.

Matt breathed in her warm, gingery smell, kicked off his flip flops and leaned against the headboard, mug in hand. "Just saw Kristin down by the pool about to do yoga."

"Oh God, she's a yoga-on-vacation person? I knew I didn't like her," Austen cracked, before taking a sip and snuggling into his side.

You're about to like her even less, he thought, despite knowing she was joking.

---

25 Coffee with milk.

"So, listen, I have a terrible theory that I sincerely hope is incorrect, and I've decided I'd like to hire you as a co-conspirator to try and get to the bottom of it," Matt announced, almost in a whisper.

Austen rubbed her eyes with her free hand. "Go on."

"I watched Kristin and Gianluca pretty closely last night, and I think they might be having an affair."

"What?" Austen bolted upright, sending her coffee sloshing in the mug.

Matt quickly pressed his fingertips to her lips. "Careful. The walls are thin."

She nodded, eyes wide.

"Will you help me observe them today, discreetly? I hope I'm wrong because it would kill Ophelia. I can't figure out why Kristin would come here with Charlie if it's true, but I saw some things last night that I can't unsee."

Austen frowned, her mouth pulling to the side in concern. "What did you see? What should I be looking for?"

"First of all, you must be subtle. They can't know they're being watched. Surveillance one-oh-one," he said. "I think they were playing footsie under the table last night."

Austen smiled skeptically and gestured between them with her index finger. "That was us. We were playing footsie under the table."

Matt laughed and leaned over to kiss her cheek. "It was also them. I'm fairly certain. I dropped a napkin at one point and when I bent down to grab it, I saw him moving away from her very outstretched and shoe-less foot."

"Okay, but you didn't actually see her foot on him?"

"I didn't," Matt acknowledged. "But I also noticed them both missing from the scene once or twice throughout the evening, like they might have slipped away together. I hate being suspicious, but I am."

"Consider me your spy," Austen said, giving him a small salute. "I'm on duty, and we'll do our very best today to put your suspicions to rest. As you say, it would be absolutely idiotic for Kristin to have come here with Charlie if she was sleeping with Gianluca."

"People are often pretty stupid when they're having affairs," Matt observed.

Austen set her mug down on the bedside table and leaned into him once again, arching an eyebrow. "Does this knowledge come from any personal experience?"

There it was again—her hesitancy to trust. "I've never cheated on a girlfriend in my life. Closest I came was standing at the door of room 209 in Dakar," he said, running the back of his hand down her cheek.

Austen took his mug from him and set it down next to hers before taking his face in her hands. "You're a good man, Matt Richmond. And I love you."

He kissed her tenderly, twirling a strand of her hair around his finger. "I love you, Austen Keller. Coffee-morning breath and all."

She buried her face in his chest and then collapsed back into the pillows. "I really hope you're wrong. About me having morning breath and, more seriously, about Gianluca and Kristin. If you're not, poor Ophelia. And at her birthday party. What a dick."

"You smell and taste like lemons, ginger and sunshine, always. And Gianluca is innocent until proven guilty. Let's give him the benefit of the doubt," Matt suggested sagely. "I don't want to be right about this."

She reached for his shirt and pulled it over his head as she moved to straddle his lap. "I think that's enough about them for this morning. Now I'd like to focus entirely on you and all the many things you consistently get right."

"Best idea I've heard all day," he replied, pulling her mouth toward his.

CHAPTER 23

Ophelia, Ibiza

The villa was still quiet when Ophelia opened the blinds, letting the early sunlight pour in. She took in the cloudless blue sky.

"Another beautiful day in paradise," she sighed, scanning the view. Something red caught her eye. "Oh crikey, looks like Kristin just finished poolside yoga. It's cruel of her to make that perfect body the first thing I see on the morning of my fortieth birthday. Why did I invite her?"

Gianluca groaned from under the pillow, mumbling something unintelligible.

"Get back in bed, you say?" she teased, sliding back under the covers. "Go on then. Yes, I suppose I will."

She pulled the pillow away from his face, meeting his sleepy eyes.

"Guess what we don't have today?"

"What's that?" he asked, scratching his beard groggily.

"Children," she smiled. "No little people will be bounding into this room at any point. Do you know what that means?"

He crossed his arms over his face, shielding himself from the light. "That we can finally sleep for once in our miserable adult lives?"

She ran her hand down his chest toward his boxers. "I had something else in mind, actually."

His hand flew down, stopping hers at his navel. "The walls are pretty thin, I think. Not sure we should be putting on a show for your friends."

Ophelia sighed, rolling onto her back. "We haven't had sex in months, Gianluca. It's my birthday. We have no children here, and I think we can be quiet."

He rolled onto his side, reaching for her arm and gently pulling her toward him. "You're right. I'm an ass. Come here." His hand traveled down her back, over her hip, and under her knee, lifting her leg over his own as he kissed her neck.

"Don't make me talk you into anything," she said, tilting her head back to let him kiss her.

"You're not. You're my wife, and I love you," he said, peeling off her tank top and lowering his head to her chest before meeting her gaze. "I know you hate hearing that, but it's your birthday, so today you're going to. But just that once. Now I'm going to shut up and bury my face between your thighs until you cum."

He pulled the covers over his head and moved down the bed, much to Ophelia's surprise and delight. He'd never spoken so crassly to her. She felt herself blush but could think of no better way to end an uncomfortable conversation. She grabbed a pillow and put it over her face to muffle her moans. *Happy birthday, indeed.*

When they finally emerged from their room an hour later, Ophelia was buzzing with happiness. She was forty, fabulous, and breakfast awaited her, alongside a small bouquet of white rock roses and lavender, clearly picked fresh from the villa's garden. *Carlos thinks of everything,* she mused.

Through the window, she saw Charlie, Jack, and Rosalie eating outside under the pergola, so she and Gianluca filled up their plates and made their way outside to join them.

"Good morning, everyone," she chimed, setting down her breakfast and a steaming cup of tea at the head of the table. "How's the Can Blanco crew doing this morning?"

Jack slid down the bench to make room for Gianluca. "Happy birthday, darlin'," he said, raising his orange juice in a toast and gesturing toward the horizon. "There are more hideous places to turn forty, I suppose."

"*Joyeux anniversaire*[26], Ophelia," Rosalie added, pushing her cherry-red sunglasses onto her head. Her lipstick perfectly matched her glasses, even at breakfast. "You look happy."

Ophelia smiled, letting memories of the morning flash across her mind's eye. "Yes, there are. And I am happy." *Just had my first non-battery-powered orgasm in ages.*

"To another fabulous trip around the sun," Charlie offered with a smile and a small salute.

"Thanks all," Ophelia graciously replied. "No sign of Matt or Austen yet this morning? I saw Kristin by the pool doing yoga earlier."

"Yep, she's showering. Should be down any minute," Charlie replied, popping a piece of melon into his mouth.

"Here I am," Kristin sang, stepping out from the house in a skintight white tank top and low-rise floral capri pants and putting her plate down in the spot next to Charlie. "I saw Matt earlier. He was up before everyone, but he disappeared back into the house when I started my workout."

Ophelia stacked ham and cheese on a piece of bread as Kristin sat down, looking more well-rested than the day before. "Your discipline is admirable. My exercise routine usually involves running after two small children. My plan this weekend is no exercise at all."

"It's a good plan," Rosalie concurred, taking a sip of coffee. "I'm also anti-exercise on vacation. Vacation is for relaxing."

---

26 Happy birthday

"It's a lifestyle choice," Kristin trilled, stirring honey into her tea. "But I get that it's not for everyone. No one has to join me."

"Okay, we won't," Ophelia laughed, tapping the table to close the matter. "I'll be thoroughly slathered in sunscreen and prostrate by the pool with a book in fifteen minutes and have no plans to move until lunch."

"Your dedication to sport is admirable," Charlie said, squeezing Kristin's shoulder. "And clearly, it pays off. Just look at you."

Ophelia felt a twinge of guilt. "Yes, bloody hell. Ignore me. I'm only jealous of your not-forty-year-old perfect body."

Kristin shook her head. "Perfect doesn't exist."

"Perfect is boring," Jack declared, standing up. "Now, excuse me while I exercise." He dropped into a plank and did one push-up before popping back up and brushing his hands together. "Okay, that was perfect. I've officially earned my pool time."

The group laughed as Jack dramatically flopped onto a lounger.

After finishing breakfast, Ophelia claimed the pool lounger beside Gianluca, closing her eyes and soaking up the sun. She only opened them and picked up her book when she heard Matt and Austen come outside.

One by one after all the breakfast plates had been cleared, everyone claimed a pool lounger, except for Rosalie who floated in the pool on a pink flamingo inflatable.

"It's so quiet," Kristin said, a while later. "Is there a sound system? I have a great playlist."

Ophelia looked up to see Kristin standing on the opposite side of the pool in an ass-bearing, hot pink, string bikini. *Crikey. That's an eyeful.* She looked over at Gianluca, lying in the chair next to her and asked, "Is there?"

Gianluca got up somewhat reluctantly. "Yes, let me show you where you can plug in your phone. It's in the kitchen."

CHAPTER 24

Austen, Ibiza

Austen rose slightly on her forearms, watching Kristin slink toward the house with her phone in hand. She and Matt were lying on their stomachs on the two pool loungers closest to Gianluca's, and as he walked away, Matt turned his head to catch Austen's eye. She noticed Ophelia had returned to reading her book, so Austen gave Matt a small head tilt toward the house, signaling she was going inside to spy. He gave her a silent, approving nod.

She quietly slipped through the patio door and saw Gianluca and Kristin standing close together in the kitchen. Kristin plugged her phone into the jack, and they exchanged low whispers. Austen couldn't make out most of their conversation but managed to catch the tail end of one bitter-sounding sentence from Kristin:

"...could hear you fucking her through the wall."

Hearing Austen's footsteps, Gianluca spun around, his eyes widening when they landed on her. He quickly tried to mask his reaction, but it was too late.

"*Hola amigos*," Austen said, pretending not to have heard. "Just grabbing some cucumber water from the fridge." She forced a breezy tone as she pried open the stainless-steel door and pulled out a pitcher. "Either of you want some?"

"No thanks, Austen. I'm all set," Gianluca replied, walking away.

Kristin shook her head and quickly looked down at her phone. "Here's a good one to start with." *What Goes Around Comes Around* by Justin Timberlake poured out of the speakers. "And, yes. I will have a glass. Thanks."

Austen poured three glasses and handed one to Kristin, who tapped her fingers feverishly on the counter, out of sync with the music.

"Is this song about being cheated on? Or being a cheater? I've never been sure," Austen asked. It was a bit on the nose, given what she'd overheard, but she kept her voice casual.

Kristin inhaled a sharp breath and stammered, "I... I think it was about Britney Spears cheating on him."

"Poor Britney. She's a mess," Austen said, starting to walk back outside. "I mean why would anyone cheat on JT, right?"

Kristin followed behind her, unamused. "Right."

When Austen returned to her pool lounger, Matt raised an eyebrow, wordlessly asking if she'd seen anything. She handed him a water glass and mouthed, *Tell you later*. Ophelia was still just a few chairs away, engrossed in her book.

From behind her sunglasses, Austen continued to observe the group. Kristin had retaken her spot between Charlie and Jack and sat cross-legged, her foot bouncing nervously against the chair. Austen wondered why, if it was true, Kristin would have come here.

This is starting to feel like some horrible reality TV show, she thought.

As lunchtime approached, Gianluca announced they'd be leaving in forty-five minutes, so Austen and Matt headed to their room to get ready. Once the door closed, they huddled together on the bed to debrief.

"When I walked into the kitchen, they were whispering and standing really close. I heard her say, '...could hear you fucking her through the wall.' She sounded pissed off. But Gianluca saw me and left. That's all I got."

Matt's eyes widened. "How pissed off? Tell me more about her tone."

"She was seriously angry," Austen said flatly.

"There's really no reason for Kristin to chastise Gianluca about having sex with his wife, unless—" Matt's voice trailed off, sounding heavy with the realization.

"Unless." Austen echoed with a sigh.

Matt rubbed his forehead back and forth. "But you didn't hear anything more. What else could it have been? Are we jumping to conclusions? Confirmation bias is a real thing."

Austen took his hands in hers, meeting his eyes. "I love your willingness to give them the benefit of the doubt, but really, what else could it be?"

Matt groaned, pulling her into his arms, his forehead resting on her shoulder. "I don't know what to do."

"If they're stupid enough to be doing this in front of everyone before lunch on day two, we'll see more before the weekend's over. Let's be sure," Austen suggested, stroking his back.

He sighed into her hair. "I'm sorry for dragging you into this."

"Don't be sorry. We'll figure it out together. If we're right, we'll support her," Austen replied firmly, the word "*if*" hanging heavily between them.

Their table on the patio at Aiyanna overlooked the sea, just a hundred feet away. They sat on rattan chairs under bright, multi-colored parasols that cast wide shadows. Ophelia, smiling contentedly in a black cotton eyelet lace dress, sat at the head of the table. Kristin sat to her left while Gianluca hesitated before choosing a seat at the opposite end, distancing himself from Kristin and his wife. Charlie sat on Ophelia's right across from Kristin, while Austen and Matt took seats in the middle, well-positioned to observe the group.

Gianluca ordered a pitcher of cava sangria and starters including grilled watermelon, steamed mussels, and artichoke flowers covered in pine nuts, lemon, and feta cheese. As soon as the food arrived, they all dug in, sounds of contentment filling the table as a light Mediterranean breeze swept through.

"This grilled watermelon is orgasmic," Kristin declared out of nowhere, licking her lips.

Austen's eyes darted to Gianluca, who quickly looked down at his plate and blew out a short breath. *In frustration?*

Charlie laughed heartily and reached across the table to squeeze Kristin's hand. "I don't think I've ever heard you use that word to describe food. Maybe we should get some to go and save it for later."

"Probably not a great idea, hon," Kristin smiled sweetly at Charlie. "I think the walls at the villa are a bit thin." Her voice landed heavily on the word "thin" as her gaze traveled toward Gianluca.

Austen glanced down the table as Gianluca let out another exasperated puff of air and scratched his beard. As soon as he did, he glanced over at Austen and caught her looking at him. She quickly looked away, pretending to admire the centerpiece of jade green succulents. *He's nervous that I overheard them this morning*, she thought.

No one else seemed to notice the exchange. Austen looked at Matt, who was watching Ophelia with concern. She seemed blissfully unaware, smiling primly as she sliced an artichoke flower.

"I have to tell the story about the first time I met Gianluca and Ophelia," Jack announced. "We were here in Ibiza, with my husband Luis, although none of us were married yet. We had a mutual friend named Philip who had organized a villa holiday."

"We were also eight that week," Ophelia added, passing the dish of mussels to Charlie. "Similar group makeup, in fact. Three couples and two singles. Jack, you count as single this weekend because Luis isn't here."

Jack continued, "We bonded over our shared love of *hierbas* and our shared horror about one of the singles there that weekend. He was this skanky little boy who blatantly flirted with Luis all week and kept trying to undress at the dinner table whenever he was sitting by him. What was that horrid creature's name?"

Ophelia covered her mouth with her hand, sitting up straighter and shaking her head. "Nicolas. He was exceptionally awful."

"Nicolas. That's right. Ugh. Such a jezebel. We'd come in from the water, and rather than change in the bathroom like a normal person, he'd make a show of shimmying out of his Speedo under some kind of flowy leopard-print caftan and be all bare-dicked at the dinner table, always sitting uncomfortably close to Luis," Jack shared, shuddering in mock horror. "It was appalling. I was utterly agog."

"It was bad," Gianluca agreed. "Poor Luis. He always looked so uncomfortable."

"Poor Luis?" Jack exclaimed, raising his voice. "He was getting propositioned while I was sitting right there. Poor me! It was like that little skank thought I didn't exist and could get away with coming onto my boyfriend right in front of God and everyone."

Austen exchanged knowing glances with Matt. *Creepy parallels to the current situation?*

"People who do that kind of shit are clearly desperate for attention," Rosalie declared, sliding on sunglasses. "It's sad, really. I feel sorry for the little skank."

The way Rosalie said it, with her charming French accent, made everyone around the table laugh—except for Kristin. Austen noticed her quietly stabbing an orange slice at the bottom of her glass with a straw.

"It's so easy to get away with things if you're subtle," Rosalie continued, casually twirling a strand of brown hair around her manicured fingertip.

"Like you and Carlos last night?" Jack teased with a crooked smile and raised eyebrow, slowly turning his head toward Rosalie.

Mouths dropped open all around the table as all eyes landed on Rosalie. Austen hadn't noticed a thing.

"Damn. I thought I'd gotten away with that," Rosalie giggled, finger-combing her brown wavy locks in front of her face, her cheeks flushed with embarrassment.

Jack leaned over, wrapping an arm around her shoulders and shaking her gently. "No, girl. You are totally busted and officially my hero. Chef Carlos was hot."

Matt chuckled. "I saw that happening too, I must admit. No one is ever as subtle as they think when alcohol's involved."

"Nothing gets past these guys. I mean it. Jack and Matt are two of the most observant men I've ever known," Ophelia declared, pointing her fork between them. "And Matt's line of work makes him something of a professional observer, so no one gets to keep any secrets this weekend. Sorry, Rosalie."

Austen looked at Gianluca, who had joined Kristin in what seemed to be a shared quest to find something fascinating at the bottom of their glasses.

Rosalie raised both palms to the ceiling. "How could I have resisted a man who cooks like that?"

"Quite right. And I did say I wanted everyone to have a great time this weekend, so well done you," Ophelia declared, raising her glass to Rosalie in a toast.

"You go, girl," Charlie laughed, raising his glass in turn. "To your carefree abandon and being bold enough to take what you want."

Under the table, Austen slid her hand onto Matt's thigh, feeling grateful to already have what she wanted. His hand quickly found hers and turned it over. Despite the heat, shivers went up her back as he traced a heart on the inside of her wrist with his index finger.

"To everyone getting laid this weekend," Jack toasted, hoisting his glass in the air.

"Everyone but you," Ophelia cracked, an exaggerated frown plastered across her face in pity.

Jack stuck out his tongue at her. "Yes, everyone but me. I'm a happily married one-man man. I plan to have my fun jamming through the waves on a jet ski after lunch. Who's with me?"

Matt raised his hand. "I could be tempted."

Just then, the waitress arrived, holding the first of the group's main courses. "Speaking of delicious temptations, who ordered the grilled octopus?"

"That's me," Austen replied, leaning back as her lunch was served.

CHAPTER 25

Gianluca, Ibiza

After everyone's bellies were full of food and sangria, the group made the short walk to the narrow Platja Cala Nova, and Gianluca rented eight sunbeds and four umbrellas for the group, arranged in two rows of four. After paying the attendant, he joined the others as Matt and Jack wandered off to investigate jet ski rentals. There was one sunbed left unclaimed, inconveniently placed in the back row next to Kristin. Ophelia, Austen, and Rosalie tucked their cover-ups into beach bags and started toward the shimmering turquoise sea.

Realizing Kristin wasn't following, Ophelia turned around. "Don't you want to swim?"

Kristin pulled out sun cream from her bag and waved it in response. "Just going to lather up. Be there in a bit."

Ophelia nodded and turned back to catch up with Austen and Rosalie. Gianluca watched as the three women ran into the water, hand-in-hand. Kristin started to rub sun cream on her body, and it took all his effort not to watch. He clenched his jaw and spread his towel on the remaining sunbed before collapsing onto it.

"You two should go in. Enjoy the water. I can stay here and watch everyone's stuff," Gianluca offered.

Charlie patted his stomach and closed his eyes. "Too full. Going to lay here and let lunch digest. But feel free to go in. I'm more than happy to stand guard—proverbially speaking since no actual standing is required."

Kristin tugged on the string of her white bikini top. "Shall we?" she asked, drawing his gaze to her ample chest.

Gianluca shook his head and looked away, glancing at Charlie. "I'm good here for a while."

Normally, he would be the first to dive into the sea. As an Italian, he was hard wired to love floating in the Mediterranean, but right now, he needed to stay vigilant.

"OK, losers," Kristin said, tossing her sunglasses onto the sunbed. "I'm going in."

Charlie raised his head and gave her retreating form a quizzical look. "Did she just call us losers?"

"She did," Gianluca confirmed, attempting a casual shrug.

Charlie turned onto his side to face Gianluca, propping himself up on one elbow. "Sorry, mate. I don't know what's gotten into her. She's been twitchy for the last few days. Maybe even longer, now that I think about it."

"It's nothing," Gianluca replied, waving a hand dismissively.

"Usually, she's more relaxed," Charlie observed. "One of my favorite things about her is that nothing ever seems to rattle her."

The word "rattle" sent Gianluca's thoughts spinning toward the baby Kristin was carrying—his or Charlie's. He knew he had to stay cool, but it was getting harder to suppress the rising panic.

Charlie continued. "Of course, at some point, when nothing ever bothers someone, you have to wonder how much they care."

Gianluca's curiosity was piqued. *Charlie thinks Kristin doesn't care about him? About anything?*

This weekend notwithstanding, Kristen had never been needy. Her aloofness had suited him perfectly, but he could understand how Charlie could find it hard to accept in a serious relationship. Ophelia, for all her reticence in expressing emotions, was always present. Her actions spoke louder than words ever could. He let his gaze drift to the sea, where Ophelia bobbed in the waves with Austen and Rosalie.

"Sorry, mate. I'm rambling. Ignore me," Charlie said, breaking Gianluca's train of thought.

He nodded and scanned the beach, seeing Matt and Jack approaching. "Are you two going jet skiing?"

"I am," Jack replied, tossing his wallet and phone into Rosalie's bag. "Matt's wimping out. Later, gents."

He trotted back toward the jet skis while Matt reclined on a sunbed next to Gianluca, his eyes trained on the sea.

Gianluca lay back, trying to organize his tangled thoughts. Kristin, who Charlie thought didn't care, was furious at him for "making her listen" to him and Ophelia have sex. He'd known she might overhear, but fear was driving his actions now more than logic. If everything went to hell this weekend, which he considered a distinct possibility, that morning might have been his last chance to ever have sex with his wife. So, he'd taken it.

He knew he'd caught Ophelia off guard with his language. They'd never been much for talking during sex. It was Kristin who'd encouraged the dirty talk, so he knew he'd slipped up when he told Ophelia he was going to bury his face in between her legs, but his thoughts in that moment had been an incoherent coupling of wanting Kristin and needing Ophelia.

She was right. It's been months since we've done it, he realized guiltily. *How did we get here? She's the mother of my children, for fuck's sake.*

"It was good of you to organize this weekend for Ophelia," Matt said, pulling him back into the present. "She deserves it."

Gianluca swallowed hard. "She does. She's a saint."

"She's the most selfless woman I've ever met," Matt added. "Always doing the right thing for everyone. It's nice to see her being taken care of this weekend."

Gianluca scratched nervously at his beard. *He's suspicious. Fuck. But he wouldn't dare bring it up in front of Charlie. And if Matt knew, he would've already put my head through a fucking wall. Just be cool.*

"It's her weekend," he said, rolling onto his stomach and turning his head in the other direction. This put Charlie in his line of sight, and he didn't want to look at him either. "I'm going for a walk," Gianluca said, popping up. "You're good to watch everyone's stuff?"

"Standing guard while lying down," Charlie saluted from his reclined position.

Gianluca wandered along the narrow beach, feeling the fine sand between his toes and trying to clear his mind. As he walked, he felt a hand on his back.

"I saw you peel away from the group," Kristin said, her voice behind him.

He jerked away from her touch, glancing back toward the group's sunbeds. "Are you crazy? Matt's already suspicious—he's probably watching us right now."

"You said we'd take a walk today, so now we're taking a walk," she snapped, crossing her arms around herself defensively. "I told them I was going to the bathroom. They're not watching, but I won't touch you, okay? I just want to talk."

He sighed, shaking his head as they approached a rocky outcrop. "I don't know what you want me to say."

"Call it mother's instinct or whatever, but I think the baby is yours," Kristin murmured. "I want you to say you love me and that we'll figure this out."

Gianluca rubbed his face, walking in silence as beads of sweat dripped down his back and the weight of the truth pressed on him. He knew she was waiting, but he didn't yet have the courage to say what was required.

Kristin broke the silence. "I'd leave him for you, you know."

Turning to look at her, he found misplaced hope glistening in her eyes and silently scoffed at her naivete. His gaze traveled down toward her still flat stomach—the life growing inside her an unavoidable presence. Her hand reflexively moved toward her navel, and he looked away. Heat rose up his neck, and not because of the Spanish sunshine beating down on them. He was angry—not at her, but at himself. He'd been so reckless, and it was time for the reckoning.

"I don't love you. I love Ophelia. I'm sorry. It's always been her. This has to be over. You should be with Charlie. This baby has to be his."

Kristin stopped dead in her tracks.

"Keep walking, please," Gianluca muttered, gesturing ahead.

They were only a few meters from the rocks that could shield them from view, but she didn't move. Her face was a storm—silent, unreadable at first, then it shifted into something raw, something that stopped him in his tracks. He knew she was unraveling. He wanted to reach out, to fix it somehow, but couldn't.

Then she began to cry.

"Please just walk with me to the restaurant so you can pull it together," Gianluca suggested, trying futilely to regain control.

"Pull it together?" Kristin screamed through her tears, finally snapping. Her hands slammed into his chest with a force that took him off guard. She reared back to hit him again and he grabbed both of her wrists, firmly but gently forcing them down.

"You cannot do this here," he pleaded, releasing her and stepping backward. "You cannot make a scene."

"Fuck you, Gianluca! You've ruined my life."

Kristin spun on her heels and stormed away, and Gianluca scanned the beach, praying no one had noticed her outburst. His heart pounded in his chest. *She'll calm down,* he told himself. *She'll go to the bathroom, wash her face and ask Charlie to take her back to the villa. With any luck, she'll be on the next plane back to London.* But as he walked further from the group, a long string of other possible scenarios—all infinitely worse—played out in his mind.

CHAPTER 26

Matt, Ibiza

Matt saw it all happen, as he'd been trailing them from a distance. As soon as Kristin stormed off, he strode with purpose toward Gianluca who had just passed the rock outcropping. Anger bubbled up in his throat as he caught up and clamped a heavy hand onto Gianluca's shoulder.

"What's going on with you and Kristin?"

Gianluca jumped, clearly startled by the sudden confrontation.

"And don't tell me nothing," Matt pressed, his voice sharp.

"Matt, ciao. Kristin just went up to the restaurant to use the restroom," Gianluca said through pursed lips, his eyes darting nervously toward the restaurant as he scratched his beard.

He shook his head disapprovingly. "This is going to go one of two ways. Either you tell me your version of this story right now, or I'm turning around and telling Ophelia mine, and then you can answer to her."

Gianluca covered his mouth with a fist, the other hand resting on his hip. He closed his eyes for several seconds and inhaled deeply through his nose, clearly contemplating his response. When he finally opened them, he stared at Matt wordlessly for another twenty seconds or so, his head shaking back and forth.

Matt knew all too well that in high stakes stare downs, twenty seconds can feel like an eternity for the man with the most to lose. So, he simply waited him out.

"Fuck," Gianluca finally exhaled, dropping to his knees in the sand. His head hung in defeat.

Without a word, Matt sat cross-legged beside him, both men staring out at the sea. Silence stretched between them, and he waited, knowing that eventually Gianluca would break it. People always want to fill a silent void. Sure enough, after a minute, the first tears fell.

"We've been having an affair," Gianluca admitted, his voice cracking. "I'm an idiot. Classic mid-life crisis."

While Matt's expression remained neutral, inside, rage seethed. His mind flashed back to his father's betrayal and the damage it had done to their family. The image of his little sister Vivienne sobbing, asking why their dad had left, replayed in his mind. He clenched his fists, desperate to protect Ophelia and her kids from the same fate.

"You get no pity from me. The only thing I want to know is what you're going to do about it."

"I'll tell Ophelia. I promise. But can you please help me not have it be this weekend that she finds out? Can you go up to the restaurant and intercept Kristin?" Gianluca begged, turning to face Matt and digging his fingers into the sand. Tears still brimmed in his eyes. "I just ended it with her, and she's upset. We have to convince her to leave and go back to London with Charlie, so Ophelia's birthday weekend isn't ruined."

Matt hesitated, returning his gaze to the Mediterranean. He didn't want Ophelia's birthday weekend to explode, but he also didn't want to abet Gianluca in covering up his affair.

"Please, Matt. I'll come clean; I promise. But it has to come from me, not Kristin. You've got to help me." Gianluca stood and extended a hand, encouraging Matt to stand as well.

Matt stared at the outstretched hand and swatted it away.

Rising on his own, he squared his shoulders and glared. "We've known each other a long time, Gianluca, so you know that I'll do whatever it takes to protect Ophelia and those kids. But right now, helping you is pretty damn low on my priority list."

Gianluca clasped his hands in front of him. "You're family to her. To us. Kristin could blow everything up. We need to get her out of here."

Matt jabbed a finger into Gianluca's chest, his voice low and dangerous. "There is no more 'we' here. You just lost the right to call me family. My loyalty has always been with Ophelia, which is exactly where yours should've been."

Gianluca stepped back, hands raised in surrender. "I'll make this right. I swear."

Matt interlaced his fingers on top of his head and pressed down, trying to ground himself. "You go deal with your mistress before she makes a scene. You've already been sitting here on your ass wallowing for too long." He shook his head disapprovingly. "Go. I'll give you a little bit of time but make no mistake—I'm on Team Ophelia."

Gianluca nodded and trudged toward the restaurant, dragging his feet through the sand.

As Matt made his way back to the group, the weight of what he'd just confirmed pressed down on him, making each step feel heavier. He took deep breaths, trying to regain his composure. The days ahead would test his strength as a friend. For Ophelia's sake, he wanted to let Gianluca handle things with as much dignity as possible. But if it came down to it, he also had to be able to look her in the eyes and honestly say he'd been one hundred percent loyal to her since the moment he'd found out. It would be a dangerous minefield to navigate.

When he reached the sunbeds, the others were basking in the fading afternoon light. Austen lay on her stomach, eyes closed.

Gently, he traced a finger down her back over the strap of her bikini. "Want to take a dip with me?"

She popped up and looked quickly around the group, getting her bearings. "Absolutely."

They strolled into the sea, and as soon as they were deep enough, Matt dove into a wave, allowing the cool water to wash away a small amount of his tension. Resurfacing, he moved toward Austen and pulled her into him, wrapping her arms around his neck and her legs around his hips. He held her close, grateful and guilty for their happiness in the face of Ophelia and Gianluca's crumbling foundations.

"I saw you follow when Kristin went after Gianluca. What happened?" she asked into his ear as the waves gently lapped around them.

"We were right. They're having an affair," he confirmed.

Austen pulled back slightly, searching his face.

"He said he just broke it off with her and is trying to convince her to feign illness and leave the island," Matt explained with a sigh, pushing a piece of Austen's wet hair behind her ear.

She squeezed him tightly with both her arms and legs and sighed deeply. "Fuck. I know how badly you wanted to be wrong. How long has it been going on?"

"I was too angry to ask," he said, stroking her back with one hand as he held her up with the other arm.

She unwrapped her legs from his waist and stood in the water, facing him, placing one hand over his heart. "What are we going to do?"

I love that she said "we," he thought.

Covering her hand with his, he shook his head. "I told him to come clean or I'd tell her myself. For now, we'll try to keep things from blowing up on her birthday, but it feels like a ticking time bomb."

"Yikes. Well, I'm here. Whatever you or Ophelia need. Just ask," she insisted, pressing her hand firmly into his chest.

Matt wasn't used to being taken care of or accepting help. It was usually him who did the protecting—whether at work, with his mom, his little sister, or past girlfriends—so Austen's willingness and capacity to help meant a great deal to him.

"Thanks, love. Let's see how he plays it. Faking like everything is one big party is going to be tough for me, though; I'm not good at faking happiness," he acknowledged.

Austen kissed him softly. "If you feel like you're going to blow, focus on me. Let me be your happy place."

"This just started to feel like a job—like Ophelia is my protectee, and I've got to do everything I can to anticipate trouble and keep her safe," Matt lamented, resting his hands on her shoulders. "I'm pretty singularly minded when I'm in this mode, but I'll try. Either way, I'm glad you're here."

CHAPTER 27

Ophelia, Ibiza

Ophelia sat up on her sunbed, hugging her knees to her chest. To her left, Rosalie and Charlie lay on their stomachs, soaking up the sun. The rest of the group was missing. Ophelia searched the water and spotted Austen and Matt entwined in the crystalline sea.

Jack approached, jogging up the beach looking wet and cheerful in his striped board shorts.

"Jet skiing was amazing. You should've come with me."

"I have children," Ophelia laughed, wagging a finger at him. "I don't jet ski. Not my cup of tea. But you look like you had fun. I'm glad."

"You're allowed to have offspring and still jet ski, my dear. These are not mutually exclusive activities. Having procreated does not rule out fun," he insisted as he toweled off.

Ophelia shook her head and pressed her dark sunglasses up on the bridge of her nose. "Those things terrify me. I don't want to die on a fast-moving water toy."

"Cutting loose a little wouldn't kill you, you know. Life doesn't end at forty," Jack lectured, stretching out onto the sunbed in the front row between hers and Rosalie's. "Listen to your elders."

Leaning over to smack his thigh playfully, she replied, "You're four months older than me. Don't pretend you're so wise."

"But Luis is five years older than us, so technically, I've been forty-adjacent for five whole years. I'm like Tyrion Lannister. I drink, and I know things," he cracked.

"How is Luis? Right as rain?"

"Do you believe we've been married for three years? Time flies." He rolled onto his side to meet her gaze and sighed deeply. "We're good, although I will say married life is different, and it's been an adjustment. There's something about the piece of paper that can make you lazy."

"Lazy, how?" she asked, reclining into her sunbed.

Propping himself up on one elbow, he explained, "Remember how when you're dating someone new, you make all this effort—buying new clothes for dates, leaving each other filthy love notes stuffed in pockets, or buying little presents just because? We stopped all that for a while."

She frowned and bit at her fingernail. "Gianluca and I have been married for twelve years. I hardly even remember those days. And we never wrote each other filthy notes."

"But you know what I mean, right?" Jack asked. "When you're dating, you want to make sure the other person keeps choosing you, so you do all these crazy things to remind them that you love them and that they'd be hopelessly lost without you."

"Sure. I remember doing stuff like that. Vaguely," she conceded, sitting up to rub more sunscreen into her face and neck.

"So, we got married, and I remember thinking, thank fuck I don't have to try anymore. Now we can just relax and be happy. I mean, we can all agree I am an intensely *trying* personality, but I honestly thought I could stop making that kind of effort. Until I realized I was dead fucking wrong," he explained.

"Did something happen?"

Jack shook his bald head. "It just hit me that we do have to keep choosing each other every day. There are so many temptations out there, so that piece of paper is pretty flimsy protection. So, I started leaving dirty little love notes in his luggage before his trips again, and then some really hot phone sex started."

"Jack," Ophelia chided, lowering her eyes and blushing slightly. "Phone sex aside, you're right. It's the little things. It's so easy to take someone for granted when you've been together for an age."

Rosalie sat up in the sunbed to Jack's left, pushing her sunglasses to the top of her head and reapplying her red lipstick. "I was only eavesdropping a little, but as I said last night, this is why things ended with my ex. He took me for granted, which I did not accept. Well, that and he wanted us to become ethically non-monogamous, which was a hard no for me."

Charlie, who'd been lounging silently in the row behind them, sat up next. "I've been full-on eavesdropping myself. The convo just turned to ethical non-monogamy, and now I'm curious."

"You're such a man, Charlie," Rosalie scolded jokingly, turning backwards to face him. "Sex is on the table, and now you're awake."

Smiling sheepishly, Charlie replied, "Guilty as charged. It's the one topic on which men want to be in on all the details. But I'm also anti-marriage, so I'm curious about society's lean toward ENM."

"I admit I don't really understand this 'ethically non-monogamous' business," Ophelia frowned. "What does that even mean? And is society really leaning that way?"

Rosalie grabbed a paisley headband to tame her hair. "It's when two people agree that they're committed to each other but also free to explore other options, either together or separately, to get their kink on. I tried it once, and it was not for me."

"Is it more common amongst the LGBTQ community?" Charlie asked.

Jack frowned. "I don't think there are a ton of statistics available on this topic, but I won't perpetuate the stereotype by saying yes. Rosalie, you brought it up so I can ask, right? Was your ENM deal with a woman?"

"No. With a man," Rosalie confirmed. "I'm very hetero despite believing it'd be much easier to fall in love with a woman. They're so much easier to understand."

"Says you," Charlie muttered, brushing sand off his feet. "I don't think I'll ever understand women."

"I got married to escape the miserable dating hamster wheel," Jack sighed, blowing out a dramatic breath. "I'm a one-man kind of a man. ENM is definitely NFM."

"I'll never keep up with all this new bloody sex lingo," Ophelia lamented, shaking her head. "What the hell is NFM?"

Jack raised an eyebrow at her and smirked. "Not. For. Me."

Ophelia laughed and then glared at Jack, frowning. "Now you're just trying to make me feel old."

"No frowning. It causes wrinkles," Jack deadpanned.

"I'm too uptight and British for that sort of thing. It all sounds quite messy," Charlie said. "Also, between managing Miles, his mum, my job, and Kristin, I've already got too much on my plate."

Turning to Rosalie, Ophelia continued, trying not to sound judgmental. "If you don't mind my asking, what was the appeal of this ENM situation for you with the first guy?"

Rosalie shrugged. "I think he didn't want the responsibility of meeting all my needs and thought I didn't want the responsibility for his, so he thought we could be happier with other people doing some of that work. I guess I wasn't totally happy but also wasn't ready to leave him."

"You did say last night that it takes a village," Jack said.

"I did, and I was open to it with the first guy, but I just ended up being jealous. The village is great for emotional support and helping out if you need someone to pick up your kid from school or whatever, but I don't want all the village people in my bedroom," Rosalie exclaimed.

"The Village People," Jack shrieked. "It *is* fun to stay at the YMCA. Personally, I was always partial to the one with the hard hat. Give me a cat-calling construction worker any day. Luis dresses up in that outfit for me sometimes. So hot."

Ophelia giggled and shook her head at Jack, who had started to sing the chorus of the song, including the arm motions to spell out the letters of Y-M-C-A. While he sang and bounced on his sunbed, her thoughts drifted to Gianluca and the idea of an open relationship. It made her feel sick. When Jack finished his performance, she said, "I don't think I could ever share Gianluca. I'd be utterly mad with jealousy."

Rosalie sat cross-legged and looked out toward the sea. "I get it. But I can see how it could work for some who are less jealous by nature. I mean, how many married people do we all know who love each other deeply but have lost all the passion in their relationship? So many. I think that if people were able to be truly honest with each other about their needs and wants and allowed for some creativity in their couplings, there might be fewer divorces."

No thanks. I don't want creativity in my coupling, Ophelia thought.

"Honesty is overrated. I think I prefer to just stiff-upper-lip it like a good Brit and carry on," Charlie admitted, collapsing back into his sunbed.

"No, I can see where it could work for some," Jack agreed. "Nothing makes you more attentive to your partner than feeling like you could lose them to whatever hot piece of ass they brought home that week. It's one way to take nothing for granted."

Ophelia's mind snagged on what people take for granted, and she looked around cautiously, making sure Gianluca wasn't approaching them. She hesitated to make the admission, but it felt relevant to the conversation at hand. "This may be a rather random segue, but Rosalie, last night you talked about how your ex always wanted you to cook. Gianluca expects that, too. And the thing is, I used to love doing it. Making meals for my family was my way of showing love."

"Food is a love language," Rosalie nodded. "Especially for Italians."

"But at some point, he started taking it for granted, and now I mostly just feel resentful," she explained. "I think that must make me a horrible person."

Ophelia's heart ached at the thought. But it wasn't just about the meals; it was the memories tied to them—the laughter, the licking of sauces off each other's fingers, the shared moments in the kitchen that had once brought them closer. Now, cooking felt like an obligation, a reminder of how their love had faded into routine. She wished Gianluca could see the toll it took on her, the way it made her question their bond.

Jack grabbed her gently by both shoulders and shook his head. "You're a wonderful person, and I'm sorry your husband sometimes takes you for granted. You should tell him how you feel and remind him that he's damn lucky to call you his. Do you want me to kick his ass? Or maybe Matt should do it with all those rippling muscles. He's definitely an ass-kicker."

Ophelia's eyes darted back to the water as Matt and Austen emerged, smiling at the group. "No ass-kicking required, but thanks for the offer, Fabulous Jack. I shall let you know if I change my mind," she said, patting his hand.

"What'd we miss?" Austen asked, squeezing water out of her hair.

Jack pointed at Matt. "You and I almost got into some serious fisticuffs."

"A proper kerfuffle," Charlie nodded.

Matt looked confused, eyes shifting between Jack and Ophelia as he settled into the sunbed behind Austen's. "Why are we fighting?"

"You're not," Ophelia insisted, swatting at the air near Jack before looking over her shoulder at Matt. "Never mind. You didn't see Gianluca out there, did you? I feel like he's been MIA for ages."

"Not in the water, no," Matt said, momentarily burying his face in the towel. "He was walking up the beach a bit earlier."

Austen wrapped a towel around her waist, sat next to Ophelia, and gestured toward the restaurant. "Anyone want anything to drink? I can make a run. Grab whatever?"

"Ooh, good call. I could go for a beer," Jack said.

Charlie raised one finger from his reclined position. "Make that two, please, Austen."

Rosalie shook her head, and Ophelia cracked a smile. "I could go for a cheeky beer. Do you need a hand?"

Austen jumped up, ready to run her errand. "Absolutely not. It's your birthday. You sit right there and look fabulous. Matt? Want anything?"

"I'm good. Thanks, doll."

"Back in a flash," she said before disappearing up the beach.

"Don't you ever take that girl for granted," Ophelia said to Matt, pointing in the direction Austen had disappeared. "She's lovely."

"Yes, ma'am," Matt agreed. "I won't."

CHAPTER 28
Austen, Ibiza

Austen entered the restaurant, scanning for Gianluca and Kristin, but neither was in sight. She made her way to the converted silver Airstream that served as a takeaway bar and ordered four beers. While waiting in the shade for her order, she spotted them emerging from the direction of the outdoor bathrooms. Kristin looked like she'd been through the wringer—puffy eyes, blotchy face. Even her hot pink tunic hung haphazardly over her perfect body.

Gianluca looked exceptionally tense, every muscle clenched tightly. They walked side by side but weren't touching.

"I'll be right back," Austen told the bartender, stepping forward to intercept them in a few strides. She blurted out, "Hi. Neither of you knows me particularly well, so I'm sorry for intruding on what is clearly a personal crisis of epic proportions. But Matt is really worried about how this will all play out for Ophelia, so if there's anything I can do to help get you out of here, Kristin, just say the word."

Kristin looked helplessly at Gianluca, throwing her hands up in frustration before wiping her nose on the sleeve of her cover-up. "Of course, he told her too. Now I'm just the pregnant problem everyone's trying to manage."

Austen's eyes widened as she looked between the two of them. "You're pregnant?"

"Kristin, for fuck's sake," Gianluca muttered, shooting her a pleading look. "Austen, please—Charlie doesn't even know yet, and it might very well be his. Please don't tell Matt. Or anyone else."

He will most definitely hear about this, she thought.

Austen suddenly felt she was in way over her head. Her heart broke for Ophelia, but instincts took over, and she slipped into problem-solving mode, formulating a plan. "How about this… I'll say I bought beers and headed back to the beach when I bumped into Gianluca. Then I decided I wanted to run to the bathroom, so he took the beers, and I went back up where I found Kristin unwell. I'll tell Charlie he should come get you and drive you home. What do you think?"

Gianluca exhaled sharply, placing a hand on Kristin's shoulder. "That's a good idea. Can we please go with that?"

Kristin jerked away from his hand and wiped fresh tears from her eyes, nodding as she stared at the floor. "Fine."

"Gianluca, there are four beers waiting for me at the Airstream bar. Go pay for them and take them down to the beach—they're for Ophelia, Charlie, Jack, and me," Austen instructed. "I'll get Kristin settled and follow you shortly."

Gianluca gave her a grateful nod, relief flashing in his eyes. He looked sympathetically at Kristin. "This is for the best," he said quietly before walking away.

Austen led Kristin to a small seating area with low-slung couches outside the restrooms, guiding her into a seat. "Do you want some water before I get Charlie?"

Kristin looked up, her eyes red-rimmed and weary. "Why are you being nice to me?"

Austen pouted. "It's just water, Kristin. I'm sorry this is happening to you, but I think we both know blowing up Ophelia's birthday weekend isn't going to help anyone."

Kristin exhaled, finally nodding. "Yes, water would be nice. Thank you."

Austen quickly returned to the bar and saw Gianluca leaving with the beers in hand. She ordered a cold bottle of water and brought it back to Kristin. "Just stay here and wait for Charlie. I'll send him right up and tell him you're unwell. The rest of the story is up to you, all right?"

Kristin took a small sip of water, her voice barely a whisper. "Yes, fine."

"Do the right thing, Kristin," Austen pleaded. "Go home."

Kristin buried her head in her hands, and Austen turned away, hurrying out of the restaurant. Her mind raced as she walked back toward the beach. *Kristin is pregnant, maybe with Gianluca's baby. But maybe not? Either way, poor Ophelia. Matt's going to flip. What a fucktastrophy.*

When she reached the beach, Gianluca handed her a beer. Ophelia, Charlie, and Jack were clinking theirs together, chatting happily.

"Hey, Charlie," Austen said, getting his attention.

He turned to her, eyes squinting against the sun.

"I ran into Kristin up at the restaurant. She's not feeling well, so I told her I'd send you up. She's waiting for you in the seating area right outside the loos."

"Oh dear. Thanks, Austen," he said, downing a final swig of his beer before tossing on his T-shirt. "Do I need shoes to go into the restaurant?"

"You might want to take all your things. It seems like she may need to head back to the villa," Austen suggested, taking the beer from his hand. "I think you'll have to drive her home."

Charlie's expression turned wary as he packed up their belongings into Kristin's beach bag. "Right. Okay. Blimey."

"What's going on?" Ophelia asked, looking over her shoulder.

"Kristin isn't feeling well. I think Charlie needs to take her home," Austen replied, trying to keep her tone light.

Ophelia's hand covered her mouth. "Oh no, what a shame. I hope it's nothing serious."

"Good thing we came in three cars," Gianluca chimed in.

Matt shot him a hard look. "Good thing."

Austen sank onto the sunbed beside Matt, handing him Charlie's beer and resting a reassuring hand on his knee.

Matt accepted the drink but didn't take a sip, instead tapping his thumb along the aluminum rim, the tension radiating off him. She could tell he was on edge, uncomfortably caught between his good friend, her philandering husband and monitoring the entire group's every move, anticipating disaster.

After a moment, Gianluca looked at his watch, cleared his throat, and scratched his beard. "I'd suggest we stay here for another hour or so, then head back to the villa to clean up before dinner. Sound good?"

"Sounds good," Austen replied, shifting her hand to rub slow circles on Matt's back in an attempt to calm him. The repetitive motion seemed to work, his tapping finally slowing.

With Ophelia, Rosalie, and Jack engrossed in their conversation a few seats over, Gianluca slipped away again, heading into the ocean alone.

Good riddance, she thought.

"What happened up there?" Matt asked, his voice low.

"I intercepted them and sent Gianluca down with the beers so I could separate them and be the one to get Charlie. I didn't think it would be good if Gianluca had done it," she explained.

"Smart. You're good at this. Want a job?" He smirked.

She shook her head. "No thanks. I've got one. But I have more bad news."

He silently searched her face, waiting.

"She's pregnant," Austen mouthed, curving her hand over her belly in an imitation of a bump.

Matt's face dropped into his hands, and he sat like that for a moment before looking back up at her, his eyes wide. "Whose?" he mouthed.

"Don't think she knows," she whispered.

Without another word, Matt laid back on his sunbed, sliding his Ray-Bans over his eyes. Austen took it as a sign that he needed time to process, so she shifted over to Gianluca's abandoned sunbed beside him and gave his hand a comforting squeeze. She started to let go, but he quickly tightened his grip, threading their fingers together and letting their hands dangle in the space between their beds. He didn't look at her or say anything, but his hold on her was firm, and she matched it, letting him know she was there.

Austen's heart sank for Ophelia, who remained blissfully unaware of the crisis brewing around her, and for Matt, who was in the trenches of his mind preparing for the worst. She wanted to support him however she could, to help him protect Ophelia, but a pang of fear twisted inside her too. How quickly life could turn upside down, she realized—one moment stable, the next, the bottom could fall out.

CHAPTER 29

Gianluca, Ibiza

The group piled into the remaining two cars for the drive back to the villa. Matt and Austen rode with Jack and Rosalie, leaving Gianluca alone with Ophelia.

He drove slowly through the dry, olive tree-strewn landscape, trying to prolong these few, unthreatened moments. Ophelia recounted some of the conversations she'd shared with Austen and Rosalie while bobbing in the sea, but Gianluca wasn't listening. His responses were automatic—small sounds and nods that implied he was listening—though his mind was a thousand kilometers away. The weight of everything pressed down on him: his father's uncertain health, the possibility of a new child, and the potential destruction of his life as he knew it. His attention snapped back only when Ophelia said, "I hope Kristin is okay."

On impulse, he reached across the console to take her hand, hoping the skin-to-skin contact might soothe his nerves. He knew his cortisol levels were too high and that he needed to do what he could to keep his blood pressure as regulated as possible. Stroking her hand with his thumb brought a sliver of relief, though he had to let go repeatedly to shift gears and navigate the island's winding roads. Every time he released her hand, fear bubbled up from deep inside his roiling gut. *I can't lose her. My life doesn't work without Ophelia.*

They arrived at the villa, and he cringed at the sight of Kristin and Charlie's car parked out front, alongside Jack's. He'd hoped—irrationally, perhaps—that they would have gone straight to the airport. But a man could hope.

Inside, they found the group idling around the common area and kitchen, dropping beach bags in corners, pulling out snacks and drinks, and chattering leisurely. Charlie sat at the kitchen counter, a beer in hand, staring blankly at his phone.

"How is she?" Ophelia asked him, her voice warm and concerned. The softness in her tone fanned the flames of Gianluca's guilt.

Charlie looked up, his expression hollow. "She's pregnant."

The flat tone of his voice—which was decidedly not that of a happy father-to-be—sent a cold shock through Gianluca's body. He saw the confusion ripple through the villa as everyone exchanged uneasy glances, trying to piece together what was happening.

Ophelia crossed the room, resting a tentative hand on Charlie's shoulder. "That's wonderful news, isn't it, Charlie?"

Charlie's chin trembled as he met her gaze, his eyes unfocused. "It would be if I hadn't had a vasectomy years ago."

Fuck. It's mine. Gianluca's stomach dropped, bile rising in his throat. Visions of his family flooded his mind—happy memories with Marco and Esme, each one extinguished in a dark flash behind his eyes. He saw Ophelia's beautiful face smiling up at him the first time he held both babies in the delivery room. Marco's first word. Esme's first steps. Now, another child, the one Kristin carried, hovered at the edge of his vision, threatening all he'd built. He gripped the counter, bracing himself for whatever was coming next, silently pleading that his name wouldn't pass Charlie's lips.

His voice a bitter rasp, Charlie continued. "I got one after Miles happened." He made air quotes around the word "happened," then took a slow sip of his beer. "I was furious about being strapped with a kid I didn't want, so I decided to get the snip. Figured I could reverse it one day if the time ever felt right."

Jack muttered, "Oh shit," stumbling back to lean against the counter.

Charlie let out a mirthless laugh, staring down at his phone. "Yeah, 'oh shit' was exactly what she said when I told her."

Ophelia slipped an arm around his shoulders, shooting Gianluca a wide-eyed glance that seemed to say, *Bloody hell, now what are we supposed to do?*

He stared back blankly at his wife, still reeling.

Leaning closer to Charlie, Ophelia continued in the soft voice she always used when one of their children needed soothing. "That's a tough blow, Charlie. I'm so sorry. What can we do?"

Charlie shook his head, clearly dazed. "I don't know. This is such a giant cock-up. Oh my God. A literal cock…up my girlfriend. That got her pregnant."

Jack stifled a laugh, pressing a hand to his mouth, and Rosalie nudged him with a sharp elbow, glancing apologetically at Ophelia, who silently pleaded for decorum.

"Sorry. I have absolutely no chill when things get awkward," Jack mumbled, still struggling to suppress his amusement.

Charlie remained unamused, staring down at his phone. "I was looking at flights, trying to get out of here. I can't even look at her. But the first ones aren't until tomorrow."

"Is Kristin up in your room?" Austen asked. "Maybe I should go check on her?"

Gianluca watched as Austen and Matt exchanged a brief, knowing glance. When Matt nodded, Austen headed quietly up the stairs. Gianluca knew they weren't helping for his sake, but he took some comfort in their efforts to shield Ophelia from this dam that threatened to break over them all.

Ophelia called her thanks to Austen and then looked around the room, biting her fingernails, clearly unsure what to do.

"Really sorry, man. You're welcome to the second bed in my room tonight if you want it," Jack offered, having regained his composure. "I can move your things over, no problem."

Rosalie propped herself on a barstool across from Charlie and looked at him inquisitively. "Sorry to ask the obvious question, but you two have been together five years, yes? How did she not know you had a vasectomy? This seems like something that would have come up."

Charlie shook his head and shrugged. "She told me she had one of those coil things—an IUD—put in before we met, so it never came up."

"Well, that makes sense, I suppose," Rosalie murmured.

Some hormonal IUDs can be effective for as few as three years, Gianluca recalled from his mental medical encyclopedia, his insides twisting.

Ophelia offered Charlie a glass of water, which he sipped absently. Shame burned through Gianluca's chest as he watched his wife attempt to comfort the man whose girlfriend he had impregnated. His guilt pressed down on him as he glanced around at the silent, uncomfortable group.

"Sorry to be such a party killer," Charlie whispered, burying his face in his hands.

Matt, who had been silently stewing, finally spoke up. "Don't apologize, Charlie. Let's try to make the best of this less-than-ideal situation. Did you manage to get a flight for tomorrow?"

"Yeah, ten o'clock tomorrow morning," Charlie mumbled into his hands.

"Okay, you're understandably upset. Would some forced distance help? Would you like us to find Kristin a hotel room by the airport? Get her out of here for tonight?" Matt suggested.

Ophelia tutted in disapproval. "We're not kicking Kristin out of the villa, for goodness' sake. She's pregnant and vulnerable."

Gianluca caught the intent behind Matt's plan and decided to jump in. "He's not suggesting we throw her out in the cold, Ophelia. But some comfortable distance might be a good idea?"

Tears began to fall down Charlie's face. "I'd appreciate that, honestly. I really can't bloody look at her tonight, and I shouldn't have to leave. I'm the wronged party here."

You and Ophelia both, Gianluca thought grimly. He watched as Matt exchanged a brief, silent look with Ophelia, as if seeking her approval to proceed. She sighed, then nodded.

"I'll take care of it," Matt said, shooting Gianluca a hard, reproachful look that he hoped Ophelia didn't notice. "Assuming she's willing to go. I'll talk to her."

Matt strode upstairs, and Gianluca's heart sank as Ophelia followed him. *Of course she wants to help; she's a saint.* Swallowing down a thick lump in his throat, he headed for the fridge. "Anyone want some cava sangria?"

A chorus of agreement rose from Jack and Rosalie, and he busied himself pulling out ingredients and chopping fruit. The task felt inappropriately festive, but he needed something to do with his hands to keep his turbulent thoughts at bay.

Surely if she'd told him it was mine—fuck it really is mine—he'd have said so, so I'm okay for now, he thought, a cautious breath of relief escaping his lips.

Jack and Rosalie busied themselves with snacks, speaking in low tones. Charlie stayed at the counter, staring blankly into his beer.

Matt eventually reappeared, looking grimly satisfied just as Gianluca poured cava into the pitcher, letting it cascade over the fruit. "She'll go to a hotel," Matt announced. "I'll make the arrangements and drive her there myself. Ophelia and Austen are helping her pack."

"Take our car," Charlie offered, tossing Matt his keys.

Matt caught them easily, nodding in thanks.

Gianluca sighed in relief, his gaze drifting to Charlie, who sat slumped under the weight of everything. He gave Matt a grateful nod, silently acknowledging the reprieve he'd been granted, however temporary. He clung to the faint hope that the paternity of Kristin's child might remain uncertain, even if just for a while longer. *Maybe, just maybe, I can make it out of this disaster alive.*

CHAPTER 30

Matt, Ibiza

Matt went directly to his room to grab his laptop and book a hotel for Kristin. He knew that getting her out of the villa as soon as possible, while perhaps unkind, was the best way to contain the risk. Once the arrangements were made, he headed down the hall, tense with the need to finish this. As he approached her room, he heard Ophelia's voice. He knocked and entered without waiting for an answer.

Ophelia sat beside Kristin on the bed, rubbing her back as Kristin sobbed into her shoulder. Austen was emerging from the en suite bathroom with Kristin's toiletries bag, which she tossed into the already packed suitcase on the window bench. She caught Matt's eye, her expression a mix of nerves and resolve.

Matt tensed. *Please, Kristin. Hold it together.* Every cell in his body was on high alert, ready to whisk her out of there to protect Ophelia from the ugly truth.

Ophelia looked up, her eyes filled with concern, before turning back to Kristin. "Matt's here. He'll take you to the hotel. Would you like to get out of here?"

"Your bag's all packed," Austen added, zipping the suitcase and setting it near the door.

Kristin's shoulders shook, her head still buried against Ophelia. She didn't respond.

Ophelia continued gently, "I know things seem bleak right now, but one way or another, this will all get sorted. If you want to be with Charlie, you'll work toward forgiveness. If it's this other man you want, then you'll figure that out too. And if you don't want to keep the baby, that's your choice."

Kristin lifted her head, her voice raw. "Charlie's never going to marry me, and the other guy's never going to leave his wife. If I don't have this baby, I'm going to end up alone."

Ophelia's brows lifted in surprise. "Oh dear. The baby's father is married?"

Desperate to stop the oncoming train, Matt intervened, his voice urgent. "Kristin, let's get you out of here."

Ophelia held up a hand, insisting softly, "Give her a moment."

Matt watched Kristin closely, trying to read the emotions that flickered across her tear-streaked face. She stared at Ophelia with swollen and bloodshot eyes, clearly grappling with a decision. *She's weighing whether to hurt Gianluca or protect Ophelia,* he thought, silently begging. *Please, choose her.*

"Yes, he's married. I'm a terrible person," Kristin sobbed.

Ophelia rubbed her upper arm gently. "You're not a terrible person."

Matt saw it unfold in slow motion. That small kindness from Ophelia broke Kristin completely.

"I *am* a terrible person," she cried, pushing herself off the bed. "Stop being nice to me. I can't handle it anymore. You should fucking hate me. Matt, please get me out of here."

"Yes, let's go," he said, grabbing her suitcase and placing his other hand on her back, ready to guide her out. His pulse hammered as if he was being pursued by an armed gunman.

"Wait," Ophelia insisted, rising from the bed. "Why should I hate you?"

Kristin turned to Ophelia, her face crumpled in anguish, her nostrils flaring as tears continued streaming down her face. A strangled sob escaped her throat.

Ophelia's face shifted as the realization dawned, her expression wavering between confusion and disbelief. "You don't mean…"

"I'm so sorry, Ophelia," Kristin choked, her slight frame racked by sobs.

The color drained from Ophelia's face, and her legs gave way as she collapsed in shock.

Matt dropped Kristin's suitcase and caught Ophelia before she hit the ground, lifting her into his arms. In that moment, she was the one who needed to be extricated from the room.

"Kristin, don't move. I'll be back for you," he commanded, his voice firm as he carried Ophelia out.

Austen followed closely, shutting the door behind them.

PART SIX

MAY

After She Knew

CHAPTER 31

Ophelia, Ibiza

Ophelia found herself sitting on the bed in her and Gianluca's room, though she wasn't sure how she'd gotten there. *Did I black out?* She felt numb, as if Kristin's revelation had cut the live wire that normally fed her frenetic energy. Now, there was nothing—just an eerie silence. Slowly, her vision sharpened, and she realized Matt was there, holding her face gently between his hands.

"Fie, I'm so sorry this is happening. I'm going to get Kristin out, and we're going to figure this out together. I'm in your corner, okay? Always."

Gianluca has been sleeping with Kristin. And she's pregnant with his child. The thoughts drifted through her mind, struggling to find a logical place to land in her now oddly still head or heart. She blinked at Matt, her focus wavering. "You knew?"

"I only found out today," he said, pushing her hair behind her ears and glancing nervously at the closed door. "I confronted him and told him I'd tell you, but he begged me to help get Kristin out, so your birthday weekend wouldn't be ruined. I'm not making excuses for him—or for myself. It sounds ridiculous now. I'm so sorry."

His words sounded muffled, as if they were traveling through water.

"How could they do this to me?" She looked down at her hands resting limply in her lap. The gold of her wedding band caught the light, and it suddenly felt as heavy as lead on her finger. She stared at it in disbelief, a wave of tears building behind her eyes.

Matt wrapped his arms around her, pulling her close. "I don't know, Fie."

She buried her face against his chest, quietly sobbing. *My husband. And my friend.* Images of them in bed together crashed into her mind, and she squeezed her eyes shut, trying to force them away. She rolled out of Matt's arms and curled into a fetal position on the bed, feeling as though all the bones in her body had melted. Nothing was holding her together, and each breath was a struggle through her tears.

"Fie," Matt said gently, "Austen's going to stay here with you while I take Kristin to the hotel, all right?"

She must have nodded because the bed shifted, and she heard the door click softly as he left.

Ophelia turned her head to find Austen standing beside the bed, her expression heavy with sympathy.

"You knew too? Am I the last person in this house to know?" Ophelia asked, her voice thick with despair as she pressed her face into the bed.

Austen sat down beside her, lightly rubbing her leg. "No, not everyone knows. Can I get you anything? Water? Vodka? A knife to chop his dick off?"

A surprised laugh escaped Ophelia's mouth which quickly devolved into sobs. She curled herself back into a ball.

"A Kleenex, maybe?"

"All of those things sound good," Ophelia managed, wiping her face on the bedding.

Austen returned with a box of tissues, and Ophelia sat up to blow her nose. She buried her face back in her hands, struggling to calm her breathing for what felt like several minutes. When she looked up at last, she glanced helplessly at Austen. "What do I do now?"

Austen took her hands, her tone steady and calm. "I know it may not feel like it, but you're in control now. His fuck up means that this just became your world, and he only gets to live in it if you allow it."

Ophelia nodded slowly, despite her total incomprehension of Austen's reply.

CHAPTER 32

Gianluca, Ibiza

Gianluca's mind was in overdrive. He'd made and served sangria, handed out snacks, and tidied up the kitchen, but now he was at a loss. Every nerve in his body screamed for him to retreat to his room, but Kristin was upstairs. Charlie remained slumped at the kitchen counter, and Jack sat beside him, talking quietly. Rosalie had retreated outside to smoke, choosing nicotine to take the edge off the tension that reverberated through the villa. He was considering joining her, if only for the distraction, when Kristin reappeared, looking utterly unhinged. Tear stains marked her cheeks, and her eyes blazed as they locked onto his.

"Cat's out of the bag, Gianluca. I told her," she declared, hands planted defiantly on her hips.

Charlie jolted out of his daze, confusion knitting his brows. "Told who what?"

Gianluca gripped the counter, feeling a surge of anger and dread. "You didn't," he growled, meeting her gaze with daggers.

Kristin crossed her arms, holding his stare, her expression stubborn. "I did."

His vision blurred before snapping back into sharp focus. He needed to play defense—and fast. He turned toward Charlie, who was still piecing it together. The moment the realization dawned, Charlie's jaw slackened, and he whipped around to face Gianluca.

"It was him?" Charlie's voice shook with fury as he leaped off his barstool, lunging at Gianluca. Jack intercepted him just in time, holding him back. Matt rushed into the room, helping Jack restrain Charlie, giving Gianluca a chance to slip out and dash toward the stairs. He took them two at a time, desperate to reach Ophelia.

He burst through the bedroom door and found her sobbing on the bed, Austen by her side.

"Ophelia, I'm so sorry," he pleaded, dropping to his knees in front of her.

Before he could say another word, Matt appeared, yanking him to his feet and shoving him against the wall. "Do you want me to get him out of here, Ophelia?" Matt snarled, his gaze never leaving Gianluca's.

"I don't know what I was thinking," Gianluca stammered over Matt's shoulder, his hands folded into prayer under Matt's forearm, which pressed firmly into his chest. "I don't love her. I love you."

Ophelia sat up slowly, her tear-streaked face showing only cold detachment as she stared at him like he was a stranger. "Yes, Matt, please. Get him away from me."

Matt didn't hesitate. He pulled Gianluca off the wall, shoving him roughly out of the room and into the hallway before slamming the door. Gianluca's ears buzzed, and everything around him felt hazy, unfocused. Through the haze, he saw Matt's face, the fury in his eyes unmistakable. A vein throbbed at his temple.

"Leave her alone, Gianluca. Go sit in my room and stay out of the way until I get your hysterical girlfriend out of here."

From downstairs, he heard Kristin and Charlie screaming at each other. It happened. His world had imploded. And he had no one to blame but himself. He stumbled begrudgingly to Matt and Austen's room and collapsed onto the floor, splaying out prostrate like a starfish.

In fight-or-flight situations, Gianluca had always been a fighter. It was one of the reasons he was so good in the ER, where running toward trouble was a job requirement. Adrenaline fueled him to fight heroically to save total strangers. But for just a moment, in the gripping fear of losing everything he held most dear, he desperately wanted to flee.

I should leave. Run as far away from this nightmare as possible.

He sat up and stared at the closed door, evaluating his options, none of which made sense. After forcing a few deep breaths, he remembered himself.

I can't leave Ophelia like this. I need to fight for her. She'll forgive me. She must. We have kids. Christ, the kids. I can't be one of those every-other-weekend fathers, missing out on their lives. What the fuck have I done?

He pushed himself up from the floor and stumbled back to his and Ophelia's door. He tried to open it, ready to beg, but the door was locked.

"Ophelia, let me in," he pleaded, knocking lightly. "Please, *tesoro*."

Pressing his ear to the door, he strained to hear the conversation inside. He caught Austen's voice, muffled through the wood, but he couldn't make out her words. He continued knocking with the slow beat of a metronome, willing Ophelia to feel his persistent desperation on the other side. After a while, he slumped down, his back to the door, continuing to knock softly over his shoulder.

Eventually, he heard a key turn in the door and leaned forward, jumping to his feet as it opened. His heart twisted with regret and self-loathing when he saw Ophelia's deeply pained face staring back at him. Strands of her black hair stuck to her face in the damp left by her tears.

None of it was worth this, he thought.

"I want you out of this villa right this second," she said. Before he could respond, she closed the door in his face.

He reached for the doorknob, desperate to plead his case, but he heard the lock turn. "Ophelia, *tesoro,* please. We need to talk," he said through the door.

"Gianluca, you heard her," Austen's voice came through, firm and unyielding. "Show some respect to your wife and give her what she wants right now, which is your absence. You'll talk when she's ready."

Defeated, he pressed his hands against the doorframe, dropping his chin to his chest. Austen was right; he couldn't force the conversation through a locked door. With that realization, his other senses kicked back into focus, Kristin's and Charlie's shouts suddenly audible from downstairs. He quickly retreated to Matt and Austen's room and locked the door.

CHAPTER 33

Matt, Ibiza

Matt could hear Kristin's sobs and Charlie's shouts even before he reached the kitchen. The anger radiating off Charlie was palpable, a stark contrast to his usual easygoing demeanor.

"What the bloody hell were you thinking bringing me here?" Charlie's voice was laced with fury. "Bringing *yourself* here when you're screwing *him*? And screwing over Ophelia, who has never been anything but wonderful to you. Who are you?"

"I'm so sorry," she sobbed.

Matt knew he should defuse the situation quickly. He entered the room slowly, trying to project calm.

"Kristin, I've booked you a room, and I've got your bag," he said, lifting it slightly when she turned to look at him.

Tears streamed down her face, but she said nothing. Her eyes searched his face in desperation. She was in shock and needed to be extricated.

"I suggest we get you out of here," Matt continued, keeping his voice low. "Quickly. So everyone can cool down."

"Well, I'm not bloody well staying here with the man who's been screwing my girlfriend," Charlie shouted, his voice echoing in the empty space around them.

Matt raised both hands, palms outward. "I get it, Charlie. I want to help. My suggestion is that you come with me and Kristin now."

Charlie shook his head, despair etched into his face. "I don't want to be with her either. I can't believe this is happening. Somebody kill me."

Matt's eyes darted to the block of knives on the kitchen counter. Even if the words were meant as a figure of speech, Matt's training caused his muscles to tense reflexively, his jaw tight.

"We can call the hotel from the car and see if they have a second room," Matt suggested, moving subtly between Charlie and the knife block. "If not, I can drop you off at a different hotel. But for everyone's sake, let's get both of you out of this house. Why don't you go upstairs and pack your things?"

Charlie leaned against the kitchen island, covering his face with his hands, his breathing labored. After a few tense moments, he straightened and nodded. "I'm going to pack." He stormed out, leaving Matt alone with Kristin.

Kristin sank onto the kitchen floor cross-legged, folded over herself and buried her face in her lap.

Matt watched as her shoulders shook with her tears. He poured her a glass of water and placed it beside her on the floor, resting a napkin on top.

Hearing the clink on the tile, she looked up, took the napkin, and blew her nose.

Matt waited, watching her cautiously. His senses remained on high alert, attuned to the sounds of the house, scanning for the next impending disaster. Both Charlie and Gianluca were upstairs—a volatile mix. Outside, he glimpsed Jack and Rosalie smoking by the pool, wisely keeping clear of the chaos within. Fewer people to manage meant fewer variables to control, which was exactly what Matt needed right now.

Kristin eventually looked up, her voice a small, defeated whine. "I'm not actually a terrible person."

He glanced at his watch, feeling an intense loyalty to Ophelia that made it nearly impossible to muster any sympathy for Kristin. He said nothing.

A few minutes later, Charlie returned, carrying his bag. "Let's go," he said flatly, patting his pockets. "Where are my damn car keys?"

"I've got them, Charlie," Matt reminded him. "Let me drive you both. I'll cab back."

Charlie sighed and nodded, resigned.

Matt extended a hand to help Kristin off the floor, picked up her bag, and guided them out to the car. Charlie climbed into the front passenger seat without a word or a glance at Kristin. Once on the road, Matt handed Charlie his phone to call the hotel. A second room was available, which he promptly booked. Matt didn't envy the night they'd spend in the same building yet kilometers apart.

The car was silent, the air thick with tension. Matt noticed Charlie repeatedly clenching his hands into fists and flattening them out against his knees, as if trying to physically force control over his turbulent emotions. In the rearview mirror, he could see Kristin, eyes closed, head leaned back, fighting to hold back tears.

"How long has it been going on?" Charlie asked abruptly, staring straight ahead.

Matt's gaze flicked to the mirror. Kristin's eyes remained closed, but her face contorted as if bracing for impact. At least a minute went by as they waited for her response. The tension in the air carried the exact weight of two broken hearts.

"A year," she whispered.

Charlie's head fell into one hand, his elbow resting on the window ledge. "Why?" he asked, his voice barely audible, filled with pain.

Matt stared straight ahead, praying to the traffic gods for clear roads so he could soon escape from this gut-wrenching conversation.

A suffocating silence settled over them. After what felt like an eternity, Charlie spoke again, his voice breaking. "Why?" he demanded, louder this time.

Kristin's voice was barely a murmur. "Every time we were together, he made me feel like I was the only person who mattered to him," she admitted. "You'll always love Miles more than you love me."

Charlie whipped around, his eyes wide with rage and disbelief. He glared at her in stunned silence, his hand gripping the center console tighter and tighter, fury visibly building within him.

"Parents *should* love their kids more than they love anything or anyone else in the world," he yelled.

"Mine didn't," Kristin retorted, lurching forward, reaching for the back of his seat as fresh tears streamed down her face.

Charlie turned away, distancing himself from her, pressing his forehead against his interlaced fingers. He sighed, a sound of utter resignation. "God help this baby."

Kristin fell backward into the seat, her sobs echoing through the car in an endless wave of sorrow. No one spoke again until they pulled up to the hotel and said goodbye.

Only when he was riding away in a cab did Matt allow himself a deep breath. In his professional life, he'd managed plenty of tense security situations, but emotionally charged ones had a unique, draining intensity. Given the choice, Matt would take "security tension" over emotional turmoil any day.

The conversation also left him thinking about children. He and Austen hadn't yet discussed whether they wanted kids. *I should bring it up some time soon,* he thought, closing his eyes and mentally adding it to his to-do list.

CHAPTER 34

Gianluca, Ibiza

When he could no longer hear anyone yelling, Gianluca stuck his head cautiously out of his hiding spot and crept down the hall, pausing in front of his and Ophelia's room. Her muffled voice seeped through the walls, although he couldn't make anything out. He placed a flat hand gingerly on the closed door and sighed deeply, feeling powerless to fix what lay broken behind it. Medical school had taught him how to identify, treat and heal disease, but no one can teach how to mend a broken heart.

Resisting the urge to knock again, he quietly made his way downstairs and peered into the kitchen. Empty. Through the windows, he saw Jack and Rosalie smoking by the pool, and he wandered outside to join them.

"Can I have one of those?" he asked.

Rosalie wordlessly handed him the pack and a lighter. He lit a cigarette, sinking into a nearby chair. "Thanks. And sorry about all this drama."

They both stared at him in silence.

"I know. I'm a bastard," he acknowledged.

"That you are," Jack replied, shaking his head. "I thought I picked up on a vibe between you two, but I refused to believe you'd do that to Ophelia. You're a real dumbass, man."

Gianluca nodded. "I know. Did Matt take Kristin to the hotel? Where's Charlie?"

"Once he found out you're the baby daddy, he didn't want to stay here either," Rosalie explained. "Matt drove them in their car, since neither was in any state to drive, and he'll take a cab back."

Gianluca exhaled a slow stream of smoke, nodding.

"We were thinking maybe we should leave too," Jack said. "Seems like you've got a lot going on here, to put it mildly."

"No, you stay. I'm leaving. Ophelia wants me gone, and she needs her friends right now. I'll find a hotel," he explained, ashing his cigarette. "Fuck. My bag. All my stuff is in our room, and Ophelia's locked herself in."

"I'll get it," Jack offered, rising. "You stay put."

Gianluca sank back into his chair, and noticing Rosalie's disapproving gaze, he laughed bitterly. "I suppose this weekend turned out differently than any of us expected. Sorry to have shocked you by being a bastard."

"You being a bastard doesn't shock me," she replied bluntly, before taking a long drag. "People cheat all the time. But it takes an exceptionally callous prick—I mean, an insanely reckless asshole—to bring his mistress to his wife's birthday weekend."

Gianluca felt the last remnants of his energy drain away. "Ophelia invited her. She wasn't supposed to come. This wasn't supposed to happen."

"I'm sure it wasn't," she exhaled. "But it did."

Jack returned moments later, dropping a weekender bag at Gianluca's feet.

"That was fast. Thanks, Jack."

"It was waiting out in the hallway. I'm guessing Austen packed it for you," Jack said. "If it were up to me, I'd have lit it all on fire and thrown it out the window."

Gianluca managed a weak smile, then stood, stubbing out his cigarette. "Okay, I'm going. Will you tell Ophelia that—"

"No," Jack and Rosalie interrupted in unison.

He picked up his bag and walked away, pulling out his phone to search for a hotel. Giving Ophelia the space she'd asked for was the least he could do. For tonight.

CHAPTER 35

Ophelia, Ibiza

"Sweetie, it's Jack," she heard through the door. "Just wanted to let you know that all the crazy is out of the house. It's just me and Rosalie downstairs now. Can we bring you anything?"

Ophelia smoothed her hair back from her face and took a deep breath. Her pulse still pounded in her ears, and the walls felt too close, pressing in on her with reminders of what had happened here—the same room where she and Gianluca had made love just hours earlier. The memory gripped her heart like a vise. "Let's get out of here," she sighed.

Austen nodded and followed her to the door, resting a reassuring hand lightly on her back.

"Thank you," Ophelia murmured to Austen, then unlocked the door and opened it to find Jack waiting. "I need booze."

Jack gave a slight bow and offered his arm. "Allow me to escort you poolside, and we shall make that happen immediately, milady."

Ophelia leaned her head onto Jack's shoulder as they walked down the stairs and stepped into the fresh evening air. The sun was just beginning to set, casting a muted light over the glassy Mediterranean. She took a deep breath, inhaling the familiar scents of pine and sea salt, willing them to soothe her frayed nerves. Jack led her poolside, where Rosalie sat, looking slightly out of place.

"Rosalie, I'm so sorry for all of this," Ophelia lamented, sounding frazzled. "You came expecting a nice weekend away and ended up in the middle of my insane family nightmare."

Rosalie shook her head firmly. "Please don't apologize, Ophelia. I told Jack I'd be fine to leave if you'd rather be alone with your friends."

"No, it's fine," she replied on autopilot.

"I'm on bartender duty," Austen said. "What's everyone having?"

After placing her order, Ophelia took a shuddering breath and sank back into a reclined lounger. Everything felt distant, her head floating like an untethered balloon just above her body. *What do I do now? How am I supposed to get through the rest of this weekend, much less the rest of my life?*

Rosalie's voice was the next thing she heard.

"I have Carlos's number if you want me to see if he'd come back to cook for us tonight? I'd be happy to make the call."

Jack chuckled. "I bet you would be, you wicked little thing," he teased, then quickly turned to Ophelia, wide-eyed and remorseful. "So sorry, Lady O. Any talk of wicked little things is wildly inappropriate right now."

Jack's attempt at humor hit too close. Sitting up abruptly, she looked at the sky, trying unsuccessfully to force the tears back. After a few moments, she felt Jack's hands on her knees and dropped her gaze to meet his. Tears spilled down her cheeks.

"Rosalie's calling Carlos. We're going to take care of everything. Whatever you need, I'm here. Not just this weekend, but as long as it takes," Jack said, gently wiping her tears away with his thumbs. "I can come to Rome to help with the kids. I don't have a job, so my job can be you."

Ophelia shook her head. "I don't want to be a job, Jack."

"You're not," he replied. "That's not what I meant. Just let me be here for you. I want to help, even if all I'm good for is a fabulously broad shoulder to lean on."

"It's a very nice offer." Austen's voice broke in as she returned with a tray of drinks and snacks. "And when a fabulously broad shoulder is offered by someone called Fabulous Jack, you should definitely accept." She handed Ophelia a copper mug. "And of course, you've got Matt's shoulders too. And mine—not as broad, but they're sturdy enough. Whatever you need, starting with this Moscow Mule, heavy on the vodka."

"Thank you, both," Ophelia whispered, taking a deep sip.

"Carlos will be here in an hour," Rosalie announced as she rejoined them, looking pleased. "He didn't guarantee the menu, but he said he'd do his best under the circumstances. And he's charging it all to Gianluca's card."

"Attagirl," Jack said, cracking a smile.

At the mention of Gianluca's name, Ophelia's heart clenched again. She stared into her drink, watching the ice cubes swirl as a million questions flooded her mind, each one colder and sharper than the last. *How long has this been going on? Months? Years? How did I miss it? He says he doesn't love her—but was that a lie too? How do I get Kristin off my team at work? Marco and Esme are going to have a sibling? How is that supposed to work?*

Austen's voice interrupted her mental spiral. "I can see you're lost in your thoughts, which is natural. Do you want to talk about it, or would you prefer a distraction? I saw Pictionary in the living room. I think it's in Spanish, which might make it even better?"

"I feel like such a fool for not knowing," Ophelia murmured.

"You're not a fool," Austen insisted. "Don't be mad at yourself. Be mad at Gianluca. He hid it well. This is one hundred percent his fault, not yours."

"And Kristin's," Jack added, scowling.

Ophelia shook her head sadly. "I can't believe this is happening. I genuinely thought she was my friend."

"I can't believe she had the audacity to come here this weekend and pretend to be," Jack snapped.

"And she's having his baby?" Ophelia moaned.

"Let's not go there. Tonight, let's focus only on you," Austen urged gently.

"Only me," Ophelia repeated, setting down her drink. "Only me needs to float."

She stood, pulled off her cover-up, and dove into the pool, surfacing near a turquoise raft. Pulling herself onto it, she lay on her stomach facing away from the group and hid her tears in the rivulets of water dripping from her hair.

CHAPTER 36

Matt, Ibiza

When Matt returned to the villa, he was relieved to find Carlos busy in the kitchen. He'd asked the cab to stop at the small *supermercado*[27] on the way back so he could pick up some wine and an assortment of meats, cheeses, and chips—just in case—but whatever Carlos was cooking smelled far better than his backup plan.

"*Hola, señor.* Good to have you back," Matt greeted, glancing around cautiously. "Everything under control here?"

"*Sí, señor.* They're all outside," Carlos replied, nodding toward the pool. "Food will be ready soon. They're on the hard stuff. Can I make you a drink?"

"Thanks, but I'm good." Matt poured himself a glass of wine and moved to the window, watching the group outside. His gaze lingered on Ophelia, wrapped in a towel with damp hair and puffy eyes. The sight tugged at a painful memory from middle school, when his own mother had looked much the same in the weeks after his dad moved out. He recalled the endless days she spent in pajamas, barely eating, barely there. A broken heart had broken her spirit, rendering many of life's simplest tasks impossible. It was

---

27 supermarket

he who had picked up the slack in those days, making many basic meals for himself and Vivienne, trying to help however he could. The experience had left its mark on all their hearts.

"Carlos, is Gianluca still here?"

"No, Rosalie told me he left. Booked himself a hotel room. I'm cooking for the five of you." Carlos's knife moved steadily, chopping potatoes. "Sounds like a lot of drama went down here today."

Matt shook his head. "You can say that again." He took a sip of wine, picked up the bottle and a few extra glasses, and headed outside.

"You're back," Austen greeted him.

Matt sat beside her and kissed her cheek, then turned to Ophelia. "How we doin', Fie?"

Ophelia rolled her eyes in reply. "Thanks for getting them out of here."

"It's not a problem," he replied, holding up the wine glasses. "Anyone want some wine?"

"Austen's been very obligingly overserving me Moscow Mules," Ophelia said, her words slightly slurred.

Matt looked at Austen who simply shrugged. "I think she deserves it."

"No judgment here," he confirmed, setting down the glasses. "But it's a good thing food is on the way. How'd you manage to get Carlos back?"

Jack raised an arm and pointed down at the top of Rosalie's head. "We invoked the powers of the waify French bohemian goddess."

"Right. Well done, Rosalie," he smiled.

"Just trying to contribute where I can, as the most random guest at this curious little gathering," she replied, raising her glass. "Happy to help."

"I think I'll take a quick shower before dinner, if that's all right?" Matt said, looking to Ophelia, who nodded her approval.

"And I'm bringing my wine."

"I'll be right behind you," Austen said, stretching. "I could use a rinse too."

Upstairs, Matt set his wine glass on the counter and stepped into the shower, letting the warm water wash away the day's sand and some of the tension in his muscles. His heart broke for Ophelia and for Marco and Esme, who would all be victims of Gianluca's idiocy. He'd been a few years older than Marco when his family drama had hit, and he remembered it with utmost clarity. When you're a kid, nothing is scarier than having your sense of security suddenly shatter.

As he wiped condensation off the mirror, a fluffy white towel wrapped around his waist, Austen entered the bathroom holding a full glass of wine.

"I want to hug you, but I'm filthy and you're all nice and clean, so I'm just going to get naked and hop in the shower immediately."

She set down her wine and slipped off her beach dress. Matt took her in. Her green eyes perfectly matched her green bikini. "Hug me anyway," he said, wrapping his arms around her tightly. "I can shower again."

She leaned into him, resting her head against his chest. "What an awful day. I can't even believe it."

He kissed the top of her head, only to feel grit against his lips. Spitting sand toward the sink, he tossed his towel onto the floor and turned the shower back on. "You really are filthy. My lips are covered in sand. Get in here with me."

Austen shimmied out of her bikini and stepped into the shower. Matt turned her back to him, working shampoo into her hair with gentle fingers. She relaxed, leaning into his touch as he massaged her scalp.

"What do we do?" she asked softly.

She said "we" again, he thought, smiling. From the first time they'd met, he'd known she could manage high stress situations, but this was the first time they'd navigated a crisis together, and he was struck by how well they functioned as a team.

"Whatever she needs," he replied, his fingers still working through her hair. "But Fie's not always great at figuring that out for herself, so I think it's going to be tough."

Austen turned, wiping water from her eyes and meeting his gaze. "Promise me we'll never be like them. If you ever have doubts, I want you to leave me before you cheat. If you're not all in, be all out. And I'll do the same. But I really hope you're all in, because I am."

He cupped her face, his eyes solemn. "I'm all in. And I promise. I have zero doubts. You and me—we're the dream team."

She kissed him but stopped as soap began dripping down her face. Closing her eyes quickly, she gripped his waist, arching back into the water to rinse the suds away.

Matt's gaze traveled down the length of her body as he lathered his hands. She continued rinsing her hair, and he began tracing slow, soapy circles over every inch between her neck and upper thighs, feeling her body respond to his touch, and his own respond in kind. She leaned forward, her eyes still closed tightly, and her hands found his ass as she quietly moaned into his neck.

"What do you need?" he asked, water dripping down their faces and steam rising all around them as they clung to one another urgently.

"I need you inside me," she breathed, rocking her hips into his.

He pressed her against the shower wall and hungrily obliged.

CHAPTER 37

Austen, Ibiza

Austen fastened her bra and took a sip of her wine. "Are we horrible people for having shower sex while Ophelia is downstairs in crisis?"

Matt stepped into a pair of boxer briefs and kissed her with a smile. "No. I think we both needed that. But we should get downstairs and tend to her needs now."

"And definitely keep our hands off each other tonight," Austen declared.

"Which would've been even harder without that little shower interlude. See? We were preparing for the hard work ahead of being good friends," he laughed.

"How'd you get to be so incredible?" she asked, brushing tangles out of her wet hair. "It's like you had a handbook on handling all of this."

"My dad cheated on my mom when Vivienne and I were kids. He moved out for a couple of months," he revealed, pulling a T-shirt over his head. "I was thirteen. So, I suppose I've seen this show before."

Austen turned to face him, surprised. That was a revelation she hadn't expected. "Jesus, Matt. I'm so sorry. I didn't know."

"How could you have? It's fine," he assured her, sitting down on the bed as she dressed. "It was a long time ago, but let's just say I've seen the shattered-mother thing. This isn't my first time helping clean up a cheating man's mess. I hate Gianluca for doing this to her."

She imagined him as a boy, watching his mother suffer, and her heart ached for him—for the innocence lost. Her thoughts then turned to Ophelia. "I wonder how long it was going on—their affair."

"A year," he said. "Kristin confessed that to Charlie on the drive to the hotel. I'm sure Ophelia doesn't know yet, though, so keep it to yourself."

Austen's eyes widened. "A year? Jesus. I'd kill him if I were her. A one-time slip I could maybe move beyond, but an entire year of lying and deceiving the woman he's supposed to love? No way. I could never forgive that. Could you?"

"No, I don't think I could. But her situation is different. They have kids together—a life that she can't easily leave." He paused, tapping a finger on the bedspread. "It's brutal. But time heals all wounds if the person wants to heal. Ophelia's got a choice to make."

"I'm so glad I never had kids with my ex-husband. I can't imagine being forever tied to someone you don't want to be with anymore, just because you reproduced," she sighed.

Matt leaned back, a serious look crossing his face as he locked his eyes on hers. "I think it probably would've come up by now if the answer was yes, but just so I'm sure, do you want kids someday?"

The question was so unexpected that it nearly knocked Austen off balance. They'd only been dating for four months, but at their age, she supposed it was a discussion that should be had quickly. Kids weren't on her agenda, so she hadn't thought to bring it up, but she suddenly realized how foolish that was. Her lack of desire for kids had effectively ended two relationships already—first with her ex-husband, Brad, and then with her Australian, Kevin.

"Um, no," she stammered. "I never have. Ophelia asked me that when we took Marco back to their house after the playground incident in Rome. I told her that at forty-two, I thought that ship had sailed." She looked at Matt hesitantly, her heart suddenly pounding. "Do you want kids?"

"Eve and I talked about it and even removed the goalie at one point, just letting fate decide. But it never happened," he admitted with a casual shrug.

Austen searched his face, trying to read anything unsaid. *Is he holding onto hope of becoming a father?* Her pulse raced as she carefully continued. "Ophelia told me she thought you'd be a great dad, and I'm sure you would be if that's what you wanted."

Matt took her hand, squeezing it gently. "I think you'd have been a great mom too, if you'd wanted that. But I respect that you didn't. At this stage in my life, I think I'd be happy either way—if it happened or if it didn't. I have Esme as a goddaughter. That's enough for me."

"Are you sure?" she asked, practically holding her breath.

"I'm sure," he nodded. "The world is a dangerous, crazy place. I don't need to bring a kid into it."

Relief washed over her, and she felt the tension drain from her body. "Two of my past relationships ended because they wanted kids, and I didn't. You kind of scared the crap out of me just now."

"Sorry. I didn't mean to." He leaned over, kissing her cheek. "We just hadn't talked about it, and with all the drama this weekend about accidental pregnancies and the possibility of shared custody agreements hanging in the air, I figured it was time to make sure we're on the same page."

"No babies for us then," she confirmed.

"We'll keep playing on Team Birth Control," he agreed with a smile.

She pointed her thumbs at her chest. "Big fan of Team Birth Control, this gal. Always have been."

When they arrived downstairs, Ophelia, Jack, and Rosalie were settling in at the table under the pergola, all looking a bit tipsy and in need of food. Matt kissed the top of Ophelia's head, then took a seat next to Rosalie as Austen slid in beside Jack.

"Wonderful. Everyone's here, so we can begin what will inevitably be the worst birthday party in history," Ophelia slurred, raising her glass.

"It's not the worst birthday party of all time," Jack insisted, filling empty glasses with wine for the newcomers. "But it's certainly one of the more memorable. Anyone else have any particularly memorable disaster birthdays? Misery loves company, as they say."

Austen raised her hand cautiously. "When I was ten, I had a bowling party. My parents drove everyone to the bowling alley, but when they got there, they realized they'd left me at home. I'd been in the bathroom when they loaded up the cars."

"Forgotten at your own birthday?" Jack squealed. "Savage."

"I had a party at the beach in Papeete one year. I think I was six?" Matt recounted. "There was a water balloon fight, and one kid picked up a jellyfish by accident, thinking it was a balloon, and threw it at another kid."

Austen's mind flashed to Thailand and her near-threesome interrupted by a jellyfish sting. *A story for another time, or perhaps never,* she thought.

Ophelia dropped her fork. "A child mistook a jellyfish for a water balloon at your birthday party?"

"Island life. It happens," Matt offered, sipping his wine. "And maybe that's why I'm not a fan of birthdays."

"Right, well I think Matt wins," Rosalie declared, digging into the paella Carlos had placed on the table.

Ophelia shook her head, scooping up some rice. "Does he, though? Does a jellyfish sting trump finding out that your husband's mistress—who you thought was your friend—is pregnant with his baby?"

"Do you want me to murder him? I could find a way," Matt replied, leaning toward her with a pointed look.

Austen shivered slightly. *He probably could,* she thought.

"I'm sure you could find a way, but if you got caught, I'd never be able to live with myself while you rotted in prison," Ophelia smiled weakly, shaking her head. "So, no. But thanks for the idea. And I may change my mind eventually."

"It's a standing offer," he declared, raising an eyebrow. "And a woman's prerogative to change her mind."

Ophelia reached out to squeeze Matt's hand. "What would I do without you?"

"You'll never have to find out," he replied, squeezing back.

Austen fell silent, looking at Matt and Ophelia's joined hands. A small wave of insecurity washed over her as she compared her and Matt's fledgling romance to his and Ophelia's decades of history and legacy of first love.

She loved Matt, and she knew he loved her. But she wasn't sure how much—if any—of the flame between him and Ophelia might have burned quietly in the background all these years, for him or for her.

Does first love ever really die? Hating herself for the insecurity and doubt, Austen wondered if, now that Ophelia's marriage was in crisis, Matt's instinct to protect might draw him back toward her.

That's the thing about love, she realized. *Once you're in it, you suddenly have something to lose.*

CHAPTER 38

Ophelia, Ibiza

"Fie, it's your birthday, and birthdays are for gifts. So, here you go," Matt said, sipping a small glass of *hierbas* over ice and sliding a silver-wrapped package across the dinner table toward her. "It's from me and Austen."

Ophelia reached for the package, forcing a smile. She opened it, revealing a delicate lace table runner. Fingering the intricate material, she looked at Matt with curiosity, waiting for an explanation.

"You told me Esme cut up your mom's table runner, and I know you don't have much left of her things," he said gently. "So, I got this for you. It was made in Bedford, so I hope it's a comparable replacement."

Ophelia stared at Matt in wonder.

"Where's Bedford?" Rosalie asked.

"It's where I grew up. And my mum died when I was very young," Ophelia explained. She reached across Rosalie and grasped Matt's hand, looking between him and Austen. "It's the most thoughtful gift I've ever received. Thank you."

"That was all Matt," Austen said, smiling at him. "Being a great gift-giver is a real art, and it seems that's yet another one of this guy's exceptional skills."

"What's the best gift any of you have given or received?" Jack asked. "Luis surprised me with a long ski weekend in Aspen for my fortieth in January—first-class tickets, the works. First class is my personal heaven."

"My sister gave me a painting by an artist I was obsessed with. I'd been raving about her work for weeks before her show at the gallery," Rosalie shared. "I thought she'd bought it for herself, but she gave it to me as a birthday gift months later. It's in my living room, and I adore it."

"Both very nice," Austen said, nodding in approval. "My college boyfriend went on a months-long trek through South America after we graduated, and I gave him an antique compass engraved with 'So you can always find your way back to me.' It got stolen while he was traveling, and we obviously broke up," she laughed. "But I still think it was a great gift."

Ophelia rested her chin on her fist. "I'm trying to remember what I got Gianluca for his last birthday, and I honestly can't. It was probably something horribly practical and boring, like a sweater. Maybe it's all my fault he ran off with Kristin."

"Fie, don't do that to yourself," Matt insisted. "This is all on Gianluca."

Jack leaned in toward Ophelia, forcing her to look into his eyes. "Also, there's nothing wrong with practical gifts. Love is doing a bunch of small things for the other person to make them feel happy and safe. Sometimes, love is sweaters."

Austen placed a hand on Ophelia's. "I think love starts as a feeling and then becomes a choice—to keep showing up for the other person in the way they deserve, even when it's hard. I've seen you with him and with the kids, and you do that. You love them well."

"I never even say the word," Ophelia murmured, her shoulders sagging.

"What word?" Rosalie asked, puzzled.

"Love," Matt replied.

Jack's brow furrowed. "You never say the word 'love'? What do you mean?"

Ophelia could feel all their eyes on her, waiting for her to explain her extreme emotional failings. "My father never said it to me, so I never learned how," she said, briefly burying her face in her palms.

"Oh, sweetie," Jack said, wrapping his arm around her.

"I know I'm broken—far from perfect. I tried therapy, but Gianluca said he knew that I felt it even if I never said it. He told me I didn't have to. And then Esme told Matt a few months ago that she didn't think I loved anything or anyone because I never say it. I've screwed everything up."

"Fie, first of all, no one is perfect," Matt said firmly. "Second, he's your husband. He's supposed to choose you, protect you, and love you, no matter what. He knew who you were when he married you. He's the one who failed, not you. And we're all going to keep telling you that until you believe it."

Rosalie nodded, smiling at Matt. "What he said, Ophelia. I've known you for maybe thirty hours, and it's already clear to me that you're a kind, generous, loving person to everyone around you. Just look at your friends here, who all love you fiercely. I believe that we get back as much love as we put out into the world, so clearly, you must have given a lot of love."

"Well said, Rosie," Jack concurred.

Ophelia looked around the table at the smiling faces of her friends and felt a wave of exhaustion roll over her. Tears pricked at the corners of her eyes, blurring her vision, which was already hazy from the alcohol.

"I'm exhausted and quite drunk. I should go to bed," Ophelia declared, standing up and swaying slightly as she clutched the table runner to her chest. "Thank you all for being here, despite the wretched circumstances."

Matt stood. "Do you need help getting upstairs, or are you all right?"

She waved him off, blowing out a puff of air. "I've got it. I'm jilted, not invalid."

"Goodnight, gorgeous," Jack said, blowing her a kiss. "This too shall pass."

"Sleep well," Austen and Rosalie chimed in unison.

Ophelia waved goodnight and made her way to her room, where she carefully placed her gift in her suitcase. She staggered into the bathroom and looked at her bloodshot, puffy eyes in the mirror as she brushed her teeth. Her friends' words echoed in her head like a mantra, even if she didn't believe them: *Gianluca's job was to choose, protect, and love me, and he failed. I'm not perfect, but this is not my fault.*

She spat out the toothpaste, drank a full glass of water, and took one more look at herself as fresh tears started to fall. *Also, forty sucks.*

CHAPTER 39
Matt, Ibiza

Matt eased the door shut behind him, careful not to wake Austen as he slipped out. The morning was still and quiet, which was a welcome reprieve after the previous day's chaos. He poured himself a cup of coffee, grabbed a yogurt, and headed outside, hoping to have a moment to think before the others stirred. But he found Ophelia already on the back porch, cradling a teacup in both hands.

She traced the rim of her cup with her thumb, her expression distant, but when she noticed him, she offered a faint smile.

"You're up early," he greeted her, giving her shoulder a gentle squeeze.

"Couldn't sleep," she admitted. "Been up since sunrise, wondering where Gianluca slept last night and hating myself for caring. And then hating him some more."

"You haven't heard from him at all?" he asked, joining her at the table.

Ophelia slid her phone to him. "He texted me last night around ten o'clock."

Gianluca: I'm so sorry. I love you.
I always and forever choose you.

"How does that make you feel?" Matt asked.

"Like I want to demand an explanation for what on earth happened to get us to this point," she replied, pushing her sunglasses on top of her head. "And like I want to punch him in the bollocks."

Matt involuntarily squirmed in his seat at the image. "Both are valid. Will you text him back?"

She pouted slightly. "You think I should?"

"If I were him, I'd probably be waiting for a clue from you on what to do next," Matt offered. "He knows he's in the wrong. He loves you, so he's probably kicking himself, trying to figure out how not to make things worse by doing or saying the wrong thing."

Ophelia considered his words. "I'm trying to decide if he even deserves a chance to explain himself. Is there anything he could say that would make a difference at this point?"

"You can be selfish here, Fie, for once in your life. Do what you want, not what you think he needs," Matt insisted.

Ophelia's gaze went skyward, trying to consider what he'd said. He sat quietly, waiting for her lead. After about forty-five seconds of silence, she pushed her mug aside, reached across the table, and took one of Matt's hands in both of hers.

"Can we please talk about anything else? I can't stand to think about it. How are things going with Austen?"

He was happier with Austen than he'd been in a long time, but he knew that no one in crisis wants another person's happiness rubbed in their face. Matt thought carefully about what to share. "I liked what she said last night about love starting as a feeling and becoming a choice. I think we're still in the 'feeling' stage, given it's only been four months, but I feel like we're going to keep choosing each other."

"She looks at you like you hung the moon. You deserve to be chosen." Ophelia squeezed his hand, released it, and then ran her fingers across her forehead under her bangs. "Gianluca said he's choosing me over Kristin, so I feel like I'm supposed to let him. Forgive him. But how can I?"

Matt had often wondered if his mother had truly forgiven his father after his own indiscretions. He assumed she had, since his father had come back, but he'd never dared to ask. Still, he remembered the extreme relief he'd felt as a kid on the day his father returned. His thoughts went to Marco and Esme and then back to Ophelia, willing there to be a good outcome for them all.

"You don't have to decide that today. This is all still very raw," he offered. "But maybe start by inviting him back here this afternoon so you can talk? If that's what you want. I can clear everyone out to give you privacy."

He looked up to see Austen emerging from the house, sleep in her eyes, and hair piled in a messy bun on top of her head. She joined them at the table, flopping onto the bench next to him with a plate of fruit and a steaming mug of coffee.

"Good morning, sunshine," he smiled, kissing her cheek.

She rubbed his back in greeting but focused her attention on Ophelia. "How are you feeling today?"

Ophelia clutched her teacup to her chest. "Well, so far my forties are definitely not my favorite decade, but I'm only one day in, so I suppose there's still time for improvement," she said with a sad smile.

"We were just talking about whether she wanted to invite Gianluca back here today so they could talk," Matt recounted.

"I'll have to talk to him eventually, so I probably should just rip off the bandage and do it," Ophelia replied.

"If that's what you want," Matt insisted.

Ophelia looked off into the distance toward the Mediterranean. "I want to not be yet another failed marriage. I want my kids to grow up with both their parents around. I want to not be forty and a single mum."

"If you can forgive him and want to stay together, then you will," Austen offered gently. "But listen, I've been forty and single. I get that the kids change the equation, but for what it's worth, these four years since my divorce have been amazing in terms of personal growth and figuring out what I really want and need in life. It doesn't have to be the end of the world. There is life after divorce—if that's what you choose."

Matt watched his current love working hard to take care of his first love, and he felt exceedingly grateful—for having both women in his life, for having clarity on what he wanted, for not turning into his cheating father, and for Austen's ex-husband's idiocy in letting her get away so he could hold on to her instead.

"And I take issue with the term 'failed marriage,'" Austen continued. "If you leave your shitty job for something better, no one calls it 'failed employment.' Life is about allowing yourself to grow, allowing your desires to change, and having the courage to walk away to improve your situation."

Matt looked at Ophelia and pointed at Austen. "What she said."

Wiping tears from her eyes, Ophelia lamented, "I thought I was happy. I thought we were happy. Maybe things have been bad so long that I've forgotten what happy feels like."

"I'm not defending him at all, Fie, but people make mistakes," Matt said, taking a sip of his coffee. "Hear him out. You don't have to forgive him this weekend or even this year if you don't want to. If you guys are meant to be, he'll fight for you, and maybe you'll come out of this even stronger."

I think my parents did, ultimately.

Austen leaned in. "And if you decide to go the other way, I can assure you of one thing: it's impossible to fail at divorce. Once you put that in motion, you're guaranteed to get it done."

"The important thing to remember is that you're in control of whatever happens next," Matt reminded her. "You get to dictate the terms."

Ophelia sighed deeply. "Okay, I'll tell him to come by later, assuming he's still on the island. Would you mind clearing out with Jack and Rosalie for a few hours?"

"You got it. Just let me know when he's going to be here, and I'll make sure we're gone," Matt agreed.

"Thanks, Richie," she said, standing up and moving to his side of the table. "And you know what? My terms for today are that I'm not going to let him see me cry. That'll be what he's expecting, and I refuse to give him the satisfaction."

Matt stood and placed a reassuring hand on her shoulder. "No matter what he's done, I don't think Gianluca would ever take any satisfaction in seeing you cry, Fie."

"I know. That's not what I meant, really. It's just that in our relationship, he's usually the one in control, and I want that to be me today," she vowed, resting her forehead against Matt's chest.

He squeezed the back of her neck gently and kissed the side of her head. "I think that sounds like a good plan. You deserve that."

CHAPTER 40

Gianluca, Ibiza

When he arrived back at the villa, Gianluca was relieved to see no cars parked out front. He wanted to face Ophelia alone without any distractions. His mind had been spinning since everything had unraveled yesterday—about what he needed to say to her, about the kids, the new baby, and all the reasons he'd allowed his affair with Kristin to happen, much less to drag on for an entire year. He hated himself for getting into this mess in the first place and was prepared to grovel for as long as it took to make things right.

At his core, he didn't believe Ophelia would leave him. He knew he'd have to work to win back her trust, but he was used to getting what he wanted, even when he didn't deserve it. The wildcard was the baby, but he'd sort that out in time. For now, his priority was keeping Ophelia by his side and keeping his family intact.

He wiped his sweaty palms on his cargo shorts and rang the doorbell. Though he still had a key, he wanted Ophelia to feel in control. His pulse quickened as he heard her footsteps approaching.

She opened the door and met his eyes without a word. The sight of her cracked his heart open—she looked like she'd spent the night crying. He hated that he'd hurt her, but there was nothing he could do to change the past, so he resolved to focus on the future and how they might get through this together. She motioned for him to come in, her arm moving as if it had no bones left in it. He'd never seen her so lifeless. He wanted to reach for her, but her body language told him not to. Hurt and disappointment seeped out of her every pore. He'd justified his affair in a million ways over the past year, but all his reasons were bullshit. He had betrayed her, and he was ready to own it.

"Thank you for being willing to talk," he said, as they moved toward the back patio. "I have so much I want to say, but if you'd rather start, I'm listening."

"Why did you do it?" she asked, her eyes dark and lifeless as she sat down at the outdoor dining table.

Gianluca was prepared to be yelled at, for tears, for hysterics. He was not expecting one calm, icy sentence from his usually spirited wife. It threw him off balance, and he teetered onto the bench opposite her, reaching toward her across the table, but she kept her hands firmly in her lap.

"There's no reason I can give you that would make it okay. I know that, so I'll not try to justify my behavior. It was inexcusable," he began, scratching at his beard. "I was weak, and she was persistent. I was a fool, but I don't want her. I only want you and our family, and I'm so very sorry it took this to make me realize that."

"Persistent?" She repeated the word slowly, her gaze steady and unblinking. "So, it went on for a while?"

He hesitated, hoping to avoid specifics. "Does it matter how long? It happened. I regret it deeply, and I'm willing to do whatever it takes to help us move past this."

Her expression remained unreadable. "I think it matters very much. I want to know when it began."

He knew better than to lie again. "The night I met her at Al Piave, after you left us alone."

Ophelia dropped her head into her hands, silent for what felt like an eternity. Gianluca watched the top of her head, desperately wondering what thoughts were tearing around in there.

When she finally looked up, cold, hard anger poured out of her squinted eyes, but her voice stayed eerily calm. "You've both been lying to my face for over a year? Were you having sex with her every time she was in Rome working for me?"

Gianluca felt shame burn through him like fire. "I'm sorry, Ophelia. It's not an excuse, but she was—is—in love with me, and hearing that felt good. I'm ashamed to admit it, but I got caught up in it. I'm sorry I needed that, but I suppose I did."

"So, this is my fault. Because I never say it?" she asked, her lips pressing together tightly.

"That's not what I meant. It's my fault, completely. I'm only trying to explain how I got caught up," he said, his voice faltering.

Ophelia let out a dry laugh, her head rolling back. "You two fell in love on night one, did you? That sounds more like lust, Gianluca. So far, your so-called explanation," she said, raising her hands in air quotes, "is nothing but a load of bollocks."

"You're right. It is. I'm so sorry. Please, just tell me what I need to do to start earning back your trust, and I'll do it," he pleaded.

She stood up and walked away toward the pool, leaving him frozen in place. Her eerie calm was unsettling. He wondered if she'd taken a sedative. It wasn't in her nature to be this even-keeled, especially in a situation this emotionally charged.

"Ophelia, *tesoro,* please talk to me," he called after her.

Turning back, she asked, "Is she the only one, or have you cheated on me with other women?"

Gianluca walked to her and took her hands in his. "She was the only one. I swear it. And I promise I'll never lie to you again."

She pulled her hands free, her gaze drifting past him to the horizon. "I changed countries for you. Left my entire life behind to fit into yours. I take care of the kids, the house. I make your coffee every morning, cook your dinner nearly every night. I spend my days trying to be what I think you need." Her voice held a quiet sadness. "And you fucked my friend and lied to me about it for a year. You promised to love me and be faithful until death parted us. Your promises are worth nothing now."

Every word stung because it was true, except that Kristin had clearly never been her friend. But there was no point in arguing semantics.

"I fucked up," he admitted, hands clasped in front of him like a prayer. "I will regret this for the rest of my life, but I never stopped loving you or our family. I'll never stop trying to make it right."

"And what about your new family with Kristin?" she asked, her expression listless, her body swaying slightly. "How are you going to make things right by them?"

Gianluca gently guided her to a nearby pool lounger and sat beside her, taking her hands once more. "They aren't my priority. You, Marco, and Esme are. I'll deal with that situation when the time comes, but right now, all I care about is you three."

Ophelia slowly pulled her hands away, tilting her head as she regarded him. "You got her pregnant, and now you're planning to abandon her? That makes me hate you even more."

"There's a fine line between love and hate, Ophelia," he said, cupping her face. "I'm your husband, and even if you never say it, I know you love me. I also know I've hurt you, but I believe we can get through this because of that love."

She turned her head, breaking his hold on her. "Sometimes love isn't enough, Gianluca. I used to love smoking. I thought I'd want that forever, but I gave it up because it was bad for me. I thought I wanted you forever too, but maybe I was wrong. Maybe I should give you up too."

Panic gripped him, and he buried his face in her lap, his arms wrapping around her waist. "Don't give up on me, Ophelia. Please. We can do counseling, whatever it takes. We belong together. We're a family, and we must fix this."

She lifted his arms away from her waist and stood, backing away. "We're not a 'we' right now, Gianluca. And I don't have to do anything."

CHAPTER 41

Ophelia, Ibiza

Ophelia looked down into Gianluca's pleading eyes. Her instinct, built and reinforced over more than a decade of loving him, was to comfort him. But she resisted. It was she who deserved comforting now. Her mind felt heavy and clouded, as though stuffed with cotton wool, and as she tried to look forward, she saw no clear path to a life that resembled "normal," whatever that was anymore. He had broken them.

She wanted nothing more than to kick him out of their family home, but she knew that would upend everything for Marco and Esme. *Not disrupting the children's lives is my priority now*, she thought. But even so, she desperately needed to reclaim some control. She remembered Austen's words from the day before: *This is now officially your world, and he only gets to live in it if you choose to permit it.*

A breeze drifted off the Mediterranean, caressing her skin, and she took a deep breath to steel her resolve.

"I want you on a plane back to Rome ASAP. Not mine. Change your flight. I'm going to stay here as planned until tomorrow night with the rest of our guests," she said, working hard to keep any emotion out of her voice. "By the time I get home, I want you and all your things moved into the guest room. I won't disrupt the kids' lives by kicking you out, but I also won't share a bed with you. That's all. Please leave now."

Gianluca's shoulders slumped, a defeated sigh escaping his lips. "Thank you for not kicking me out. I don't deserve your kindness, I know. And I understand and respect that you need time. You'll have as much as you need. But I will be fighting for us and for our family every step of the way. That, I promise."

"I'm done listening to you today, Gianluca. Get out." Her tone was calm, though her blood felt as though it had reached boiling point. She had to summon every ounce of her inner strength to maintain her composure. He stood and moved toward her, one arm outstretched, but she held up her hand as a barrier.

"You no longer have permission to touch me."

"Okay. I'm leaving." He stepped back, hand dropping to his side. "I'll see you back in Rome tomorrow night. Please tell everyone I'm sorry for the chaos."

Ophelia shook her head. "No. I won't apologize for you. Just leave."

He hung his head, nodding, and walked away, leaving her alone by the pool. She stood unmoving until he was out of sight. Then, she dropped like a lead balloon onto the pool lounger, pulling her knees to her chest and wrapping her arms around them, making herself as small as possible. Her breathing came in shallow, ragged gasps, and when she heard the crunch of his car tires on the gravel driveway, the dam that had been holding back her tears finally broke.

She buried her face in a pool towel to muffle the sobs and catch the tears and snot that poured out as her shoulders shook. She briefly considered going inside to cry in their bedroom, but the idea that they might never share a bedroom again tore through her and rooted her in place. Everything he'd said replayed in her mind, and she fought a mental battle between the hope in his promise to fight for her and a raging anger over his betrayal. She wasn't sure which she should hold onto more tightly.

Finally, when the tears slowed and her soul felt empty, she gathered herself and went inside to find her phone. She pushed her damp hair away from her tear-streaked face, blew her nose, splashed cold water on her face, and typed out a message.

> Ophelia: He's gone. Come back whenever. No rush.

Matt: You ok? Want us to pick anything up for you? We're at the beach now with Jack and Rosalie. Want to join us? I can come pick you up.

> Ophelia: I'm ok. And no. Don't need anything. See you when you're back. Xx

Matt: Ok. See you soon. Call if you change your mind. X

Ophelia put her phone aside and wandered upstairs to take a shower, ready to wash away her tears and the general sense of despair that clung to her. This was their last night in Ibiza, and she didn't want to mope—not with her friends here. She scrubbed herself clean, applied cooling gel eye patches, dried her hair, and put on makeup along with a simple black strapless dress. The eye patches couldn't perform miracles; she still looked like she'd spent the past twenty-four hours crying. But her guests had flown here to be with her, and she intended to make an effort for them.

When she returned downstairs, she found Jack, Austen, and Matt seated at the outdoor table, munching on olives and drinking rosé, their skin sun-kissed and glowing from the beach.

"Well, check you out," Austen said, grinning as Ophelia approached. "Great dress."

Ophelia forced her best smile. "It's our last night on the island, and we're going out. I called Sunset Ashram, and they have a table waiting for us at seven-thirty."

"Are you sure?" Jack asked, reaching for her hand and pulling her to sit down next to him. "Do you want to talk about what happened with Gianluca? Rosalie is upstairs showering, so it's just us."

She took a deep breath before giving the most concise update she could manage. "I told him to fly back to Rome and move into the guest room before I get back. I want to throw him out, but I can't do that to the kids. At least, not yet."

"How'd he take it?" Matt asked, pouring her a glass of rosé.

She nodded in gratitude and took a sip. "He thanked me for letting him stay. Said he was going to fight for us."

Austen leaned in, resting her chin in her palm. "Is that what you want?"

Ophelia sighed as her gaze drifted to the sky. "It's too fresh. I don't know what I want other than to get my mind off it for a few hours tonight."

"Then that's what we're going to do," Jack said, nodding firmly. "Your wish is our command, and the rosé will flow as steadily as required to keep you sane—or comfortably numb. Your choice."

Matt reached across the table and took her hands in his, squeezing them gently. "Fie, obviously no one knows what's going to happen here, but remember this: you're a wonderful, smart, capable woman and mother, and we all love you fiercely. You're never alone."

She closed her eyes, letting Matt's words settle over her. *I am capable*, she silently repeated like a mantra.

He continued, "I think this situation, as hard as it is, is going to bring out a strength that you didn't even know you had. And I think that's going to be beautiful."

Ophelia squeezed his hands back, feeling her heart constrict at the notion that any beauty could emerge from this nightmare. She'd never thought of herself as particularly strong, but as she looked at her friends' earnest faces, she wanted to believe that Matt could be right. She knew it would take every ounce of mental fortitude she had to maintain a brave face for the kids once they returned to Rome, but she was determined to keep their world intact, even while hers had been shattered.

"Thanks, Richie. At least I didn't cry when he was here," she said softly. "I was proud of myself for that."

Matt smiled approvingly. "Good girl. I'm proud of you, too."

Ophelia squared her shoulders, pressing her palms flat against the table. "You three go get cleaned up, and let's have a good night."

"Yes, ma'am," Austen replied as they all rose from the table and headed off.

Once alone, Ophelia poured herself another glass of rosé and let out a deep sigh. The truth was, she wanted nothing more than to crawl back into bed and cry herself to sleep. But she couldn't—not with her guests here. She may not have thought of herself as particularly strong, but she had always prided herself on being genuine and showing up for others. Now, with Gianluca's betrayal cutting deep, that resolve felt as shaky as ever.

I suppose the "fake it until you make it" stage of my life starts now, she thought, downing the wine.

CHAPTER 42

Austen, Ibiza

Sunset Ashram was a round, open-air restaurant with sand floors and a thatched roof, boasting a perfect sunset view over sea. A deejay mixed dance music that drifted through the air as their party of five settled into a semicircular booth. They had cleaned up nicely, dressed in their best boho beachwear. Ophelia sat in the center, flanked by Jack and Matt, while Austen and Rosalie occupied the outer seats. Austen watched as the waiter poured cava over mixed fruit before serving their umpteenth pitcher of sangria.

"We're gonna need another bottle. Actually, just keep them coming," Ophelia said with a fake smile before looking both ways at her friends. "So, what did you all do today?"

"Jack and I went to Los Enamorados for lunch, where he failed spectacularly at trying to flirt with the waiter," Rosalie said, grinning.

"Excuse me, pot. Meet kettle. You were an absolutely wretched wing woman," Jack countered, throwing his head back dramatically. "This guy was definitely at least bi-curious, and Rosalie was flirting with him too. I think we scared him off because we couldn't stop giggling and watching his very cute ass scurry around the restaurant."

"I wasn't flirting. I have plans later with Carlos, so I honestly wasn't even trying," Rosalie replied, inspecting her fingernails with exaggerated nonchalance. "I was just being French. We don't flirt. We simply smolder while acting aloof, and men are drawn to it like moths to the flame."

"French women do indeed do that," Austen confirmed, sipping her sangria. "It's a skill."

"Well, I wasn't really trying either," Jack declared, leaning his head on Rosalie's shoulder. "I enjoy a fun flirt sesh, just to make sure I've still got it. But in this case, I blame you entirely for distracting him."

"It may have also had something to do with their super garlicky aioli. We're probably both still breathing fire," Rosalie added, covering her mouth with both hands.

"You can't win 'em all," Austen said with a grin. "My strategy before Matt, of course, was always to have high hopes and no expectations when I was on the prowl. That was how I stayed sane through all the little disappointments."

"High hopes and no expectations," Ophelia repeated thoughtfully. "I like that. It's a good strategy for life in general, I think. Impossible to be disappointed if you expect nothing."

"Gosh, I don't know," Austen said, tilting her head to one side. "No expectations from life sounds like depression, no? No expectations from dates was just a coping mechanism for the bad behavior that dating apps have normalized, like ghosting or random dick pics. But I wouldn't extrapolate it beyond the dating realm."

"So, what *do* you expect from life?" Ophelia asked, clearly in a contemplative mood.

Austen considered the question carefully. Ophelia appeared to be holding everything together, but Austen couldn't imagine how she possibly could. "Life is unpredictable. The pandemic made that clear. And sometimes it's chaotic, between work, friends, family, and other obligations pulling you in a million directions," she began. "My expectations—or perhaps my hope—for my life is that it be joyful chaos. I loathe the predictable, so if life is joyful, I think I must be doing things right."

Matt smiled at her quizzically. "Joyful chaos? I've never heard that one before."

"I just made it up," Austen smiled, trying unsuccessfully to wrestle her hair into submission in the sea breeze. "But I'd rather be joyfully chaotic any day of the week than bored and shooting for some kind of impossible, curated perfection."

Ophelia gave a satisfied nod while scooping burrata covered in pine nuts and pesto onto a piece of bread. "I like it. Joyful chaos sounds like a great goal to me."

"To joyful chaos," Jack toasted, raising his glass. "Lady O, I suspect your life might be quite chaotic in the coming weeks and months, and joy might be a bit hard to come by. But if you ever need an escape, you're always welcome at our place in New York."

As Jack spoke, Austen caught Matt watching Ophelia. Acting on instinct, she jumped in with her own offer. "You're welcome in Paris, too. Anytime. Not to take anything away from Jack's lovely invitation, but I've got the best girlfriends in the world, and I can guarantee pampering, shopping, champagne, and whatever else you need. When was the last time you had a proper girls' weekend?"

Austen's motives were both genuine and defensive. She sincerely liked Ophelia, but in case the upheaval in Ophelia's relationship resurfaced any lingering feelings for Matt, Austen wanted to abide by the age-old adage of keeping her friends close and her enemies closer. She hated even thinking it, but she hoped that spending more time together would help her overcome the doubt.

Ophelia scratched her cheek, sipping her drink as she considered. "The last time? I'm not sure. For one, flying terrifies me, so I usually avoid it. But it may have been before Marco was born. So, maybe a decade ago? Good Lord. That's pathetic."

"It's not pathetic," Austen reassured her, taking a bite of sea bass ceviche. "But it sounds like you're way overdue. Come to Paris soon and let me and my girlfriends spoil you. You deserve it."

"A proper girls' weekend in Paris is hard to argue with," Jack conceded. "Luis and I are happy to have you, but as we require a trans-Atlantic flight and you hate flying, I will happily defer to Madame Keller."

"You should do it, Fie. Austen has quite the crew there. You'd have fun," Matt said, resting a hand on Austen's thigh before turning to give her a warm smile.

The gratitude she saw in his eyes eased her nerves. Austen willed herself to extinguish her lingering fears and show up for both Ophelia and Matt with her full heart. *Trust this love,* she told herself. *He's done nothing to cause you to doubt him.*

Austen returned her gaze to Ophelia.

"I think life puts certain people in your path at certain times for a reason, and I've just got a feeling that you should come to Paris and recharge with us," she said. "Listen to Audrey Hepburn. Paris is always a good idea."

"I'll think about it," Ophelia promised. "It's a lovely offer. Cheers, Austen. A girls' weekend sounds brilliant. Gianluca can take care of the kids for a few days. I guess I can get him to do whatever I bloody well want for the foreseeable future, eh? Might as well take advantage of that."

"I think your hall pass will be valid for some time," Jack agreed.

When the waiter arrived to clear their appetizer plates, Matt leaned close to Austen, his voice low. "Want to take a quick walk on the beach before the rest of the food gets here?"

She nodded and slid out of the booth.

"We're going to pop down to the beach for a few minutes," Matt announced as he stood.

"Sure thing," Ophelia said, turning back to Jack and Rosalie.

Matt led her out of the restaurant and down the sandy, wooden stairs to the beach. The sun had begun its slow descent into the sea, painting the horizon in shades of orange and pink. Lacing his fingers into hers, Matt led Austen along the sand, their steps sinking lightly with each stride.

"Your joyful chaos plan and offer for a girls' weekend put some light back into her eyes for the first time since yesterday. Thanks for doing that."

"Of course. It's nothing," Austen said with a small smile. "It's what friends do."

"I know, but she's my friend first, so I just wanted to say that I really appreciate you embracing her the way you have," Matt explained.

His earnestness made Austen's heart tighten. She tugged on his hand and pulled him to face her. Taking a moment to purse her lips tightly, she then spoke. "I have a confession."

Matt tilted his head and raised an eyebrow. "A confession. Should I be worried?"

Austen hesitated, debating how much to disclose. The warmth of the fading sunlight caught his open, curious expression, and her words spilled out. "Last night, I started to worry that there may be some lingering feelings between you and Ophelia."

Matt frowned, scrunching his nose. "I thought we put this issue to bed a long time ago. Why is it back?"

Austen bit her lip, weighing her response. "Heightened circumstances. Heightened emotions. Men like to feel needed—to be the one saving the damsel in distress. And some women like to be saved."

Matt shook his head, resting his hands on her shoulders. "You're mistaking me for someone with a hero complex. I love you. I want you. And I've never met a woman less in need of saving. So no, that's not who I am. I want this. Us. The end."

Sometimes, simply hearing the words you've been craving is enough to make them real. Austen rested her forehead on his chest, letting his assurances soak deeply into her heart. After a moment, she met his gaze assuredly and spoke. "Okay. It's forgotten. The girls and I will pull out all the stops to spoil her rotten if we can get her to Paris."

Matt pushed a strand of hair behind her ear, his gaze wandering toward the horizon. "I wish my mom had had a good friend around when she was going through the affair with my dad. I've been thinking about it a lot today, for obvious reasons, and I suspect she felt very alone during that time."

Taking his hand, Austen fell into step beside him as they wandered farther along the craggy beach. She thought about the road ahead for Ophelia and tried to imagine what Matt's mom had endured.

"Kids never know what's going on in their parents' lives. And even if you had, there wasn't anything you could've done."

"I know," he conceded, kissing her hand as they walked. "But I think that experience shaped me—made me want to take care of people. Right now, I want to cover Ophelia in bubble wrap to protect her."

"You're taking great care of her. And of me," Austen said with a soft smile.

"It's different with you, though," he replied.

Austen looked up at him curiously. "How so?"

Matt walked in silence for several moments, his gaze fixed on the boats bobbing gently in the tide. Eventually, he spoke again. "You know how sometimes your head is in control of how you move through the world, but sometimes it's your heart?"

She nodded, encouraging him to continue.

"When I was with Eve, and even with Ophelia, I think I was always in my head, thinking about how to protect them. It was almost like work—focusing on taking care of the physical body." He paused, turning to her. "With you, it's all heart."

Austen raised an eyebrow. "I don't think I really want to hear about how you prioritized your ex-girlfriends' bodies."

He laughed, grabbing her waist and pulling her close. "I didn't mean it like that. I just want to protect your heart."

"Well, good, because I love you so much that sometimes it feels like my heart could explode," she said, before pressing her lips firmly to his. Pulling back, she gave him her most sultry look. "And for the record, you do a pretty good job of taking care of my body too."

As the sun continued its descent, casting rainbow hues across the water, Matt pulled her close, kissing her deeply, his warmth spreading through her. When they finally broke apart, he said, "The disaster of this weekend has made me feel very lucky that you're mine. This feels like a partnership—like I'm with an equal—and damn, it feels good."

Austen, who had been searching for her equal since her divorce from Brad, felt her heart swell. Here he was, standing on an Ibizan beach at sunset, promising to protect her heart.

"It feels better than good," she murmured, threading her fingers through his hair. "I'm so grateful to be yours. Opening myself up to you has honestly been terrifying after having my heart broken a few times, but you make me feel safe."

"You're safe with me," he promised softly, his hands gliding lazily across her back, in rhythm with the waves lolling against the beach. "And I feel very lucky to be yours too."

Austen let her body fully relax into his, resting her head against his chest and wrapping her arms loosely around his waist. Her backless halter dress allowed his caresses to be skin-to-skin, and she reveled in his touch. His hips shifted slightly and deliberately into hers, making her suddenly aware of his arousal. She pulled her head back to meet his gaze with a knowing smile.

"And rather than promise to take care of your body in my usual professional way, I will promise to worship your body. Every day.

In the least professional way possible," he teased, tracing a finger from her bottom lip, down her chin and neck, between her breasts, and around to her back.

"I'd drop down to my knees and worship yours right here and now if we weren't on a public beach," she shot back with a wink, giving his ass a playful squeeze.

He let out a dramatic groan and adjusted himself before taking her hand and steering them reluctantly back toward the restaurant.

Austen had never felt more in tune or more in love with anyone in her life. It was going to take every ounce of her willpower to wipe the giant, lovestruck grin from her face when they rejoined the decidedly less joyous group.

CHAPTER 43

Matt, Ibiza

Matt slid back into the booth beside Ophelia, scanning her face for clues to her real mood. Jack was talking animatedly, his arm draped casually over the back of the booth behind Ophelia, while Rosalie snapped pictures of the fading sunset, the sky and sea melting into a deep, tranquil blue. He could tell Ophelia's calm demeanor was an act, a shield she was working hard to maintain, and he didn't blame her. He might have done the same in her position.

"What'd we miss?" he asked.

"We were just extolling the virtues of traveling with friends," Jack said, popping a piece of fried calamari into his mouth. "I'm back to lobbying for Ophelia to come to New York."

Ophelia sighed, brushing a loose strand of hair from her face. "It's crazy how once you have kids, you never travel anywhere without them again. It's boring, but I hate leaving them—this weekend notwithstanding. Crikey, can you imagine if they'd been here? They'd be scarred for life. They might still be, depending on how this all unfolds."

"Kids are resilient, and you'll manage it," Matt assured her, keeping his tone light but confident. "I've told you about my dad's affair, right? It didn't scar me—it just made me resolve to be a better man than he was."

As the words left his mouth, memories of Marco and Esme collided with flashes of his younger self and Vivienne back in Papeete. He could still hear his mother's muffled sobs through the walls and remember the helplessness that had swallowed him whole. Vivienne had been relentless with her questions. "Why did Daddy leave? Did we do something wrong? Doesn't he love us anymore?"

All Matt had known how to do at the time was distract his sister from the pain: games, made-up stories, dragging her outside, or turning the radio up to drown out the noise. He imagined Marco stepping into that role for Esme, protecting her from the fallout as best he could, and he hated the necessity of it. His mind conjured a vivid picture of his thirteen-year-old self wrapping a protective arm around Marco's ten-year-old shoulders.

"I think I need to switch to tequila," Ophelia announced, breaking into his thoughts as she searched the room for a waiter.

Rosalie raised her hand to flag someone down. "I'll take care of that for you."

Ophelia gave her a slight nod of thanks, then turned to Matt with a weary sigh. "I just keep wondering how I missed this—how I didn't know he was running around with Kristin behind my back for an entire bloody year." She pressed her forehead into her palm.

Matt's arm instinctively went around her shoulders, pulling her closer.

"A year?" Jack's voice rose in disbelief. "Jesus Christ on a popsicle stick. How do you know it went on that long?"

"This morning, he decided to become Mister Honesty," Ophelia replied dryly, shaking her head.

Austen, who had been unusually quiet, shifted beside Matt. "I just keep wondering why on earth she came here this weekend. It makes no sense."

"Gianluca told Rosalie and me yesterday that he and Kristin had agreed she'd cancel last minute," Jack said, glancing at Rosalie. "But obviously, something changed her mind. Sorry, Ophelia—I wasn't sure if I should bring it up, but I figured every detail might be relevant now."

Ophelia's fingers tapped absently on the table. "Yes and no. What do the details matter? I just wish I could wipe it all out of my brain."

Matt's mind drifted back to his own family's temporary unraveling. His father's affair had come to light when the other woman knocked on their front door one day when he was at work. She didn't say where they'd met—only that he'd lied to her about being married and she felt his mother deserved to know. Matt and Vivienne had been in the next room, listening as the bomb dropped. His father claimed it was a one-time mistake, and Matt had often wondered if they'd all have been better off never knowing.

His long-standing curiosity on his mother's behalf edged him forward.

"Would you really rather not know?" he asked. "If I could give you a mind eraser right now, would you take it?"

The bass from the DJ's set reverberated through the restaurant, yet the table fell into a contemplative silence.

"It's tempting," Ophelia confessed. "Life must've been simpler when marriage was a business arrangement and wasn't made messy by emotions." She popped a *patata brava* into her mouth, chewing slowly.

Rosalie exhaled through her lips, her expression thoughtful. "In France, affairs aren't shocking. Practically everyone has them, so husbands and wives often just look the other way. It's not romantic, but c'est la vie sometimes. People are imperfect and so is love."

"The French are just so damn... French," Jack cracked, rolling his eyes dramatically. "In puritanical America, it does not work that way."

"It's a personal choice," Austen said, setting down her half-eaten croqueta. "How you choose to love only needs to make sense to you and your partner. There's no wrong way to be in a relationship, as long as it's honest."

"But Gianluca wasn't honest," Ophelia pointed out, tossing back her tequila shot.

"No, he wasn't honest—right up until he was," Matt said carefully. "I'm not saying he deserves your forgiveness. That's for you to decide. But whatever happens next, your relationship is in a new phase. You both have to decide what that looks like, and I think it'll take a lot of brutally honest, probably painful conversations."

"So, no to the mind eraser," Ophelia said, pushing the remnants of her food around her plate. "I suppose it's better to move forward, eyes wide open, into whatever fresh hell awaits."

"And maybe—just maybe—leave open the possibility that something good could come out of it," Matt added, his tone hopeful.

As if on cue, the sun slipped below the horizon, and cheers erupted from the restaurant as the patrons celebrated the end of another sun-soaked day. The DJ cranked up the music, neon lights illuminated the thatched roof, and the crowd swayed to the beat.

"Tonight, I just want to get drunk, dance, and forget," Ophelia declared, surveying the crowd of revelers.

Matt filled her glass. "You're in the right place for that."

"And with the right people," Jack agreed, draining his glass and handing it to Matt for a refill. "We're in Ibiza, and it's Saturday night, for Christ's sake. It's time we shake our asses."

Ophelia picked an orange wedge from her sangria and ate the fruit from the rind, wincing at its tartness. "I can't remember the last time I shook my arse on a dance floor. And it is my birthday."

Jack's hand shot out to grasp Ophelia's. "I have a brilliant idea! Let's find you a revenge fuck. This place is crawling with singles, and I will wingman the shit out of you if you want. You pick a target, and we'll get him—or her, no judgement—for you as a birthday present."

Rolling her eyes, Ophelia replied, "Creative as ever, Fabulous Jack, but no thanks. Not my style."

"Suit yourself," Jack nodded. "But we're going to get you another tequila shot, then get that ass of yours shaking. Drink up, and let's get our dance on, people."

Glasses clinked across the table, and Matt's eyes shifted toward the vibrating crowd near the DJ booth. Twenty-somethings in various states of undress and sobriety bounced to the beat, their movements chaotic under the swirling lights. He set his glass down without drinking, his instincts telling him to stay alert. With Jack egging her on, he had a sneaking suspicion he'd be carrying Ophelia off the dance floor before long.

CHAPTER 44

Ophelia, Ibiza

Ophelia woke on Sunday morning face down on her bed, her fringe stuck to her forehead and her mouth as dry as the desert. Spotty memories of dancing and far too much alcohol meandered lazily through her mind as she forced herself to flop onto her back with a groan. Dragging her wrist toward her face, she squinted at her watch through bleary eyes and saw it was nearly eleven o'clock. Check-out from the villa was at noon.

She sat up slowly, relieved to find a glass of water and an ibuprofen on the bedside table—thoughtfully left by someone. Swallowing the capsule and downing the water gratefully, she let herself bask in the small comfort. She couldn't remember coming home, but the warmth of the memories—however vague—left her with an unexpected sense of peace. All things considered, she chalked it up as a win.

When she eventually lumbered downstairs, she found the whole gang eating a late breakfast by the pool. No one looked as green as she felt.

"I hope I didn't do anything dreadfully embarrassing last night," she croaked as she sank into a chair. "I have only the spottiest memories after those tequila shots. Thanks for nothing, Jack."

"You're welcome, darlin'," Jack replied with a wink, pouring her a cup of tea. "Here to serve. And for the record, you did nothing embarrassing. You danced your little ass off, and you were fabulous. I left Advil for you. Did you take it?"

She leaned her head onto his shoulder, letting her tea steep. "Yes, thanks," she murmured. "And thank you all for making the most of this epic disaster of a birthday weekend. At least no one will ever call it unmemorable."

"That we will not. How are you feeling about heading home?" Austen asked.

Ophelia straightened in her chair and reached for a piece of toast, spreading butter as she replied. "I can't very well hide here forever, as tempting as that sounds. I do miss my kids. So, I suppose I'll do my best British thing—keep calm and carry on."

"I'm going to text you a few possible weekends for Paris as soon as I'm back and can coordinate with my girlfriends there," Austen said, stirring milk into a fresh cup of coffee. "You really should come."

"I'll try to make it work," Ophelia promised, placing her palms flat on the table. "We need to check out by noon, though, chaps. Sorry about that. As much as I'd love to sit here for ages and nurse this massive hangover with you lovely people, I'm going to take my tea and toast to-go and get packed up."

Back in her room, Ophelia's eyes fell on the new lingerie she'd purchased especially for the trip. The tags were still on. She sat down on the bed and let her fingers run over the delicate black silk and lace, her stomach twisting as memories bubbled to the surface.

They'd had sex hours before everything fell apart. She'd practically begged him for it, and yet once they got going, he'd even told her that he loved her—something he never did, at her own request. Now, though, she could only see it as guilt. *He must've been so severely on edge, knowing Kristin was in the next room,* she thought. His mouth had been uncharacteristically dirty that morning, which had both shocked and aroused her.

She frowned, the memory now tainted. *Kristin probably taught him that. I bet she loves talking dirty. Maybe that was the real Gianluca, and Kristin brought it out of him in a way I never did.* The thought of Gianluca's mouth on Kristin's body made bile rise in her throat, and her fingers tightened around the lace. *I could've been that girl if I'd known that's what he wanted or needed. I might've even enjoyed it. Everything might've been different.*

She wiped away her tears and shoved the lingerie back into her bag, forcing herself to focus on the tasks ahead. Thoughts of Marco and Esme took over as she began folding clothes. How would she explain Gianluca sleeping in the guest room? A white lie seemed like the best option. She hated lying to her children but protecting them had to come first. They needed happy parents. The question that weighed heavily in her mind was whether she and Gianluca could ever be happy together again—or if she would have to learn how to be happy without him.

The return to reality after a holiday was always difficult, but her reality had turned upside down and inside out during her time on The White Isle. Three days ago, she'd anticipated a weekend of sun, fun, and friends. Now, as she zipped her suitcase, her heart ached with sadness and dread.

CHAPTER 45

Gianluca, Rome

Gianluca arrived back at their flat in Rome well ahead of schedule. He decided to leave the kids with his parents for a few more hours while he moved his belongings into the guest room. The room was cramped and impersonal, but he barely noticed as he hung his suits in the tiny closet, his motions mechanical and his mind elsewhere. His phone buzzed on the nightstand.

K: Are you ever going to talk to me?

He sighed. A conversation was unavoidable—better to get it over with before Ophelia got home.

Gianluca: Can you talk now?
K: Yes! Call me.

He sat on the floor, leaning against the guest bed. For a long moment, he simply stared at the screen, his thumb hovering over the call button. He'd rehearsed this conversation all morning, but the weight of what needed to be said sat heavy on his chest. Finally, he pressed the button.

Kristin picked up after one ring. "Do you hate me?" she whispered.

He ran his fingers back and forth across the rug, his head low and his energy lower.

"You dropped a fucking bomb on my marriage, Kristin. How do you expect me to feel?"

"Tell me you didn't mean it when you said you didn't love me."

His sigh was deep and slow, the sound of defeat. He scratched his beard, struggling to find the right words.

"I don't love you," he said at last, making sure his tone carried the regret he felt. "I'm sorry."

Her voice pitched higher, raw with emotion. "Then what the fuck have you been doing with me for the past year?" she screamed.

Gianluca reflexively jerked the phone away from his ear but could still hear her rage bleeding through the line.

"You made me fall in love with you, and now you've ruined my entire life."

Her anger ignited his own. It burned hot and fast—at her, at himself, at the fact that his father might have cancer, and that he was sitting on the floor of a guest room in his own flat. His blood boiled.

"And you ruined mine in return, so I guess we're even," he snapped, the words cutting through the tension like a blade. Forcing himself to take a deep breath, he steadied his voice. "Listen, I'm not going to tell you what to do about the baby. If you decide to keep it, I'll support you financially. But I can't be part of this kid's life. Or yours."

The line went silent, but he could still hear her uneven breathing. She was speechless.

"I'm sorry," he said quietly. "This must be over. A clean cut. It's the only way I can see forward. I'm almost fifty, Kristin. I have two kids already. I can't create space for another."

"I never thought you could be so cruel," she whimpered.

"You only knew me in fancy hotel suites where life was sexy and carefree," he replied, pity lacing his words. "That was never real life. And real life is brutal. Sexy fantasyland disappeared when you got on a plane to Ibiza and blew up my life."

"If you'd answered any of my calls or texts before the trip, I would've told you then," she argued. "Why didn't you answer? It could've all been different."

He rested his forehead on one knee. Her question lingered heavily in the air. Finally, he said, "I would've ended it anyway. I was always going to choose Ophelia. She's my wife."

"I hate you," Kristin sobbed.

"You should," he replied, drained of fire. "I hate me too."

The line went dead. Gianluca let the phone slip from his hand and sat motionless on the floor. His head fell back against the bed as he closed his eyes. He'd always seen himself as a powerful man, capable of bending circumstances to his will. Yet now, he felt powerless. Kristin had torpedoed his life, but he knew the blame lay squarely with him. And now, there was an innocent child caught in the wreckage. His child.

Hours later, the sound of the front door opening roused him from his stupor. Gianluca stood quickly, brushing himself off as he walked into the hall. Ophelia was kicking off her shoes when he rounded the corner.

"Welcome home," he said, as he awkwardly picked up her luggage. "Let me take your bag up to our—I mean, your—room. I've moved my stuff to the guest room like you asked."

"Where are the kids?" she asked, looking past him.

"I didn't tell my parents I came back early, so I'll pick them up later tonight, as planned. I texted them to confirm."

"Fine," she declared, still looking anywhere but at him. "I've decided that we'll tell the kids you're in the guest room because you're snoring and I can't sleep. We'll put up a united front when they're around. I want them to feel like nothing has changed. Is that clear?"

"Yes. Clear."

He stood there uncomfortably, painfully aware of the charged silence stretching between them. The anger radiating from her was palpable. For the first time in their relationship, he had no idea how to appease her.

"What happens when they're not around, Ophelia?"

She shrugged and finally met his gaze with tired eyes. "I don't know. We'll take it day by day. All I know for sure is that today, I want nothing to do with you."

"I want nothing to do with me either," he said, lowering his gaze. "I hate myself for putting us in this position, and I promise you, I'll spend every day for the rest of my life trying to make this up to you. You're the best thing that's ever happened to me. I don't … I don't know how I lost sight of that. But I never will again."

"I hate you too," she said simply, walking past him into the kitchen.

He carried her bag upstairs, guilt-racked and feeling like his heart had been torn from his chest. In their room—her room now—he set the luggage on the bench at the foot of the bed. His eyes lingered on the space, every detail a reminder of the life they'd built together, their happy memories each a more brightly tinted hue than the other. *How could I have been so blind? Risked it all for someone I never truly loved?*

CHAPTER 46

Ophelia, Rome

Gianluca had left for work before Ophelia had emerged from their—her—room that morning. She returned to the flat after work on Monday with trepidation, uncertain how their first full night in their new normal would unfold.

Entering the house, she found the familiar chaos of the children running around, their laughter mingling with Stefania's gentle reminders to be careful. For a fleeting moment, the scene brought her comfort.

After sending Stefania home, Ophelia began cooking dinner, the routine grounding her as the kids' footsteps echoed from upstairs. As her pasta sauce simmered on the stove and she sipped a glass of *Montepulciano*, the sound of Gianluca unlocking the front door sent her pulse racing. Reflexively, she ran her fingers through her fringe and adjusted her apron. Old habits lingered, tethered to muscle memory, even as her mind wrestled with the enormity of their new reality.

When he stepped into the doorway, his expression mirrored her unease.

"Ciao. Can we talk?" he asked.

Her grip tightened around the wooden spoon she was using to stir the sauce.

"The kids are upstairs," she whispered, her gaze fixed on the pot. "I don't want them overhearing anything."

"It's not about us. It's about my dad."

The weight in his voice froze her mid-motion. She turned to him, eyes wide.

"Is he okay?"

Gianluca shook his head, his jaw tightening. "He has a mass in his stomach and is having a biopsy. They told me when I dropped the kids off before Ibiza."

Her breath caught, the words slamming into her. "Why didn't you tell me?"

He let out a bitter laugh, scratching his beard—a telltale sign of his anxiety. "They asked me not to. They didn't want to ruin your birthday weekend."

The irony of his response hung heavy between them. Her body wanted to step forward, to offer him comfort, but the angry tempest in her mind beat back her sympathy. Her feet stayed planted, her body paralyzed by the tension of conflicting emotions.

Gianluca revered his father, and the realization that he had been silently carrying this burden all weekend—on top of everything with Kristin—left her reeling.

"When's the biopsy?" she asked, her voice steadier than she felt.

"Wednesday." His shoulders sagged as he spoke. "It's Doctor Conti, so he'll expedite the results for me, hopefully before the weekend. I'll go with him to the appointment to make sure everything goes smoothly."

"Do you want me to come?" The words slipped out hesitantly. She loved Gianluca's father deeply, but she wasn't sure if her presence would ease or complicate matters.

He smiled a weak smile. "Thank you, but no. You don't need to. I just thought you should know because my parents will probably expect to hear from you."

Ophelia nodded, swallowing the lump in her throat. "I'll call them tonight. But let's not say anything to Marco and Esme until we know more. I hate keeping secrets from them, but at this point—" She trailed off, unsure how to finish the thought.

"What's one more secret?" he said with a pained frown, his tone laced with self-recrimination.

Their eyes met, holding in a shared, sorrowful silence.

PART SEVEN

JUNE

Escape

CHAPTER 47

Gianluca, Rome

"The incision looks good, Papà," Gianluca said, pulling down his father's shirt. "You're healing very nicely."

The surgery had removed a large portion of the tumor in his stomach but revealed the cancer had spread aggressively to the liver. His father had been resting at home for ten days, but the prognosis looked bleak. Gianluca had visited their house every other day since he'd returned from the hospital, checking on both his parents. On the days he didn't go, Ophelia went instead. They had agreed to this arrangement to avoid arousing suspicion but also because neither wanted to fake normalcy in front of his parents. Pretending for the kids' sake was taxing enough.

"I told you I'm fine," his father replied stubbornly, batting away Gianluca's hands. "You should've gone to Paris with your wife this weekend. Your mother and I don't need you hovering."

Gianluca hadn't been invited to Paris. As soon as his father's surgery was done, Ophelia informed him that she was going to visit Matt and Austen. He couldn't remember the last time she'd gone away for a weekend without him, but he understood her need to escape. She'd shown up for his parents with unwavering grace through his father's medical ordeal, as though their marriage wasn't falling apart. In front of the kids, she was putting on an

Oscar-worthy performance as a happy mom. But as soon as their bedtime routines ended, she retreated to her room and locked the door behind her.

He spent his evenings on the couch alone, alternating between reading, watching TV and replaying every mistake he'd ever made in his head. This weekend, she hadn't just locked the door, she'd left altogether.

Brushing off his father's comment, Gianluca helped him settle back into his chair before heading to his car. As soon as he fastened his seatbelt, his phone buzzed in his jacket pocket. Fishing it out, he froze when he saw the message.

K: I lost the baby.

His phone slipped onto his lap as his head fell back against the headrest. He shut his eyes as a tidal wave of relief washed over him. He felt like he might cry tears of joy, but quickly wondered how Kristin was feeling. *Reprieve? Sadness? A combination of the two?* He had prayed for this outcome—not that he'd admit that to anyone.

I should call her. That'd be the kind thing to do. He hesitated. Kristin might need support, but he worried how Ophelia would feel if she found out they'd spoken. Still, he couldn't ignore the message. He picked up his phone and tapped the call button.

It rang twice before the line clicked open and Kristin's quiet sobs filled the silence.

"Are you okay?"

"I lost the baby," she said, barely above a whisper.

For the first time since she had told Ophelia the news, he felt a flicker of tenderness toward Kristin—an echo of their past connection.

"I know. I got your text. Are you in hospital?"

"Yes. I started bleeding this morning and rushed here, but it was already gone. They're working on my discharge papers now."

She paused before continuing, her voice cracking. "You're probably relieved, aren't you?"

Gianluca hesitated, his guilt and relief battling within him.

"Are you?" he asked haltingly.

He heard only her sobs in response and sat quietly on the phone, waiting. After about a minute of silence, interspersed with sniffles, she finally spoke.

"Yes. Does that make me an even more horrible person than I already was?"

"No," he said shaking his head softly. "You're not a horrible person, Kristin. You never were. We both made some horrible choices, but now we can move on, start over, and try to do better. This is for the best—for both of us."

"I know," she conceded. "I would've wanted the baby if I had you with me, but once I knew I didn't, I was so scared. It felt like my life was over. And now I guess I get it back, but it still hurts."

Her sobs grew louder, and Gianluca waited patiently on the line, his sense of relief growing with each passing minute.

When he heard her breathing steady, he spoke again, trying to infuse kindness into his voice. "A fresh start will be good for you. You deserve that. Take good care of yourself, okay? Be happy."

He knew there wasn't anything else left to say.

"Yah, you too. Bye Gianluca," she said softly before the line went dead.

He tossed the phone onto the passenger seat, gripped the steering wheel with both hands, and rested his forehead against it. It was over. No more baby. With that threat gone, he felt more hope than ever that he could pull up from this nosedive his life had taken and get his wife back. The blood that had been sluggishly pushing through his body in recent weeks suddenly felt cleaner, oxygenated.

But the feeling of reprieve was short-lived. Looking up at his parents' building, he felt the weight of his father's terminal prognosis pressing down on him. He'd seen the charts, read the reports.

He knew the odds. *Is my father's life the price of my desperate wish for my baby's to end?* Alone in his car, he let his tears fall freely, grief and relief pouring out in equal measure. When they finally ran dry, he wiped his face with his sleeve and shifted the car into drive.

He'd text Ophelia the news later. For now, he just needed to go home and hug his kids.

CHAPTER 48

Matt, Paris

Matt opened his apartment door to find Ophelia looking worn and frazzled. Her black maxi dress clung limply, her jet-black hair poking out in all directions beneath the sunglasses perched on her head. Whatever she'd been through on the flight or before it, Matt could see stress and exhaustion etched into her face.

"Welcome to Paris, Fie. How was the flight?" he asked, kissing both her cheeks and reaching for her suitcase.

"Dreadful. But I'm here now," she exhaled, catching her purse as it slipped off her shoulder.

He rolled her small suitcase into the apartment, pushing it toward the guestroom. "Welcome to *chez moi*[28]. The wine is chilled, and we have a dinner reservation at eight at Chez Marcel—it's classic Parisian. Owned by one of Austen's friends. You'll love it."

Ophelia wandered toward the windows, admiring the view of the top of Sacré-Coeur, its white limestone facade gleaming in the late afternoon sun.

"Sounds perfect. This little *chez toi*[29]—this is not too shabby. And the flowers are beautiful." Her fingers traced the delicate black

---

28 My house
29 House of yours

orchids and white calla lilies arranged in a low cylindrical vase by the window. "Black orchids are my favorite."

"They're for you. From Gianluca," Matt said, cautiously handing her the card. "He had them delivered earlier today."

He watched as Ophelia opened the card, read it, and then shoved it back in its envelope, slipping it into her pocket without a word. Her face gave nothing away. Gianluca had texted him earlier in the week, asking for his address so the flowers could be sent. Matt hadn't asked questions.

"Very happy we made this little visit happen," he smiled, moving into the kitchen and pulling a bottle from his wine fridge. "So, how have the last six weeks been since Ibiza?"

She plopped onto a bar stool and sighed deeply as he opened the wine. "He hates himself. I hate him too. We're both trying to see if we can get past it. Jury's out," she admitted, blowing her bangs out of her eyes and resting her chin in one hand as she leaned into the counter.

"He sent me an email a couple of weeks after we all got back, apologizing for having created such a mess and thanking me for helping with… everything," Matt said, cautiously, pouring her a generous glass of the crisp white Sancerre.

"Did he?" she replied, slowly shaking her head in bewilderment.

"I was surprised too," Matt admitted, then watched as her eyes drifted back to the flowers. "We don't have to talk about it if you don't want to. We can just have some wine and a laugh, or we can talk it out and have a cry. Whatever you need."

"If only I knew what I needed," Ophelia mused, holding her glass aloft to him. "But this glass of wine and being here with you and Austen this weekend is a good start. How is she?"

"She'll be here tomorrow around noon to collect you. She's great. We're great," Matt smiled, placing a bowl of olives on the counter between them before taking a sip from his glass. "I don't want to rub it in your face though, given everything you've got going on."

Ophelia shook her head earnestly, raising a hand in protest. "Don't be ridiculous. You can be happy even if I'm bloody miserable. I don't need you to be down here in the mud with me."

Matt's mouth pulled into a tight line. "That's what friends do—they crawl into the mud and sit there with you when you're down."

"I appreciate that," she replied, squeezing his hand across the counter. "But I still want to hear about you and Austen and your work and everything—life in Paris."

He gathered the wine and olives and led her to the living room couch. "Things with Austen are good. It's only been five months that we've been together, but to be honest, I think I would've already asked her to move in if I thought she was ready for that. But I don't think she is."

"Why's that?"

Matt sipped his wine, weighing his words. "You know me. I trust my gut. She's got a big job and a big life that in no way revolves around me—which I love. I think she worked hard to build that up for herself after her divorce, and it means she's got a fierce independent streak. I can't see her wanting to give it up."

"Cohabitation doesn't require the end of independence, you know," she retorted, popping an olive into her mouth. "It's possible to share a roof and a life and still have your own interests."

"I know that. I think I need to let it feel like her idea. Right now, every time she comes over she still brings—and then takes away—her toothbrush and other toiletries. She never leaves anything here," he told her.

Ophelia gaped at him, eyebrows raised. "Have you told her she could leave some stuff? Cleared out a drawer for her?"

He cocked his head to the side, frown lines deepening. "I gave her a key. Doesn't that say 'make yourself at home'?"

"It couldn't hurt to make that offer explicitly. You're still in the early days of coupledom—learning each other's boundaries and habits. No one wants to be the arsehole who oversteps and accidentally stumbles into the abyss of drama from relationships past," Ophelia cracked. "Space in your heart and space in your apartment aren't necessarily the same thing."

"But shouldn't it be blazingly obvious that if you've got the former, you can have the latter too?" Matt asked rhetorically, considering it. "Maybe you're right. I'll tell her."

Looking satisfied, Ophelia popped another olive into her mouth. "Is Paris starting to feel like home yet?"

It had been six months since Matt had moved to Paris to work for Omar. He'd only been in town for two weeks when he reconnected with Austen that night at the Louvre. He'd instantly slotted into her circle of friends, who he liked, but between her and his work, he'd not yet had much time to make any friends of his own. He was just starting to not feel like a tourist in Paris, which felt like a good milestone.

"Work is going well. Omar keeps me busy," Matt replied. "And when I'm with Austen, it feels like home. But I'm still working on making it mine. When she's away or with her friends, I realize how little time I've been here."

"You need art on the walls," Ophelia observed, gesturing at the sparsely decorated apartment. "Love in the halls and art on the walls are what make a house a home. Sounds like you've got the love part covered."

Matt nodded, looking around the room. "Rosalie's on the hunt for some pieces for me. The apartment's a work in progress for sure."

Ophelia smiled ruefully. "I'm glad you've stayed in touch. That's one positive outcome of an otherwise disastrous Ibiza weekend."

"I need a good drinking buddy or two for boys' nights out in Paris," he said, trying to steer her mind away from Ibiza. "Austen's friends and some of their boyfriends or husbands are great, but I need people that I chose myself—like you. That takes time. So as one of my oldest friends, I'm really happy you're here."

"People you choose," she repeated, her voice dripping with sadness. "I'm so glad we chose each other too, all those years ago. But then I chose Gianluca. And then he chose Kristin, who he got pregnant. And now he says he wants to choose me again and reject her and their child. People can make some quite crap choices, can't they?"

Matt scratched the gray fabric of his couch, eyes downcast. "They really can. I wish he'd been a better man this past year. You don't deserve any of this."

He struggled to understand Gianluca's choices—particularly the decision to reject his and Kristin's child. Matt couldn't imagine abandoning responsibility like that, even if it cost him greatly.

"How do you feel about Gianluca rejecting the baby?" he asked.

Ophelia took a deep breath, then a sip of wine. "I think he's a terrible prick. But I know he's doing it to try to minimize the impact to our family, so I'm torn. I can't bloody imagine trying to make room in our life for this kid, but I also know it's not the kid's fault, and he or she will be the one who suffers if we don't. It's an impossible situation."

"The fact that you're torn shows what a wonderfully huge heart you have. I think most women in your position would be relieved—if you're still committed to holding the marriage together," Matt replied.

"And isn't that the big 'if' of the moment," she sighed. "I decided that his rejection of the baby means he isn't—and maybe never was—in love with Kristin. Love is supposed to catch you when you fall, and she's been summarily dropped."

"It's solid logic," Matt agreed, refilling her glass.

"So, he's just a fool, but not a fool in love. I suppose that's better in some weird way, but also worse. He jeopardized our family for what … some basic sex? With someone I thought was my friend? It makes me furious, but I know people make mistakes."

Her voice trailed off as she gazed out the window, a finger mindlessly tracing the rim of her wine glass.

"Impossible question, I know, but would you forgive him if you were me?"

"Oh, Fie, I can't answer that for you. No one can," he frowned. "You just have to listen to your heart and trust your instincts."

She turned back to him, her eyes glazed, as if searching for a memory. "Remember in Ibiza when I said life must've been easier when marriage was about survival and had nothing to do with feelings?"

He nodded.

"You can trust your instincts when survival is at stake," she continued. "Self-preservation is human nature. But I swear, navigating complex emotions sends logic right out the window. The heart and the head are constantly locked in a truly epic battle."

"That's why we bodyguards can't fall for our protectees," he said, nodding. "I get it."

CHAPTER 49

Ophelia, Paris

When they walked into Chez Marcel, Ophelia was immediately charmed by the small, warm, and quintessentially Parisian bistro. Its art-covered walls, delicate lace curtains, delicious smells, and crisp white tablecloths lent the restaurant a cozy charm. Pierre, the owner, greeted them warmly, saying he'd saved them the best table in the house. Settling into her seat across from Matt, she felt ready to enjoy their meal.

Pierre was pouring a pinot noir from the Languedoc-Roussillon region when her phone buzzed. She always kept it nearby in case anything came up with the kids. Glancing at the screen, she saw a message from Gianluca.

Gianluca: Kristin miscarried. There's
no more baby. I found out tonight
and thought you should know.

Hope you have a great weekend in
Paris.

She stared at the phone, her mouth falling open. Time seemed to slow as the words settled in her mind. Her own heartbeat thudded steadily in her ears. For six weeks, she had tortured herself trying to mentally piece together an image of their new "blended family"—Gianluca, herself, Kristin, Marco, Esme, and a baby.

Now, with one text, that image shattered like glass. The baby was gone. Kristin was gone. All that remained in her mind's eye was her family of four—whole again, though she knew they weren't whole. Not yet. But maybe now they could be.

Matt's hand on her forearm pulled her back to the present. His forehead creased with concern as he leaned toward her.

"What is it, Fie? Is everything okay?"

Speechless, she turned the phone screen to show him the text.

Matt read the message, his brow furrowing as he leaned back in his chair, sucking in air. "Wow. That's big news. Good news, right? For you guys, I mean. How do you feel?"

Ophelia set the phone down on the table delicately, as though it might break under her touch. She glanced back at the screen to make sure the message was real, then met Matt's gaze. "Like an absolutely wretched person," she replied, shaking her head in shame.

"What? Why?" he asked.

"Because I hoped this would happen," she admitted, picking up her wineglass and taking a long sip. "I'm awful."

Matt shook his head and reached across the table to grasp her arm again. "You're not awful. You're human. This situation was impossible. Now it's a different game. This changes everything."

"The goalposts have definitely moved," Ophelia said, a sliver of hope escaping with her voice. She covered her mouth with her hand, staring wide-eyed at Matt as the news sank in further.

Matt's lips twitched slightly to one side. "But if he wasn't going to have the kid in your lives anyway, does it actually change much for you, tactically speaking?"

Rubbing her fingers across her forehead, Ophelia confessed something she'd never dared say aloud, for fear of being right.

"I never believed he'd actually reject the baby once it was born. He rejected the idea of the kid, but ideas are abstract, easily ignored. His own flesh and blood wouldn't have been." She exhaled sharply. "He's not actually a horrible person, most of the time. I figured he'd eventually make space for the child in his life. In our lives."

"And now he doesn't have to," Matt concluded, crossing his arms over his chest. "And neither do you."

Relief flooded through her body, loosening the tension she had carried for weeks. She exhaled deeply, her shoulders finally relaxing. But the relief was quickly followed by a heavy feeling in her chest.

"Poor Kristin," she whispered.

Matt cocked his head. "Poor Kristin? Not sure she deserves your sympathy."

"No woman deserves a miscarriage," Ophelia said, glaring at him.

Matt raised his hands in surrender. "Of course. But I think you're allowed to feel relieved and happy about this. Who knows? She might feel relieved too. And don't forget, she was pretending to be your friend while sleeping with your husband."

"I haven't forgotten, but I don't have the energy to be angry at two people. Anger is such a heavy emotion to carry. I've decided to focus mine solely on Gianluca. He was the one who vowed to love and protect me. The affair is on him, not her. If anyone should be mad at her, it's Charlie."

Matt laced his fingers together and rested his chin on them. "You're one of the kindest people I've ever met, Fie. And if you feel that this news clears a path forward for you and Gianluca, then I'm thrilled for you. Are you going to write him back?"

Ophelia glanced back at her phone, considering her reply. What could she possibly say? Congratulations? Thanks for the update? Thank God? Sorry? Is she okay?

She began to type.

>Ophelia: Thanks for letting me know. Hope she's ok.

Gianluca: She's fine. In hospital but fine.

>Ophelia: I admit, I feel relieved.

Gianluca: Me too. Exceptionally relieved. It's over and now I will never need or want to speak to her ever again. All I want is you.

She handed Matt her phone across the small table as their food arrived.

He read the exchange and raised his eyebrows expectantly. "He sounds resolved. And happy. A lot of the complexity just fell away."

"But not all of it," Ophelia replied, taking back her phone. "I mean, don't get me wrong. I'm relieved on so many levels. That there's no more baby. That he says he never wants to speak to her again. That he isn't racing to London to be by her side. But—"

Matt cut into his pistachio sausage and looked at her quizzically. "But?"

"Trust takes forever to rebuild," she sighed. "And the affair lasted so long. My boss removed Kristin from my vendor list after Ibiza. I think she requested it, but officially her agency called it an internal reorganization. Without me as a client, she doesn't have any reason to return to Rome." She hesitated. "But absence often makes the heart grow fonder."

Matt pursed his lips. "Do you think they've stayed in touch? Obviously, the baby news needed to be shared. But other than that?"

"No," she said quickly, then more softly, "but how would I ever know? He's proven rather adept at hiding things."

"I understand. Once that seed of doubt is planted—"

"The thing is, he's really trying to put my mind at ease. He found us a relationship therapist who we started seeing two weeks ago.

He leaves his phone unlocked, always in plain view. He's never said so explicitly, but I'm certain he's trying to show me that he doesn't have anything to hide. I know he's trying, but I'm so hurt and so angry. I'm scared I won't be able to open my heart to him again," she explained, peeling razor clams from their shells with her fork.

Matt chewed his food and nodded solemnly, silently encouraging her to continue.

"We've talked about it a lot, obviously, over the past six weeks, and without making excuses, he's tried to explain his behavior the best way he can, which is in medical terms. He claims Kristin was an addiction he's now beaten."

"Addiction is a slippery slope," Matt declared.

"It's not the most brilliant analogy there ever was, but if we continue it, I suppose removing the temptation is the best way to stay on the wagon," she sighed, taking a bite of clam.

"To the wagon," Matt said with a smirk, raising his wineglass.

"To the wagon," she sneered, clinking her glass to his.

The next morning, Ophelia luxuriated in the childless quiet of Matt's apartment. She turned her pillow over to the cool side as her thoughts drifted between Gianluca, Kristin and their narrowly averted blended family. Growing up as an only child, she'd often fantasized about having a big, eclectic, crazy family, but an unexpected love child was taking "crazy" one step too far. The shredded mental picture of their family of four slowly started to coalesce. *Maybe we will survive this after all.*

She had tea and croissants with Matt and was in her room putting the finishing touches on her makeup when she heard Austen arrive.

Matt's hands were tangled in Austen's hair, clearly about to kiss her, when Ophelia rounded the corner. He released her reluctantly, but Austen's face was bright and welcoming.

"So nice to see you. Thanks for letting me steal him last night," Ophelia said, kissing Austen on both cheeks. "Sorry to break up whatever was just happening there."

"Don't be silly. *Bienvenue à Paris*[30]. How was dinner?" Austen asked, perching on the side of Matt's couch.

Ophelia watched as Matt leaned into Austen and wrapped a hand around the back of her neck, under her hair. They never seemed to be without one hand on the other. It made Ophelia long for those days with Gianluca when everything was simpler.

"Memorable," Ophelia responded, smiling at Matt. "I'll fill you in over lunch."

"You ready to go?"

Ophelia nodded at Austen and grabbed her purse off the table. "I'm all yours."

"Let girlie day begin," Matt faux cheered, raising one hand in a fist.

"He keeps calling it a 'girlie day,'" Austen laughed, picking up her own purse. "I think he's imagining pillow fights and us braiding each other's hair."

"Is that not what's happening?" Matt replied, sounding disappointed as he walked them to the door.

"We'll be back after dinner. Probably a bit late. Don't wait up for us, unless you want to, of course. I was planning to stay here tonight. I brought a bag." Austen gestured to a small overnight bag in the entryway.

Ophelia looked at Matt knowingly, silently telling him to clear out a drawer for Austen. He rolled his eyes slightly and nodded in response.

"Great. You two have fun," Matt said, opening the door for them and giving Austen a quick peck on the lips. "See you tonight."

---

30 Welcome to Paris

They took the Metro to the Left Bank, heading to Mon Square, a cozy restaurant nestled in the shadow of the neogothic Basilique Sainte-Clotilde. Under a yellow awning that shielded them from the June sun, they sipped icy Saint Germain spritzes garnished with fresh mint as Ophelia finally broke the news about Kristin's miscarriage.

"I feel quite happy to have learned that news via text," Ophelia reflected. "Because if I'd been there with him, I think I'd have thrown myself into his arms from sheer relief. I've not allowed him to touch me since we've been back from Ibiza, to punish him, so that would've been bad."

Austen furrowed her brow. "It wouldn't have been bad if that's what you wanted. Be careful that you don't end up punishing yourself trying to punish him. You're allowed to feel relieved and to celebrate one less obstacle to getting your life back—if that's what you want."

"I grew up without a mother. I don't want my kids to grow up without their dad around full time," Ophelia lamented, pushing her sunglasses on top of her head.

"I get that's what you want for them, but what do you want for you?"

Ophelia leaned back in her chair, gazing up at the yellow awning for several moments. She hesitated before speaking, deciding to share something she hadn't dared discuss with anyone else. "Can I tell you something entirely too personal that I just need to talk to another woman about?"

Austen firmly nodded. "Of course. Anything."

Ophelia leaned forward across the table, her cheeks reddening, and whispered, "The morning before the bomb dropped at the villa, Gianluca and I were having sex, which we hadn't done in a while, and out of nowhere he brought out some proper dirty talk. That's never been our thing. I was shocked and yet, I found it very exciting. And then, of course, afterward, I figured it must have been his thing with Kristin."

"Ouch," Austen exhaled, crinkling her nose.

"Gianluca and I have been together for twelve years, and naturally some of the spark has gone out of that part of our relationship. But that incident really got me thinking—for maybe the first time ever and not without irony—about what I really want in the bedroom," Ophelia explained. "And when we were in Ibiza, you very helpfully reminded me that I'm now in charge of what happens in this relationship."

"Damn straight," Austen nodded encouragingly.

"I've spent my whole life putting other people first, but you know what the problem is with that?" Ophelia asked, cutting into her tuna steak. "I've accidentally signaled to anyone who's watching that my needs can come last. I don't want to do that anymore."

The physical relief she felt as those words left her lips was unexpected, and she embraced the feeling with a deep, cleansing breath.

"I support that one hundred percent," Austen said, raising her glass in a toast. "Soooo, what are we talking about here? You thinking about becoming a dominatrix or something? Should we head over to the Marais and buy you some leather and whips and chains?"

Ophelia burst into laughter and covered her blushing face with her hands. Peeking back through her fingers, she shook her head. "God no, that's not what I meant. I'm so sorry. This whole conversation is wildly inappropriate."

"*I'm* sorry. I'm absolutely not making fun. I'm just not sure I'm following you," Austen explained, cutting a piece of her grilled octopus. She extended her fork with the skewered tentacle. "Want to try?"

Ophelia leaned forward and accepted the bite. As she chewed, she looked down at the feet of the people at the next table.

Austen continued. "You can tell me anything. This is a judgment free zone, and you're allowed to want whatever you want."

She kept her voice low so only Austen could hear. "I've spent my whole life trying to be whatever I thought the person in front of me needed me to be. I kept the real me hidden, scared that she wasn't all that worthy of love. I want to be done with that."

"That's fantastic, Ophelia," Austen said, beaming. "I think our forties are the decade where we can finally stop giving a fuck what everyone else thinks and accept who we really are. And if someone in our orbit doesn't like that person, then they shouldn't be in our lives. It's as simple as that."

Nodding and clinking their glasses together, Ophelia said, "Cheers to that. Thank you. I think that somehow in losing him, I'm starting to find myself."

"I learned a lot about myself, my desires, and what I was capable of when I left my husband," Austen replied. "This level of turmoil in a relationship often has a way of creating clarity when all the dust finally settles. And maybe you haven't lost Gianluca. Maybe this experience will end up being a blessing in disguise—*un mal pour un bien*, as we say in France. A bad for a good."

Ophelia traced lines on the tablecloth with her fingers as Austen's words rattled around in her head. "I think I do want to work through this, but I have no idea how. Right now, I'm still too angry."

"It's only been six weeks. It'll take time and a lot of honesty from you both," Austen said.

It was so easy to blame everything on Gianluca, but she was imperfect in plenty of ways. She knew she had to confront her own role in their relationship's unraveling and to understand herself and her own heart better, before anything between them could be put right.

"I want to set a better example for my kids—one where my voice matters more and I'm not ashamed of wanting things for myself," she declared.

"Especially in bed," Austen smirked.

"It's as good a place to start as any, I suppose?" Ophelia grinned.

"All joking aside, honest communication is the key to happiness. I truly believe that," Austen said, picking up her spritz. "How do you think Gianluca will feel about you taking more control in the relationship?"

"I suspect for the 'in bed' part, he'd be delighted," Ophelia replied with a small laugh. "For the rest, I'm not so sure. He's said he'll do anything I want to fix things, which I desperately want to believe. But all I know for sure is that we can't go back to the way things were before."

CHAPTER 50

Austen, Paris

After lunch, Austen and Ophelia made their way to the Free Persephone Day Spa, where Chiara and Daphne were already checking in at the front desk. Baby Sylvie was strapped to Daphne's chest, and both women greeted Ophelia warmly, welcoming her to Paris as they were shown to a row of four comfortable floral armchairs for their pedicures. Chiara and Daphne sat on either side of Ophelia, with Austen on the end to Chiara's left.

Austen smiled as they all selected their nail polish colors, watching Ophelia slot into the group as if she'd always been there.

"We want all the gossip. What was Matt like when he was at university?" Chiara asked. "We heard you knew him way back when."

Austen had never dared to ask too many questions about Ophelia's university days with Matt, so as the warm water filled the basin below her feet, she leaned in, grateful for her friend's boldness.

"Exotic," Ophelia replied. "I was a frumpy kid from the English countryside, and he was this beautiful guy from South Africa or Tahiti, depending on how you phrased the question. Having never been to either place, he seemed like the most interesting bloke I'd ever met."

"Exotic is dead sexy. I've just started seeing this Viking carpenter, and he feels very exotic to me," Chiara said with a grin.

"You're dating a Viking carpenter?" Ophelia asked quizzically, glancing at Austen for assurance that this was a real thing.

Chiara cackled, tossing her head back gleefully. "I met him about a month ago, falling off a wall at the climbing gym. Practically landed on him—not on purpose, I swear. He's Norwegian and just finished work on rebuilding Notre Dame after the fire. Viking ancestry, muscles for days. You get the picture."

"That does sound exotic," Ophelia marveled. "How remarkable, working on such a historic building and creating something with your hands. I work in event marketing, which feels so insignificant in comparison."

"Chiara works in fashion, and Daphne is a pastry chef, so they're creators too," Austen said. "You and I deal in words and the digital realm. They're our analog counterparts, making actual stuff in the real world."

"I used to make pottery as a hobby, before the kids," Ophelia reminisced. "I wasn't very good, but I enjoyed it."

"Who cares if you're good?" Daphne said. "That's the whole point of a hobby—to enjoy it. Make time to create. There's something soul-satisfying about it."

"Maybe I should start again," Ophelia muttered. "Probably a better choice than the nunnery."

"I'm sorry, the what?" Chiara shrieked, looking aghast.

Ophelia blinked, startled. "Oh goodness, did I say that out loud? Sorry. Shakespeare reference. Hamlet told Ophelia, 'Get thee to a nunnery.' Since my husband seems to have recently lost his ever-loving mind just as Hamlet did, I've been thinking about my namesake and all the possibilities of what I might do next."

"Austen mentioned things have been rough on the home front," Daphne said kindly. "Sorry you're going through that."

"Wasn't it also Hamlet who said, 'What a piece of work is a man'?" Chiara asked.

Ophelia nodded. "Indeed."

Chiara reached over and squeezed Ophelia's arm. "Your husband is obviously a piece of work, because you're absolutely lovely. Men are often idiots, but we love them anyway, despite ourselves."

"Let's go ahead and keep you out of Shakespearean tragedies and any nunneries," Austen said, a smile tugging at her lips. "Given our conversation over lunch, I suspect the latter may not be your best bet."

"What conversation over lunch?" Chiara asked eagerly.

Ophelia shot Austen a wide-eyed look, clearly begging her not to repeat it.

Thinking quickly, Austen said, "Ophelia always wears black, so I was joking that she might become a nun. Or, as an alternative, start wearing more color. We voted for color, which is now our mission for shopping later."

Ophelia gave her a grateful smile.

"Brightening your wardrobe after emotional turmoil is cathartic," Chiara said, lifting her foot from the water for the pedicurist. "I wore black all the time after my divorce, like mourning, until I snapped out of it and started adding pops of color."

"I didn't know you were divorced too," Ophelia said, looking between Chiara and Austen. After a brief hesitation, she continued, "Can I ask how you both knew it was the right choice?"

"Mine cheated, and I decided I couldn't forgive him for it," Chiara said, sounding apologetic. "Sorry. Austen told me a bit about what happened with you, so this might hit close to home."

Ophelia shook her head. "No need to apologize."

Austen stepped in, trying to inject some optimism. "Let's say marriage is a fifty-year relationship. There will be hard years—years where your lives' paths seem to diverge." She crisscrossed her hands in the air, illustrating diverging paths. "The question is whether, at the end of fifty years, you still want the same things out of life." She then moved her hands back into alignment. "If your paths are headed to the same place, you stick it out and fight for it. One bad year—or even two or three—are nothing in the grand scheme of a fifty-year marriage."

"That makes sense," Ophelia said. "Do you think if a man cheats once, it's inevitable he'll do it again?"

Daphne shifted Sylvie to her other knee. "I think the only inevitabilities are death and taxes. Everything else depends on the person. Look at his character. Is the affair evidence of deeper flaws or just a massive mistake?"

"It wasn't just once," Ophelia admitted, her voice heavy with sadness. "It went on for a year."

"But remember what Austen said—one year in a fifty-year marriage is nothing," Daphne reminded her. "The question is whether he's truly sorry and whether you're willing to forgive."

"He's been on his knees begging for six weeks," Ophelia said with a sigh.

"For what it's worth," Austen said, "I remember hearing you two tell the story of how you first met when we were together in Rome, and very clearly feeling the love between you."

Ophelia nodded, considering. "I know he loves me. But how do you quantify the right amount of begging to make up for a year of lies?"

Austen watched as Daphne and Chiara reached out, each taking one of Ophelia's hands. Ophelia smiled sadly at them.

"Listen to your heart. And your head. And your friends," Austen said. "Sooner or later, for better or worse, you'll know."

Daphne headed home after the spa to put Sylvie down for a nap, leaving Austen, Chiara, and Ophelia to continue to Le Bon Marché for some shopping before their dinner reservation. They wandered up to the shoe department on the top floor, where rows of elegant shoes were displayed under intricate gold latticework and sprawling skylights. Sunbeams flooded the open space, giving it an almost magical glow.

It didn't take long for Chiara to zero in on the new season's collection from Louboutin.

"Oh my God, look at these freaking fabulous snakeskin disco ball stilettos," she squealed, snatching up a particularly iridescent and impossibly high pair of red-soled heels. "Don't you just love love love them? I must try them on."

"Chiara love love loves many shoes," Austen teased, taking a seat as Chiara darted off to find a salesperson. "You might want to settle in," she added, glancing at Ophelia.

Ophelia sat beside her, quietly scanning the displays of extravagant footwear. After a moment, she said, "Did Matt tell you about the conversation he had with Esme when you two were in Rome? About how she thought I didn't like to love?"

Austen nodded slowly. "He did. I hope that's okay."

Ophelia waved her hand dismissively. "Of course. I'm always amazed at how easily the word comes to others—love. Chiara loves those crazy shoes so much she said it three times."

"Well, you know how Italians are. You're married to one. They're very passionate. But just because you're quieter about it doesn't mean you're doing it wrong," Austen said. "I've seen you with your family, and it's obvious you love them. You're a bit like my dad, I think. His way of showing love is quiet—it's in his actions more than his words. Chiara's like my mom. She loves loudly, with her whole body and many words. Both are real."

Ophelia looked thoughtful, letting her gaze wander. "I like the idea of quiet love," she said finally. "Thanks for that."

"Of course," Austen replied, glad to have struck a chord.

"You love loudly too, I think," Ophelia observed, her lips curving slightly. "I'd bet your love language is words of affirmation. Am I right?"

Austen chuckled. "I'm an exceptionally loud, complete, and total love whore. I want it all. Words of affirmation—bring 'em on. Physical touch—yes, please. Quality time—must have. Acts of service," she paused for effect. "You know, the first time I thought I might be in love with Matt was when he took the trash out at my apartment."

"The trash is what did it?" Ophelia laughed.

"No, actually. The first time I told him I loved him was when he was folding my delicates. I guess I *am* an acts-of-service kind of girl after all," Austen said with a grin.

"Laundry? That was the clincher?" Ophelia asked, still smiling. But her expression darkened. "I've done every load of Gianluca's laundry for the past twelve years. Wasn't enough for us, apparently."

Austen's heart tightened at the bitterness in Ophelia's voice, but she was determined to keep the mood light. "Can I make a suggestion?"

Ophelia turned to her, her eyes wide with expectation.

"Teach that man how to use the damn washing machine," Austen said, deadpan.

Light returned to Ophelia's face as she grasped Austen's hands. "I should do. I will do. That's the best suggestion I've heard in a while."

"And actually," Austen added, her tone softening, "now that I think about it, I realized I was in love with Matt because of an incredibly thoughtful gift he got for you—the lace table runner. He explained the ties to your mom and all the trouble he'd gone through to get it for you, and I thought, *Wow, this is the kindest, most wonderful man in the world.* It burst my heart open."

Ophelia squeezed Austen's arm. "I feel honored to be part of your love story in some small way."

At that moment, Chiara returned, teetering on the heels with a wide smile plastered across her face. She turned one ankle and then the other, letting them admire the shoes from every angle. "What do we think? Love? Love love? Or do we all love love love them?"

"Love love love," Austen said with a nod, giving Ophelia's hand an extra squeeze. "You pay, and we're going to wander on. Come find us."

Chiara nodded and sashayed off to the register, while Austen and Ophelia strolled past the myriad displays of high heels, sandals, and flats.

Admiring a black slingback pump perched on its gold shelf, Ophelia said, "I'm glad you and Matt are happy. It's such a fun stage—being this new in a relationship."

"He's pretty exceptional," Austen acknowledged, giving her a thumbs up on the shoe. "I dated a lot before I met him. People say there are plenty of fish in the sea, but there's also a lot of trash floating around out there. All that wading through the nonsense makes you really appreciate the good ones when they come along."

Not wanting to overplay her happiness, Austen added, "Although, being in love requires a lot of vulnerability, which hasn't always been my strong suit."

"How so?" Ophelia asked, returning the shoe to its perch.

"We all put up walls to hide the parts of ourselves we think might be unlovable. With my ex-husband, it often felt like we were in competition. We worked in similar fields, and my career was going stronger than his, so every time I had a big win, I felt like I had to downplay it to avoid making him feel bad. I think I got smaller in his presence," Austen said, brushing her fingers across a shelf of strappy sandals.

She continued, "But Matt celebrates everything about me. He wants me to conquer the world—to take up all the space I deserve. It's amazing but allowing him to see the full-on real me has been scary."

"I'm not even sure I know who the real me is," Ophelia revealed, her gaze falling to the floor.

Chiara reappeared, her eyes sparkling. "Ophelia, we need to find you a dazzlingly colorful revenge dress. I'm an excellent revenge shopper."

"Lead the way, my new favorite fashion guru," Ophelia laughed, extending an arm forward.

Chiara looped her arm through Ophelia's and guided them toward the racks of dresses. Austen trailed a step behind, watching as Chiara lifted a bright orange dress and held it against Ophelia.

"It's crazy how long I've only worn black," Ophelia said, clutching the fabric to her body and eyeing it warily. "My life has become a vintage Dolce & Gabbana ad."

"Dolce & Gabbana does color just as well as black," Chiara insisted. "And this color lights up your face. You look ten years younger. Try it on. Trust me."

Reluctantly, Ophelia took the dress, checked the size, and headed to the fitting rooms.

Austen gave Chiara a grateful squeeze. "Thanks for being here. I think she really needs this."

"Don't be silly. We'd be doing this anyway—it's great to have her along. The more, the merrier," Chiara said, gripping Austen's arm. "But you're right. That poor girl needs some serious merry—and some serious color—in her life. And bubbles. We're definitely getting champagne after this."

"Have you met us? How could we not?" Austen grinned.

CHAPTER 51

Ophelia, Paris

Ophelia zipped up the orange dress and studied her reflection in the fitting room mirror. Chiara was right—the color lightened and brightened everything about her. She barely recognized herself. Her hands traveled down her sides, smoothing the fabric as she turned slowly, examining every angle, searching for signs of the woman she knew.

"How is it?" Chiara asked from the other side of the curtain. "Can we see?"

Ophelia emerged tentatively from the fitting room and was immediately accosted by Chiara's gleeful shriek.

"Well it's simply perfection," she declared.

Austen smiled warmly. "You look amazing. How do you feel in it?"

"Beautiful. And lost," Ophelia quietly replied.

Chiara's face fell. "What do you mean, lost?"

"I don't know who that lady is," Ophelia replied, pointing at herself in the mirror. "She looks like someone fun and carefree who wears orange. Is that really me?"

"If you want it to be, then it can be," Austen assured her.

Ophelia took a deep breath and examined her reflection further. "This dress reminds me of the woman I was before having kids. Now don't get me wrong—I wouldn't trade them for the world. But once upon a time, I was colorful and sexy and spontaneous. But now? This doesn't look like me. I suppose I lost that other version of myself somewhere along the way."

"Was the colorful, sexy, spontaneous version of you happy?" Austen asked. "Because happy should be the goal."

"She was," Ophelia confirmed, studying her reflection in the bigger mirror.

"No reason you can't find her again," Chiara replied. "Buy the dress."

"I'm trying to imagine what Gianluca would think if he saw me in this," Ophelia wondered.

"Who cares," Chiara declared. "Don't buy it for him. Buy it for you. Consider it your bright orange beacon to help you find your way back to the happiest version of yourself."

"Sold," Ophelia smiled. *If I can learn to truly know and love myself again, maybe we can rebuild,* she thought. *Maybe we could even come back stronger.*

By the time Ophelia, Austen, Chiara and Daphne were seated at La Compagnie—a classic Parisian bistro near Matt's apartment in the seventeenth arrondissement—Ophelia felt both exhausted and energized. Between lunch, pedicures, shopping, and a cheeky glass of champagne at a nearby bar before arriving, it had been an exceptionally full day—her first proper "girlie" day, as Matt called it, in years. Being with these women had helped her forget the shambles of her life in Rome—if only for a few fleeting moments.

As waiters bustled around the restaurant with silver trays, Ophelia found herself thinking about Paris and Rome. Both cities had burned and been rebuilt countless times, yet they always rose again, more beautiful than before. *A phoenix always rises from the ashes,* she thought.

Some instinct told her she should try to rebuild her life with Gianluca, but it was the "should" that bothered her. The question she battled in her mind was whether she *wanted to*, in her heart and soul. She'd spent so much of her life doing what she thought others wanted her to do, so she struggled to get in touch with that core part of her that knew what she really wanted for herself.

From her years of therapy, she knew the behavior was deeply rooted in her childhood when she had constantly worked to not be a burden on her widowed, single father. She had learned to stay small, keep her emotions in check, and never call attention to herself. That instinct was one reason she always wore black.

"Ophelia?"

She blinked, realizing Austen was speaking to her.

"*Saint Emilion* is okay for you? Red wine?" Austen asked as the waitress hovered nearby.

"Oh, yes. Fine. Whatever you recommend," Ophelia replied, flustered.

Daphne sighed and sank back into her chair. "A pedicure and a girls' night where I can expect no one to barf or poop on me. Hooray. I needed today," she grinned. "Thanks for coming to town and giving me an excuse, Ophelia."

"The pleasure's been all mine," she replied. "I remember those baby days. Hard to find time for yourself. Honestly, my kids are ten and eight, and I still struggle. But today's been a good reminder of how refreshing some quality girl time—and not being barfed or pooped on—can be. And adulting in Paris really is dreamy."

"The dreamiest," Austen agreed.

When the waitress returned with the bottle of *Saint Emilion,* Ophelia tentatively raised a finger. "Actually, madame, can I get a glass of Chablis?"

"Oh, sorry—I thought you said red was okay," Austen apologized.

Ophelia shook her head. "I did say that, but I said it because I was being me and trying not to be intrusive. My homework from my therapist is to work on knowing and saying what I really want. So, I thought I'd try it out. Easier with you lot than with Gianluca," she conceded.

"Get the bottle. I'll drink white with you," Chiara offered. "Those two can drink the red."

"No problem here—I'm definitely pumping and dumping tonight," Daphne said. "Jean-Marc has graciously offered not only to stay home with Sylvie tonight but also to let me sleep in tomorrow."

When the Chablis arrived and everyone's glass was filled, Austen raised hers. "To Ophelia, and to knowing, saying and getting exactly what you want—because you deserve it."

They clinked glasses, each woman intentionally meeting the other's eyes to avoid the French curse of seven years of bad sex that allegedly came with toasting *sans*[31] eye contact.

"Here's what I want," Chiara announced, grinning. "An excellent meal here with you lovelies. A marvelous shag later with Magnus the Viking carpenter, probably while wearing my new snakeskin disco heels. A long lie-in tomorrow with coffee and croissants in bed. A free lifetime supply of La Roche-Posay eye cream—that stuff is magical. A vacation house on the Amalfi Coast. And an unlimited spending account at Le Bon Marché."

"Is that all?" Austen teased.

"I'm manifesting. You toasted to getting what we want, so we might as well put it out there, no?" Chiara cackled. "The universe is always listening, and you don't get what you don't ask for."

Daphne raised her hand. "Okay, my turn. I want one night of eight consecutive hours of sleep. Sorry no—one night *a week* of eight consecutive hours of sleep. I want Sylvie to grow up happy. A

---

31 without

standing invite to Chiara's Amalfi house. No more cavities—hazard of being a pastry chef. To inexplicably love vegetables. To qualify for the Paris Marathon. And also the Bon Marché thing, please."

"Excellent lists from you both," Ophelia clapped. "Austen, your turn."

Austen cocked her head to one side, contemplating. "Is it terribly cheesy to say I've got everything I've ever wanted already?"

"Boring," Chiara shrieked. "And you're making us look bad."

"But I mean it," Austen insisted. "All I ever wanted was a job I enjoy, amazing friends, to travel, and to love someone who loves me back. And I have all that." She wavered, glancing at them. "Okay, fine. The Amalfi thing and the Bon Marché account sound good too. And I don't need to wish for the good shag. That's guaranteed," she winked.

"There's my girl," Chiara giggled, slapping her hand down on the table and sending the wine sloshing in their glasses.

Ophelia could feel their eyes turn to her, waiting for her list. She sipped her wine, wrestling her thoughts into something she was willing to share, and finally spoke. "Okay me. I want to make the right decisions about what happens next with Gianluca. I want my kids to grow up well-adjusted despite living in a chaotic world that makes absolutely no sense," she nodded at Daphne in mum-solidarity. "I want friendships like these—with kindness at the center. I want Chiara as my personal shopper. I want to be happy in whatever my new normal looks like. And I want to be better at playing this crazy game called love."

All four women grasped hands around the table, forming a circle.

"I think love isn't a game to be scored. I think it's about building a self-sustaining circle of happiness and growth within ourselves and with our loved ones—friends, family or lovers—that feeds our souls and makes our lives richer," Austen offered, looking at Ophelia with extreme kindness in her eyes. "I also think that can come in many forms—that there is no such thing as 'normal' in this nonsensical world. There's only the love we choose."

They squeezed hands before raising their glasses once more.

"To the overwhelming normality of absolutely nothing being normal," Chiara said, smirking.

"And to choosing love," Daphne added.

Ophelia clinked each glass in turn, feeling tears prick her eyes. Maybe, just maybe, these women were onto something.

CHAPTER 52

Matt, Paris

The Sir Winston was one of Paris's oldest English pubs, so Matt chose it for Sunday brunch as a nod to Ophelia's roots. It sat just off the Étoile which housed the Arc de Triomphe, and he liked it for its sliding doors which opened onto the street, creating an airy indoor-outdoor dining experience and an easy escape route—not that he expected to need the latter.

Over scrambled eggs, sausages, potatoes and green detox juice, he asked, "Did you four buy out Le Bon Marché? Solve all the world's problems yesterday?"

"I got a pretty spectacular orange dress which I have no idea when or where I'll ever wear, but also these," Ophelia said, lifting one leg to show off a light blue suede sneaker. "We decided it may be time for color to make a comeback in my wardrobe."

Matt nodded his approval. "The girls took good care of you then."

Ophelia smiled and sipped her tea. "Chiara and Daphne were delightful as promised. Austen was a marvelous hostess. Not sure we solved all the world's problems, but it was a great day. And I think we made some progress on my problems."

"Oh yah?" Matt asked, skewering a potato. "Any decisions made?"

"Not really. Just a reaffirmed commitment to putting myself first occasionally, rather than always last," Ophelia said, leaning back against the wicker chair. "I'm going to try to take some control back and not be a doormat."

"No one ever said you were a doormat," Austen insisted.

"I said it. I've been a doormat. I feel exhausted all the time which leads to me letting people walk all over me. I don't know how to fix it, but I'm sure as hell going to try." Ophelia took a breath, her index finger absentmindedly running along the edge of her plate.

She seemed to be looking for the words that could carry the weight of her thoughts. Matt had always known Ophelia to be quick to speak. She rarely seemed to have time for lengthy reflection, and he wanted to allow for it. Noticing Austen was about to jump in, he reached under the table and gently placed a hand on her leg, pulling her gaze toward him. He nodded discreetly in Ophelia's direction and pursed his lips closed, trying to communicate silently to let her think.

Austen nodded, and he gave her a grateful smile, pleased that they'd reached a stage where they could understand each other, even without words.

Eventually Ophelia spoke again. "Bloody hell. In truth, I can't decide if I need a shag, a hug, a bottle of wine, an espresso or two weeks of sleep."

"Maybe all of the above?" Austen smirked.

Matt shook his head, smiling at both women. "I've heard more complex solutions to smaller problems."

Proceeding carefully, Austen continued. "Serious question for you, Ophelia—do you think you're exhausted or depleted?"

"What's the difference?"

"Exhaustion is solved by sleep. Depletion can only be solved by doing the kinds of things that fill up your individual cup—things that bring you joy," Austen explained, sipping her juice. "I suspect you're more depleted than tired and that some serious self-care is exactly the right cure."

Ophelia took a slow breath, looking earnestly back and forth between them. "It's more than exhaustion. It's like I've been running on this endless loop, trying to be everywhere for everyone. And somehow, I ended up nowhere and alone."

Her admission was delivered with a simple, unembellished honesty that resonated more deeply than Matt had anticipated.

"You're not alone, Fie," he insisted, shaking his head. "And Austen's right—filling your own cup is smart. Any ideas on what might do it?"

Ophelia's eyes drifted to the colorful tiles on the restaurant's ceiling as she considered the question.

"I want to find a pottery class and get back into that. I used to love that feeling of wet clay on my hands and creating something out of nothing. And probably yoga too," she replied. "My mind is always on some kind of frantic overdrive like coked-out hamsters are running in the hamster wheel that is my brain, so I think I need to do things that calm me down."

"Nobody likes a coked-out hamster," Matt deadpanned.

"Were truer words ever spoken?" Austen laughed, cutting into a piece of grilled haloumi. "Maybe a little meditation would help too."

"Something to consider," Ophelia agreed, refilling her cup with hot water from the porcelain teapot. "What about you, Richie? How was your day without us?"

"Good. I think I made a new friend at the gym," he replied, looking satisfied. "He's a Kiwi named Oliver who moved here recently for work. We made plans to meet up for a beer this week."

"You made a beer-drinking friend," Austen exclaimed, squeezing his shoulder. "That's great."

"Fab," Ophelia added with a genuine smile. "And on the topic of friendship, thank you both for curating this utterly escapist weekend. It's done me a world of good."

"Anytime. We love you, Fie," Matt replied. "We just want you to be happy and safe—whatever you decide to do."

"Seeing you two happy has been a great reminder of what 'happy couples' look like, and I think I needed that too. I'd lost sight of it—somehow forgotten how good things can be when they're right," Ophelia admitted, pouring honey over her Greek yogurt. "Gianluca always talks about wanting *la dolce vita*. For him, that seems to mean things going his way, which I've always accommodated. But I think it's high time I decided what 'sweet' means to me and find ways to reconstruct our lives so we're both getting what we need."

"Remember when I told you that I thought this situation was going to help you find your own strength and that it was going to be beautiful?" Matt asked.

Ophelia shook her head, quizzically.

"I said that in Ibiza," he clarified. "And I think it's happening."

"That whole weekend's a blur, to be honest. But I'm glad you said it again." She paused, taking another sip of tea. "The flowers Gianluca sent to your place weren't random. My wedding bouquet was black orchids and calla lilies." She pulled a card from her purse and read it aloud.

Ophelia, I researched black orchids. They represent strength, determination, and power—all things you have in spades—which I took for granted. I won't ever again. Calla lilies symbolize faithfulness, and you have mine. I know I failed you spectacularly, but my heart is now and will forever be yours. I'd marry you again today and every day. I love you.
Gianluca

"He's trying," Austen replied, her forehead creased. "You've got to give him that."

"He is," Ophelia agreed, tucking the card back into her purse and looking at them both with a furrowed brow. "I've been thinking a lot since I got here about these three words he invoked—strength, determination, and power. To be honest, I don't think I'd have ever chosen any of those words to describe myself, and now I'm wondering why it took his affair to bring them up."

Matt quietly pondered the question. For as long as he'd known her, he'd always thought of Ophelia as selfless—someone who tried to keep the peace, to be unobtrusive, to accommodate the needs of others. He wouldn't have instinctively called any of those three traits to mind describing her either, yet to have left her life in London and started over from scratch in Rome, she had to have at least the first two—strength and determination.

Power, on the other hand, was relative. At work, Matt had full authority to dictate how and when Omar traveled and could veto potential new staff members based on his security assessments. But that authority only went so far—Omar could fire him tomorrow if he wanted. In his personal life, Matt knew he and Austen shared equal power, a balance that allowed them to help, heal, build, or—if mishandled—break one another.

The power dynamic between Ophelia and Gianluca had certainly shifted when his affair came to light. She held all the power now.

He leaned in, resting his forearms on the table. "The day after you found out—when Gianluca came back to the villa—you told me you didn't want to cry because that's what he'd expect. And you didn't. Have you since?"

"No. I haven't let him touch me or see me cry since," she sighed. "I feel like he's turned my heart to stone."

"I think you've put your heart into a stone box to protect it," Matt said gently. "And that's serving you well. You've probably surprised him with your steel on this—and me too, if I'm honest. Your strength is undeniable."

"I have to be strong for the kids," Ophelia said, shrugging as she buttered a piece of baguette.

"No, it's more than that. The kids weren't there in Ibiza when you decided not to let him see you cry. That wasn't for them—that was for you. And that's power." He pushed his plate aside and dropped his napkin onto it. "You're a force to be reckoned with, Fie."

"Says you," Ophelia shrugged.

"Our partners become mirrors, reflecting back what they see. Gianluca sees strength, determination, and power in your resolve, and that's a testament to both you and him," Matt said.

"What exactly is he getting credit for here?" Ophelia asked, raising one hand in a sign of skeptical questioning.

"He's seeing you in a new way. Maybe it's because you're becoming a new and stronger version of yourself, and he recognized it before you did," Matt theorized.

Austen sat up straighter in her chair. "Remember yesterday when we were talking with the girls about trying to find your old colorful, spontaneous self? Maybe you aren't supposed to be looking for old you. Maybe you've already become a new you—a stronger you."

"No one evolves in reverse," Matt reasoned.

"So, to survive this I have to keep my heart in a stone box and be some steely version of myself that can't cry?" Ophelia moaned.

Matt shook his head. "Fie, no. The stone box is a temporary shield. You protect yourself in a fight, but every fight comes to its natural end. When that happens, you'll take down the shield, and your heart will still be intact."

"Gianluca has always had the power in our relationship," Ophelia said, sounding defeated. "I don't know if I can win that fight."

"From where I sit, you have all the power now. And I don't think you're fighting *against* Gianluca. You're fighting *for* your family," Matt insisted.

Ophelia dropped her head back, eyes to the ceiling as she let the thought sink in. After a few beats, she snapped her gaze back to Matt and declared, "That's a fight I bloody well want to win."

"Then you will," Matt replied with certainty. "It's written all over your face."

EPILOGUE

Ophelia, Rome

One year later

Ophelia stood at her kitchen table, dressed in a bright blue sleeveless summer dress patterned with large black flowers. She set a forest-green ceramic vase on a large sheet of bubble wrap and picked at a roll of tape with a French-manicured fingernail. Six months earlier, she had enrolled in a Saturday morning pottery class, where she delighted in shaping plates, cups, and vases from wet clay. Her creations had steadily improved, and she'd completed this particular vase just yesterday, in time to gift it. Pushing her fringe—which was still in the awkward stage of growing out—from her face, she smiled at the vase before carefully wrapping it and placing it in a box for shipping.

Sunday mornings were Gianluca's time with his parents, as his father's health continued to decline. They all knew the end was near. As the eldest son and a doctor, Gianluca had taken on the responsibility of weekly grocery deliveries and helping with tasks his father could no longer manage.

Couples' therapy had made one thing clear: family was their highest shared priority. Gianluca's dedication to his parents in the face of his father's illness had softened her heart to him, creating space for forgiveness that she might not have otherwise found. But therapy had also helped her begin to rediscover and love herself—the person she was beyond simply being Gianluca's wife and Marco and Esme's mother.

While she focused on healing, she'd held Gianluca at arm's length physically, and emotionally. The first sign of détente in that stand-off had come after a particularly heartrending therapy session when they delved deeply into her childhood and her lifelong difficulty saying "I love you." She'd left that session drained, and while waiting for the elevator, Gianluca reached for her. Having grown accustomed to not being touched by him, she recoiled and then burst into tears, burying her face in her hands. Seconds later, she felt his arms wrap around her, and she'd lacked the strength to pull away. He held her so tightly that day as she cried into his chest, that she thought he might never let go. Whispering "I love you" repeatedly into her hair, he'd held her until her tears ran dry and then cautiously released her without another word. For the first time in a year, she'd felt genuine gratitude toward him—for holding her, for not forcing her to talk about it, and for not trying to make it into something bigger than it was.

That moment had started to crack open the stone box around her heart. The cracks had grown ever-so-slightly wider with each of three subsequent hugs over the past four months. She had initiated the next hug after one of Gianluca's father's checkups had yielded only bad news. The second was after a standing ovation at their children's school play. Neither had been discussed, but Ophelia recognized them both as the result of shared emotions—sadness and pride, respectively—which came from a place of familial love. She knew that would always exist between them, regardless of whether they found their way back together as a couple.

The most recent was a spontaneous embrace after dinner at home. She was doing the washing up at the kitchen sink, and he came up behind her, rested his forehead on her shoulder and put his hands lightly on her hips. Even now, she wasn't sure what had prompted him to do it. Without thinking, she'd dropped the sponge and turned, wrapping her arms around his neck, soapy water still dripping off her hands. He'd responded immediately, wrapping his arms around her waist and pulling her tightly into his body. They'd stayed like that wordlessly for roughly one minute, their bodies frozen in place, locked in the embrace, but her thoughts swam furiously in her head, wondering what it might mean. When he released her, he hung his head and walked away without ever making eye contact. The air fled the room with him, and she found herself both missing his touch and dreading needing it again. She'd been processing those dueling emotions ever since.

Now, as she addressed the box that was covered in excessive amounts of tape, *Mr. Bodyguard* by The Mighty Diamonds rang out from her phone. She turned on her heels and leaped to answer it.

"I just finished wrapping up a birthday gift for Austen that I'll ship to her tomorrow," she said.

"You didn't have to buy her a gift," Matt replied, his tone filled with grateful and therefore unconvincing reproach. "And hello to you too."

"Didn't buy it," she clarified, excitedly rocking on the balls of her feet. "It's a vase I made in my pottery class. I hope she'll like it."

"I'm sure she will. That's very good of you. What's going on over there at the mad house? How are the kiddos?"

"Marco has become completely football-obsessed, and Esme's recently learned the lyrics to every Taylor Swift song ever written. I'm starting to worry there's no room left in her brain for school. But everything's right as rain, really. You've caught me in a rare moment of calm. They're both at friends' houses playing. What's cooking with you?"

"I proposed, and she said yes."

Ophelia gasped, jumping in place. "You're getting married! Oh, Richie, that's such wonderful news. The best news I've heard in an age. Congratulations, my friend. When and where will it be?"

"Thanks, Fie. We're really excited," Matt replied. "Probably next Spring in Paris. You'll be here, yes? Austen wants Esme to be a flower girl and Marco to be a ring bearer, even though they don't really do that at French weddings. I guess ours is going to mix in some American traditions."

"They'll both be over the moon. Wild horses couldn't keep us away," Ophelia declared, pulling out a chair and settling in for the story. "How did you ask her? Spare no details."

"We went to dinner at this place near the Louvre to celebrate getting the keys to our new apartment, so afterward, I suggested we walk for a bit and led her toward the glass pyramid at the entrance. I wanted to do it there since that's where we first reconnected after I moved to Paris," he explained.

Ophelia propped her feet up on the chair opposite her, smiling. "I remember."

"She stopped to take a picture, and when she turned around, I was down on one knee—which I don't recommend on cobblestones—but luckily, she didn't leave me down there for long. It was a quick yes," he recounted.

"You had a ring?" she asked, excitement bubbling in her voice.

"Of course. What kind of heathen do you think I am?" Matt scoffed.

Ophelia nodded her approval, a smile spreading further across her face. "Good man. Was she surprised?"

"Very. There were happy tears once the shock fell off her face," he laughed. "We'd talked about it in passing but never seriously. But I knew she'd say yes. I've known we were endgame for a good long while."

"It sounds perfect. Well done you," she beamed.

"So, for the wedding, do you think you might bring a date?" he asked haltingly.

She tapped one finger on her chin and cocked her head sideways. "Is an immediate RSVP required?"

"Of course not. Take your time," he confirmed. "Let's talk again soon?"

"Absolutely. Send Austen my love and congrats. No, scratch that. I'll call her myself soon."

Ophelia hung up the phone and continued to beam, thinking about the Parisian wedding to come. Her thoughts then drifted to her own wedding to Gianluca, nearly thirteen years prior. They were married at a villa in Tuscany in early fall, surrounded by family, friends and enough food and wine for a small army. She'd been clad in bridal white and carried a small but stunning bouquet of black orchids and white calla lilies which stood in brilliant contrast to the fall hues of the foliage that surrounded the villa. Until her kids were born, it had been the happiest, most gorgeous day of her life. She was young and full of hope for what she'd only imagined as their blissful life ahead, building the kind of boisterous and happy family she'd always longed for as an only child raised by a single and sad parent.

She had wholeheartedly and lovingly leaped into their life together all those years ago, folding her life into Gianluca's in a way that, she now realized, had allowed her to lose her sense of self. She'd put him and then the kids first at every turn, and in the last year, she'd begun to reclaim her agency through pottery classes, therapy, and several new female friends that she'd made through work and the kids' school. The question that lingered stubbornly in her mind was whether she was strong enough to maintain her sense of self if she allowed herself to fully reintegrate back into her couple.

The sound of the front door opening pulled her from her thoughts. She rose and smoothed her dress, turning to the kettle to boil water for tea. Gianluca entered and seeing what she was doing, pulled out her favorite mug—a Christmas gift from Austen that read "Do epic shit." Ophelia found it oddly motivating.

"How was your day?" he asked, leaning against the counter. "You look happy."

"I am," she acknowledged with a small nod as she filled the kettle at the sink. "I just got off the phone with Matt. He and Austen are getting married."

Gianluca smiled, crossed his arms over his chest and looked down at his feet. "Good for them. They're a great match."

Ophelia flicked the switch on the kettle, setting it to boil. She let the silence hang in the air as she plucked fresh mint leaves off their stem. Gianluca often took his conversational cues from her these days, waiting to be spoken to before speaking. He'd steadily grown more attentive and thoughtful throughout these incredibly trying months, and it hadn't gone unnoticed. Every day, he'd shown up and given her space—dialed in but never pushy.

He stood a few feet away, and she watched him out of the corner of her eye as she stuffed the mint into her small glass teapot. His salt and pepper hair had gotten saltier in the past year, but it only made him look more distinguished. At this precise moment, she felt an invisible yet undeniable pull toward him.

"It got me thinking about our wedding," she admitted softly.

His brown eyes flew up to meet hers, his lips parted. She saw color creeping up his neck—hope blooming on his face. He hesitated only for a second before standing up board straight and speaking.

"Our thirteenth anniversary is coming up soon. Lucky number thirteen. I looked it up the other day—the traditional anniversary gift for thirteen years is lace."

She eyed him skeptically, her brain unexpectedly thinking about lingerie. They hadn't even kissed since Ibiza, but her brain suddenly flooded with thoughts of sex. "And what of it?" she asked, hoping she wasn't blushing as she tried to push those thoughts down.

He almost stepped forward but stopped himself. He started to speak, slowly and cautiously. "It's meant to represent the deepening intricacies of marriage. Intricacies. Complexities. Call them what you will. We've had them, and I know I've put us through the ringer, but Ophelia, I want so badly for you—for us—to be happy again," he said, pausing for a beat and folding his hands in prayer in front of his chest. "I remember every detail of your lace dress at our wedding. You were a vision. I didn't think I could love you any more than I did on that day, but I was wrong. I love you more today."

She was a split second away from throwing herself into his arms when the kettle whistled, causing her to jump to turn it off. She poured the now boiling water into the teapot and breathed in the fresh mint scent as it diffused, feeling her muscles relax and her heart start to pound against her ribcage simultaneously. Austen's advice, given on her trip to Paris, popped into her mind—*Don't get so caught up in punishing him that you end up punishing yourself too*, she'd wisely said. *Take the leap*, her heart screamed.

"I still have the dress," she said, taking her still empty mug into both her hands and re-reading its emboldening words. She set the mug down gently and turning to face him, took a leap. "And I still love you."

Gianluca stared at her in awe. She'd said it. She had to put 'still' in there to take the edge off those three words coming out in sequence, but she finally said it, and as she did, she felt the remaining pieces of the stone box around her heart crumble and float away. And her heart beat on, pumping a shy smile across her face.

He immediately closed the distance between them. Taking her face gently in his hands, he whispered, "Marry me. Again. I love you now, and I will love you forever. Wear lace for lucky number thirteen, and let's renew our vows."

Tears fell from Ophelia's eyes, which Gianluca wiped away with his thumbs while searching her face. "Are these sad tears or happy tears?"

"Both?" she shrugged, wrapping her arms around his waist and pulling him to her, burying her face in his neck. She took in his familiar scent of Acqua di Parma cologne and let herself fully relax into his touch as his arms encircled her tenderly.

He whispered into her ear, "We can still have it all, Ophelia. Please come back to me. My life doesn't make sense without you."

Ophelia pulled back, wiped tears from her eyes, and rested her hands on his chest. He continued to hold her by her hips, his thumbs tracing her hip bones in a gentle caress. They stood in their kitchen, staring at each other in silence for what felt like an eternity, Ophelia's mind whirring as she felt his heart beating under her palms. It was entirely synched with her own. She knew the next move was hers, and despite the fear that came with it, she finally knew what move she wanted to make.

"You hurt me," she said, looking deeply into his brown eyes which so closely mirrored her own.

He hung his head, resting his forehead on hers, and gripped the fabric of her dress, twisting it into his fists. "I know. I'll never hurt you again. I promise."

Ophelia pried his hands loose from her dress, interlacing their fingers, palm to palm. "But what doesn't kill us makes us stronger."

"You're so strong, Ophelia. You've blown me away this year," he said, releasing one of her hands to tuck a strand of hair behind her ear before cupping her cheek. "I'll be stronger too. For all of us."

She took a step backward, releasing herself from his grasp and pressing both hands into the counter behind her for stability. "You and the kids used to be my whole world, but I lost myself somewhere in it."

Gianluca's shoulders dropped, and his lips pursed in consternation, bracing himself for whatever was coming next. Ophelia's heart thundered in her chest.

"I've been working really hard to find myself and love myself enough to love the rest of you well. It's a journey," she explained, locking her eyes onto his. "But I want you on this journey with me. I want us to be a family. Forever."

"You do?" he asked, stepping cautiously toward her but not daring to reach out.

Ophelia took in the earnest, desperate, searing love that was etched across his face, waiting for her to confirm her wishes. He was holding his breath in anticipation.

"This is love. It's imperfect. It's hard. It can hurt. It can heal. And it's worth fighting for. So yes, I do. And yes, I'll marry you again," she smiled, as tears started to fall.

Gianluca's mouth crashed into hers, and she felt every ounce of their collective desperation, love, heartache, and healing cascading through her body as their tongues, tears, limbs and lives twisted back together, building the new road that would carry them forward.

THE END

Acknowledgements

I must start by thanking Amy Snook of Parea Studios for believing in me as a writer and being my book industry guru since the very beginning of my journey into publishing. Without her, I'm not sure I'd have even dared to dream about writing a second book. Thank you, Amy, for making me believe that writing was something I could and should do as a profession, for everything you did to help me get the word out about *Will There Be Wine?* which built up an invaluable fan base for this sequel, and for your smart, early input on this book's evolution.

On a related note, thanks to Corley Hughes for introducing me to Amy after seeing my LinkedIn post in the fall of 2022 which said something like "I wrote a book. Now what? Anyone know anyone in publishing who can help me figure out what to do next?" It's worth noting that I hadn't seen or spoken to Corley in probably ten years or more when she replied, and that set everything on the right path. Never underestimate what the right introduction can do for someone in your network, no matter how far removed.

My other most critical thank you is to Rozi Doci, my fabulous editor with whom I've now worked on both of my books. I'd have been lost without her on both and now simply can't imagine writing another without her impeccable guidance. I hope this book will be the second of many on which we will collaborate.

Sincere thanks to Laura Doerre for coming up with the title of this book. I met Laura, a friend of a friend who was visiting Paris, once and only once over lunch, at a time when I was struggling to name it. Her suggestion was so obviously the right one that it was unbelievable to me that I hadn't come up with it on my own. That meeting was clearly serendipity.

Un très grand merci à Olivia Bourgeois for the long conversation during our holiday in Sardinia in the summer of 2023 that sparked the initial idea for this book.

On a lighter note, I want to thank Liz Jarvis for inviting me into her Ibiza summertime crew, and to her, Colleen Theis and Neil Blanket for introducing me all those years ago to Aiyanna, Sunset Ashram, and Ibiza villa life, which inspired Ophelia's birthday weekend.

To my fabulous friends and earliest readers—Tom Pilla, Ketty Bucca, Erica Guries, Julie de Widt-Bakker, Jill Petersen and Eve Hill-Agnus—a huge thank you for your early, enthusiastic feedback on this book, which helped shape it but more importantly, encouraged me to continue. Special shout out to Ketty for correcting my Italian and to Julie, as well as Katleen Dewaele, Karen Hammeren and Vibeke Hansen for being my first "live audience" and letting me read you the first seven chapters over those two lovely nights in Waimes, Belgium. I'll never forget your audible gasps and shocked faces as I read the final sentence of the prologue. That excitement carried me all the way to the end of the editing process.

Thank you as well to Claire Brown, my cover designer, for the fun collaboration, and to Laura Boyle for the interior typesetting.

Last but not least, thank you to every reader who has left or will leave a positive review for *Will There Be Wine?* and/or *Will There Be Love?*. Particularly for independent authors, those reviews mean the world and help fuel the desire and motivation to keep writing.

About the Author

Whitney Cubbison is a dual American and French citizen living in Paris since 2009. She grew up in Texas and California and graduated from UCLA with a degree in French. She started her career in Communications working for high-tech PR agencies in San Francisco and eventually joined Microsoft where she worked for sixteen years, thirteen of which from the Paris office. During that time, she held various international roles that encompassed public relations, employee communications, executive speechwriting, and social media.

She left Microsoft in July 2022 to focus on completing her first novel, *Will There Be Wine?*, which she self-published in January 2023. The story, while fiction, was deeply inspired by Whitney's own experiences as an ex-pat divorcée living in Paris and trying to navigate the cultural minefield of dating in a foreign country. Despite the ongoing trials and tribulations of this navigation, she remains a hopeless romantic.

When she's not writing, Whitney can be found sitting in Parisian cafés and restaurants with her friends, drinking wine. For more, including links to all Whitney's social media sites, please visit https://www.datingdisasters.paris/.

For anyone who is a fan of visual storytelling, don't miss Whitney's Instagram @whitneycubbisonwrites where she shares her own photos and anecdotes from many of the places her characters visit in both *Will There Be Wine?* and *Will There Be Love?* including Paris, Rome, Ibiza and more.

Printed in Poland
by Amazon Fulfillment
Poland Sp. z o.o., Wrocław